also by Anthony Burgess

novels
The Long Day Wanes
  Time for a Tiger
  The Enemy in the Blanket
  Beds in the East
The Right to an Answer
The Doctor is Sick
The Worm and the Ring
One Hand Clapping
A Clockwork Orange
The Wanting Seed
Honey for the Bears
Inside Mr Enderby
Nothing like the Sun: A Story
  of Shakespeare's Love-Life
The Eve of Saint Venus
A Vision of Battlements
Tremor of Intent
Enderby Outside
MF
Napoleon Symphony
The Clockwork Testament;
  or, Enderby's End
Beard's Roman Women
Abba Abba
Man of Nazareth
1985
Earthly Powers
The End of the World News

for children
A Long Trip to Teatime
The Land Where the
  Ice Cream Grows

verse
Moses

non-fiction
English Literature: A Survey
  for Students
They Wrote in English
Language Made Plain
Here Comes Everybody: An
  Introduction to James Joyce
  for the Ordinary Reader
The Novel Now: A Student's
  Guide to Contemporary
  Fiction
Urgent Copy: Literary Studies
Shakespeare
Joysprick: An Introduction to
  the Language of James
  Joyce
New York
Hemingway and His World
On Going to Bed
This Man and Music

translator
The New Aristocrats
  (with Llewela Burgess)
The Olive Trees of Justice
  (with Llewela Burgess)
The Man Who Robbed Poor
  Boxes
Cyrano de Bergerac
Oedipus the King

editor
The Grand Tour
Coaching Days of England
A Shorter Finnegans Wake

ANTHONY BURGESS

Devil of a State

HUTCHINSON
London Sydney Auckland Melbourne Johannesburg

Hutchinson & Co. (Publishers) Ltd

An imprint of the Hutchinson Publishing Group

17–21 Conway Street, London W1P 6JD

Hutchinson Group (Australia) Pty Ltd
30–32 Cremorne Street, Richmond South,
Victoria 3121
PO Box 151, Broadway, New South Wales 2007

Hutchinson Group (NZ) Ltd
32–34 View Road, PO Box 40–086,
Glenfield, Auckland 10

Hutchinson Group (SA) Pty Ltd
PO Box 337, Bergvlei 2012, South Africa

First published by William Heinemann Ltd 1961
First published as a Hutchinson Paperback 1983
© Anthony Burgess 1961

Printed in Great Britain by The Anchor Press Ltd
and bound by Wm Brendon & Son Ltd,
both of Tiptree, Essex

ISBN 0 09 153381 3

TO

GRAHAM GREENE

. . . Quei preti han presagito
che il paese passo passo
sarà presto incivilito;
rimarrà come un babbeo
             l'Europeo.

          —GIUSEPPE GIUSTI

It is better to marry than to burn.

          —I CORINTHIANS vi. 19

CONTENTS

Part One
3

Part Two
73

Part Three
141

Part Four
193

Part Five
243

PART ONE

I

At slow but regular intervals, in the rhythm of a Roman water-clock that knew the Empire would last for ever, the gathered globule of sweat at the end of his nose fell into the telephone mouthpiece. Down the nose from the watershed of the forehead, the leisurely wait at the tip for a drop heavy enough to drip, drop and break, and, then, at the other end of the line, an infinitesimal *plonk* unheard in the huge indifferent office. And again. And again. Till, desperate, Lydgate yelled fit to shatter the diaphragm:

"The key! The key! Somebody *must* have the key!"

Carruthers Chung stood by him, cool. Glasses, a moustache whose every hair could be counted by Lydgate as he waited, could he but see through the sweat, could he but be calm enough to wish to count, a James Joyce beard. Carruthers, the orthodox might say, was not a saint's name. Some day, Carruthers Chung had said, it might be. Carruthers Chung said, "Evelybody is looking for the key. That is the histoly of Western Philosophy. Flom Alistotle to Bertland Lussell. But the key is not there."

A New Zealand voice at the other end now said: "The Electrical Department has the front-door key. The other keys are inside the house. Including the spare front-door key. The Electrical Department are on their way back from the house now to the Electrical Department. They've turned on the juice. Rather, they've turned the master-switch on. There's a juice cut at the moment. If you go

3

to the Electrical Department now you'll just about catch them before the mid-morning break. They've got the key." The voice hung up. Lydgate hung up, and now the residual drop fell slowly from the instrument on to the magnificent marble floor of the marble halls of the Post Office. Across the road the Public Works Department truck waited, as it had waited since dawn, as it might still wait till dewy eve, a summer's day, with the workmen waiting too in the shade of Lydgate's house, if you could call it a house. It was really a kind of shelter, all woven like a big basket. It was to something like a real house that Lydgate was now to move, a slow step up in the evolutionary scale of housing. From the amoeba to God, or the gods, the gods being in a Valhalla of mansions up the hill, Lydgate now having achieved a dwelling perhaps fit for a mammal, certainly fit for a vertebrate. But he had to get the key. He saw, cruising by the Government Building and the half-built Civic Centre, a yellow-topped taxi driven by a Chinese youth he knew.

"I must get the key," he said to Carruthers Chung who was licking stamps, big proud stamps as big as the blade of the tongue that licked. Carruthers Chung finger-and-thumbed delicately out a limp scene of river and jungle (STATE OF DUNIA: ONE DECEM) and said: "Continue your search. The key to leality." He smiled sadly. "Do not forget our blidge party tonight. I shall call for you. We shall play together."

"*Taksi!*" called Lydgate. He ran with fifty-year-old stiffness down the slope of brown grass, scorched his hand on the door-handle of the taxi, winced as his thin buttocks met the oven-top of the front passenger-seat. The youth nodded and nodded, greeting Lydgate with one harshly projected word:

"You."

4

Then, as they went down Caliph Road, turned into General Mark Clark Avenue, side-streeted towards the Electrical Department, the youth gave a monotoned commentary on the sights of the town. It was a dull recital of the self-evident. To pretend that his passengers were blind gave the youth some obscure Chinese satisfaction:

"Woman cross road now. Two black woman go in shop. Dog sit bite foot. In market fish smell. There two Patu's mans." (Patu was the local nationalist leader. The two men were in Nazi jackboots, dirty shirts, on bicycles, crinkly hair long uncut, wild beards long unshaven. It was a vow; to remain hairy till Independence was achieved.) "One India man drunk. He drink brandy. There white woman very thin." The youth with great force gathered his phlegm together and gobbed out of the taxi window. "There Hillman Minx. It number D437." Sated of the animate, the youth now kept strictly to vehicles. "That Land Rover. Number DG98. That left-hand-drive car. Very big. Number D724." Then he announced, without satisfaction: "Here Lectric. All mans go out drink beer."

Lydgate gave a picture of the Caliph to the youth, legend: STATE OF DUNIA: ONE BUCK. The youth left, nodding gravely as in conspiracy again to share a frightful catalogue of the town's sights. Lydgate passed a vast silence of generators to enter the Electrical Department offices. There were small boys and refrigerators. Only one man had kept to his post this mid-morning, and that was the State Electrical Engineer himself. He, an urbane Indian with a cigarette-holder, smiled at Lydgate over a plate of curry. (Heavy sustenance at eleven o'clock was essential, breakfast having been eaten at six.) "All of my men have gone out, I'm afraid. If you search the coffee-shops you will probably find some of them. It is, I know, difficult to enter a house in the normal way without a key. And a key, of

5

course, is such a small thing, easily mislaid, forgotten or overlooked." The voice had the high pitch of a film Lama.

Wearily Lydgate went the rounds of the coffee-shops. Men of many racial groups sat round tables in party spirit, toasting, laughing, calling for unbelievable dishes—ox-brains in sour sauce, goat's innards, plain unseasoned vermicelli, cucumber and chilli, the gravy of stewed buffalo. Directions and advice were cheerfully given to Lydgate.

"Mr. John has the key still in his pocket. I saw him take it out when he took out his packet of Lucky Strike."

"Camel."

"The brand is immaterial. He wondered, I know, what the key was for, being forgetful, but he certainly returned the key to his pocket. His right-hand trouser pocket."

"But who is Mr. John?" asked Lydgate, his handkerchief saturated. "And where is he?"

"His race is not sure," said a black man, heavily tattooed. "But he will be in the Dunia Hotel. He will eat there with men of his own rank of foreman." Then a song started. Lydgate left, looked about him for an instant in the hot, hot sun. Scaffolding was everywhere, blue sky peeped in patches through the ribs. The richness of the state's uranium deposits was everywhere being proclaimed in half-built temples to Commerce, to Transatlantic Cinema, to the Broadcast Word, to Allah. How magnificent the new Mosque was to be: its cupolas gleamed like oranges in the distance. Why did mineral wealth and Islam go together? The Middle East, Borneo, here in Dunia. There must, somewhere in the Koran, be a fulfilled prophecy: "For, as Allah Most High has denied you in this world the solace of the fatness of pigs, so He has made the earth to yield a most spiritual fatness, wherewith your loins shall

6

be larded and those of the fruit of your loins, and the richness thereof shall spout heavenwards to His glory."

The youth with his yellow-headed taxi had been circling like a buzzard. Exhibiting no told-you-so triumph, he alighted on Lydgate and opened the door for him. As they made slowly for the Dunia Hotel he resumed his catalogue monologue, now rarefied to the purely arithmetical.

"There two man. There four woman. There five, six, seven dog. Chase one dog, woman dog. In shop there see two new ice-box come today. One ship come in today from Aden." Indeed, masts stood high above the Customs House. But there was no heartening smell of the sea here; the river sang and stenched of inland, spoke of being lost in the river-web of the colossal continent, never to see home again. "Outside Dunia Hotel two, three cars. No room park. You get out here." Obediently Lydgate got out by the bank of the river. Across it was a village sparkling in the sun. Village women were coming over in a ferry to the town, some of them naked above an ornate waist-throttling belt, the gleam of breasts answering the gleam of the distant cupolas. The youth counted impassively. "There five woman. That make ten." Lydgate gave the youth another picture of the Caliph. The youth nodded sadly, conspiratorially yet again.

The interior of the hotel reminded Lydgate of the interior of a Centre of Rest and Culture he had once seen in a small Spanish town. There culture had meant many pictures of Franco, here it meant even more pictures of the Caliph. Here, as there, rest meant very hard chairs. Food and drink came from behind a screen, whence too came noises of rage and impatience. And on the very hard chairs, round square unlovely tables, the mid-morning break prolonged itself. So also did the power-cut, for the ceiling-fans were still and silent. Near the door were men known

7

to Lydgate, good-hearted young unstable men in whom the mingling of blood had gone as far as it conceivably could. One was tiny and delicate, like a bird, but with a huge face scrawled with the lines of the agony of a Christ. He was Filipino, Chinese, Scottish, unsure of his allegiances, ready to weep over Old Glory or Union Jack as the drink took him; then, as the drink took him further, all for red blood and the crunch of bones. His name was Sebastian Hup. With him sat an Anglo-Burmese dashed with the blood of an Arab trader, a suspicion of Malayalam, a single drop of Portuguese. He looked handsome and English in his uniform of an Inspector of Vehicles, two pips on each shoulder, but his name was Dominic De Cruz, and his arms were covered with tattooings—hieroglyphs of Syrian secret societies for which he had worked as strong man, a sentimental back-view of a fat-bottomed toddler, a winsome pouting head labelled "Pixy Face". And standing, ready to go and supervise his Municipal Dog Catchers, was another tattooed man—Sudu, Potok, Danish, Chadi, English —called David Lloyd-Evans. On the table were chopsticks and the remains of an ample meal. Their quarrel, in this limp air, after food taken in great heat, was growing languid.

"I still say," said Dominic De Cruz to Sebastian Hup, "I still say that you've no right to sell information you get from the confidential files. And to sell that information about me was not a friendly act."

"But you were ready enough to drink on the money I got," said Sebastian Hup, frowning as in the agony of a difficult stool. "Besides, the information wasn't really confidential. Everybody knows that you were thrown out of Nigeria for fighting. True, not many people know you were thrown out of Kenya for fighting. But one thing is the same as another. It's the fighting that's the main point.

And it wasn't big information. It was worth what I got for it, no more and no less. Five bucks."

"But you lost your own confidential file, didn't you?" said Dominic De Cruz. "That, of course, was very convenient." He tapped the table with a chopstick. "I, if I were less well-disposed, could tell some stories about you that would have got you out on your ear. Sit down, Mr. Lydgate," he said courteously. "There was the case of the two thousand bucks from the Madagascar Company, wasn't there?"

"You ought to forget about that," said David Lloyd-Evans gravely. "It doesn't do any good to bring up the past. Besides, you got your cut, remember."

"Oh, and you didn't, I suppose."

"It was a small cut. I wasn't involved in anything as you were. You ought to bury the past."

"What is the past? The past is five minutes ago. In five seconds, in one second even, this will be the past. This," he added and made a fairy bell-stroke with his thumb-nail on a plate. On his thumb-nail he, or somebody else, had drawn eyes, nose and mouth with a Biro.

"Stop getting metaphysical," said Lydgate. "Please, please, which is Mr. John?"

"There." Everybody pointed in the same direction; everybody agreed as to the identity and locality of Mr. John. And Lydgate saw a man like President Nasser drinking beer and gesticulating fiercely. His table-companions were, like himself, not easily assignable to any known ethnic group. The fact of the brown pitted complexion established, one had to digest a vision of some tract of land like the Gobi Desert which produced a hieratic fruit— brown plump men born to be chief clerks, superintendents of meter-readers, store-supervisors, assistant district engineers. They were a class rather than a race; though, if a race had to be looked for, it could conceivably only derive from a trapezium whose corners were Ankara, Kirgiztan, Kabul and Yemen. Yet each guarded jealously—like a bank-book—a British passport.

"I understand, Mr. John, that you have the key to my new house. I believe that you were good enough to switch on the electricity." Lydgate's voice dropped wearily to nothing.

"What Raschid says is neither here nor there," Mr. John was saying. "The meeting had already ruled out of order any censure of the hon. treasurer. It was expressly ordered to be expunged from the minutes."

"The key."

"I have myself never been anything of a real stickler for procedure. The meeting was there to get a job done and it got the job done. Expeditiously. Those were elected who obviously had to be elected and no opportunity was given for other nominations. That had been agreed upon before the meeting took place. But to censure the hon. treasurer was out of order. There has to be a wide margin for legitimate expenses." Mr. John turned on Lydgate a great false smile. "We broke the seal, Mr. Lydgate. The electricity is now on. Potentially, that is. I gave the key to a man from the water-works."

"But surely the main cock is outside the house."

"So it is." Mr. John slapped his thigh in high merriment. "What a fool the man was. He should have known that. But so few people here know their jobs."

"And where is this man from the water-works?"

"He spends his morning break at home. He goes to bed for an hour. Sleep, he says, is more important than either food or drink."

"And where does he live?" The words were almost inaudible.

"On the Paku road. The third milestone." Mr. John smiled brilliantly in dismissal and returned to his off-duty interests. "So if Raschid has anything to say perhaps he had better say it to me. Not that I think he will. I know Raschid of old and Raschid knows me, and Raschid, though a fool, is not such a fool as to try anything on that he can't get away with." He thought for a moment and amended this statement. "With which he can't get away."

Outside the hotel the heat was mounting. Lydgate began to whimper very softly. A taxi appeared, and the youth said, "You."

There was little to describe on the Paku road, on the way to the third milestone. The youth, who now wore sunglasses, became inarticulate in the face of so many natural objects—palms, sandy mounds, dried bushes, an arid watercourse. But once or twice he essayed a mystical language, apt for the description of things beyond even number, formless essences. "Ger," he said once, and, much later, "Roft."

The man from the water-works lay naked on a bed. Children crawled over him like flies. He received Lydgate with dignity. His woman offered tea. "I returned the key," said the man, "to the Public Works Department. It was put on a hook behind the desk of the Architect. There it will be now. But," he said, lying back, showing shaven arm-pits, "there is no water. It is the lack of rain. There may perhaps be water this evening at seven. There has never before been such a drought." He stretched himself as it were in pain, like a dusky Fisher King.

The taxi-youth had gone, perhaps scared by so much naked nature. There was no vehicle in sight. Lydgate groaned, wishing to God he had his car. It was still in his old station, Shurga, having major repairs. For weeks now it had been promised in just two more days' time. He began to walk, shuffling up dust, back towards the town. In great dust a lorry passed, on it many workmen cheering and jeering. They had formed a square about what Lydgate knew, from loud squawks and crowings, was a cockfight. Cock-fights were forbidden to be held in any place, but a moving lorry was not a place. Cheers, jeers, coco-ricos passed townwards in dust.

At length an Indian pedlar appeared in a Morris. He stopped by Lydgate, and Lydgate, in relief, was ready to climb aboard, but the Indian pedlar would have none of that. Not yet awhile. In the scorching sun, on the scorched sandy grass by the roadside, he displayed some of the more unsaleable of his wares. Lydgate bought a soapstone Buddha, Japanese chopsticks in a box, a set of plastic napkin-rings. Then, with great courtesy, he was offered a lift to Dunia Town. On the outskirts of Dunia Town a youth in a yellow-topped taxi honked at him like a goose. "I follow," called the youth. "You not pay."

And so Lydgate arrived at the point where he had started, the Post Office. Opposite, the woven strands of his temporary dwelling scorched in the sun. The Public Works Department van was still there, and the men slept in the shade. All except one. Lydgate, peering with attention, saw that this was not a man after all, but one of the large local simians called a *chopi*. It wore a loose denim suit. He wondered how long it had been on the pay-roll and who normally spent its wages. He rang up the general office of the Public Works Department and was answered by a soft shy epicene voice.

"This is Lydgate. Is Mr. Henryson there?"

"Oh, no."

"It's about the key to my new house. Have you got it? Has it been returned to you?"

"Oh, yes, I have message. The key not fit. No need for key. The door open all the time."

Lydgate, feeling his age, crossed the road, seeing before him his absurd elongated shadow in shorts, the ridiculously swinging thin shadow-arms. As he came to his old dwelling—which smelt of burning grass—the denimed ape began to gibber and dance up and down. "Down, sir, down," said Lydgate. The ape danced down and stopped and then began, with urgent chatterings, to wake its colleagues. Its colleagues woke. Soon, the ape chewing a cigarette donated by one of its keepers, work commenced. The ape thought the furniture had to be moved as well as the sewing-machine, the box of books and the old group photographs. "You have done this work before," a man patiently explained in Sudu. "The furniture belongs to the Public Works Department. It stays here. He is not all that clever," he added, to Lydgate. "He is, after all, only an ape."

There was not a great deal to be moved. Wajak, Lydgate's mistress, had taken many things to the up-river village where she now abode, awaiting a baby. She had even taken the battery-radio as—so the village letter-writer had recently told Lydgate in a curt progress report—"Her mother want hear news big world over sea." Lydgate's possessions, now broiling in sun and dust on the lorry, looked pathetically few, not much to show for fifty years of life. The denimed ape, gibbering to the world, held up a photograph of Lydgate in New Guinea, Lydgate with poor dead Jack Dunbar and little Corcoran who was now a British Resident somewhere, strange morose Arthur Pitt who had made his packet and gone mad, a couple of reformed cannibals with Semitic noses. The ape elevated and lowered the picture often, genuflecting to the sun.

They moved off, Lydgate sitting next to the driver, down

13

Caliph Road, past the hospital, past the Australian nurses' quarters, past the Potok Girls' School, past busy building sites, over a small bridge, past a large waste patch of scrub, past the fine house of the local nationalist leader, past a shop called 'Chong, Glass Grocers and Frame Maker', and ended their journey at a row of mean houses set in grass-stitched sand. The door of Lydgate's new house swung in a sudden dry breeze, swung in a curiously deformed way, as if no longer firmly anchored to the jamb. Lydgate entered and began to weep dry tears (twenty-four years since he had seen England) at the cheap insult of the housing board's allocation. No fan, no power-points, termite-hollowed chairs, a table as rough as a butcher's bench, a floor with loose boards, damp on the walls and ceiling. He sat down, his trembling hand on the arm-rest. The arm-rest crumpled like paper. Men and ape entered with his chattels. Lydgate stood up and lost control. "God curse them!" he told the ceiling. On the ceiling rain had made a brown silhouette of the Prince Regent. "I'll get them, I'll get them!" he said to a gold and pearl and black spider. Then, feeling his heart hammer with a kind of after-click he could taste in his throat, he sat down again. The other arm-rest crumpled like paper. On the floor the men dumped Wajak's sewing-machine, the small bachelor refrigerator, the few books, the two suitcases of clothes, the framed photographs. The ape would not let go of the New Guinea group; he clasped it to his chest, showing formidable teeth. "It's mine," said Lydgate; "give it to me. Let go of it, you damned idiot." He stood up, towering above the ape, and the two of them began to tussle for the picture. The workmen stood round, ready to lay bets. Then Lydgate saw himself, a mature man, a much-married man of fifty, a man who had, several times in Europe, Africa and the East, had his own office, once with a secretary and two telephones, a man of dignified appearance though in shorts, grey-haired and grey-moustached, sufficiently genteel in manner and speech, with a self-taught gentility, tearfully struggling with an ape for an old yellowing picture. Ashamed, he desisted. He gave a ten-buck note to the chief workman and walked out into the sun. A youth in a yellow-topped taxi hovered. "You," said the youth and opened the taxi-door. "You too," snarled Lydgate as he got inside. "Take me to the Kool Kaffi."

"In Kool Kaffi," said the youth, "once I drink four beer. Once I drink two beer. On Chinese New Year I drink five brandy. Christmas I drink three whisky." Well-pleased with these reminiscences, he drove towards the town, emitting several times a drawn-out satisfied "Aaaah."

2

The Kool Kaffi (Bar and Restaurant) lay—on a north-south line—between Podmore and Company, General Importers, Incorporated in U.K., and the Chin Chin Cinema. West arose the smells of the market; east, of the river. There was a barren garden enclosed by a high prison-camp fence, and in the garden were many empty bottles which the Municipal Garbage Disposal Department refused to collect. The Kool Kaffi (Bar and Restaurant) had the swing-doors of a frontier-town saloon. Lydgate swung them in with angry vigour. On his entrance, as at a signal, the ceiling-fans whirred back to life and the refrigerator resumed its humming. A Chinese bar-boy, in whose mind stirred some ember of neolithic philosophy, rushed to a tap. But a derisive choking airy gurgle stated that fire and water were not germane.

All along the bar, meaty buttocks overflowing the stools, sturdy legs dangling, sat Australian road-builders—engineers and foremen. The Cockney voices of the hell-ship pioneers rang out in a richness that drowned Lydgate's order. Lydgate's voice had always had a muffled, vaguely adenoidal, quality. Yet again, he asked for brandy and water. But there was no water.

"Tike your choice," said a road engineer called Clout, "water or champigne. They haven't got either." He was thin and wore glasses, looked like a parody of an intellectual.

"What does Jeff do with the water?" asked another

man of the roads. (Jeff was the State Water Engineer.)

"Flogs it to the Syrians." This was a squat blond man from Bunbury. "Have to shive in ginger ile again tonight."

Lydgate drank his brandy-soda in one gulp, then ordered another. He was going to see Mudd, chairman of the housing board. He could not go unfortified; his heart would beat too much, a red curtain would come down, he would stutter. "And again," he said to the bar-boy breathlessly.

"Here." Collie, a man from Bridgetown, stood before Lydgate. His belly was clad in a sweat-shirt, his chunky thighs in black shorts. His head, decollated, could rest on a desk like a paper-weight and never topple, so vast and leaden was the chin. "Here," he said, "what's this I've been hearing about what you're supposed to have said?"

"Yes?" said Lydgate.

"You said that no Aussie dare ever go and have a swim."

"Did I say that? The currents are treacherous, you know, especially——"

"It was nothing to do with the currents." ("Or the rizens," said Clout.) "What you said was that we were frightened of tiking our socks off."

"I don't think I ever said that," said Lydgate.

"Yes. Frightened of tiking our socks off because we were ashimed of showing the marks of the convict's chines."

"The convict's——?"

"Chines. Did you say that?"

Lydgate looked round uneasily. The Antipods, as he sometimes called them to himself, were always ready to burst. The immobile grin, the clutched glass, the slight sway. Do him in, the Pommy bastard. The trouble was that they knew too much; knew that he loathed his second wife and that his second wife was Australian. One of these road-men (was he here now?) had said that he had met

17

Lydia in Romano's in Sydney when he was on leave between contracts and that she was bonza and dinky-die. He
had not known, he had said, at the time that she was Mrs.
Lydgate, but she had, in the course of several evenings, told
him all about her Pommy husband and how they had split
up and whose fault it was. What she had said had made
the road-man go crook and he had passed these things on
to his compatriots in Dunia and they had gone a bit crook
too. A fine Austrylian girl like that and this Pommy with
his phony high society accent dishing her for the sike of
a bit of black sharp and blunt.

"Did you sy that or did you not sy that?" asked Collie of
Bridgetown.

"I did not," lied Lydgate, "say that."

"Say," announced Clout in a very clear and beautifully
forward-placed British film accent. "Say, oh I say, Horace."

"Brandy," said Lydgate breathlessly to the boy. "No
soda."

"Now then, you, old man," said Collie. He spoke to an
Australian sitting nervously at a table nursing a child. The
Australian was unbelievably ragged—patched shorts and
a dirty shirt—and his beaky nose and sharp chin were
shaded from the ceiling-fan by an Aussie hat. With him
was his wife—a Chadi of whom, when she had a bun in
the oven, he had made an honest woman. The child he
nursed was the love-child of his wife and Maximilian Hup,
brother to Sebastian Hup. The child was a most curious
colour, almost mulberry. Another child, gold as an angel,
sat on the floor pulling a cream cake to pieces. "Are you a
liar," said Collie, "or are you not a bloody liar?"

"I don't know what you mean, Georgie," smirked the
patched Australian.

"Did you sy that he said it or didn't you sy that he said
it?"

"Brandy," said Lydgate again. "No soda."

"I suppose he did sort of sy it in a wy. But he might have been sying what somebody else had been sying." Maximilian Hup's love-child got down from his knee. He poked his half-brother in the eye.

"And another thing, old man," said Collie. "When he said that did you do anything about it, eh?"

The patched Australian, whose name was Forbes and who came from Marmion, New South Wales, licked his lips, smirked with nerves, and began very rapidly swinging the right leg that sat on his left knee. He was terribly torn. Drawn towards a man who, like himself, had dark meat in the larder and curiously coloured children, he was at the same time deeply ashamed of his ostracism. Any little door that his compatriots would open for him, however low the lintel, he was ready to crawl through. 'Let me not,' his heart said, 'be altogether rejected. Throw me not completely out of the bed where the great Australian dream is snored. I will cling to the edge, shivering without blankets, if only you will show me, by a word or smile, that I have a place there. My wife can sleep on the floor if you will let her. The children can sleep on the landing.' Forbes smiled. "Well, Georgie," he said, "I told him that that sort of thing was the sort of thing that'd mike any good Aussie go a bit crook, I said. And I said that not everybody kime to Austrylia in the prison-ships. And then he sort of said how he was only kidding."

"Well, old man," said Collie. "My people kyme over in the early dyes."

"Brandy," said Lydgate.

"And I'm not ashimed of them. They started the country off, chines round their ankles or not. We still have a picture of the old man at home. He used to sy that the old country wanted to get rid of its real men. He used to sy that the old country was throwing buckets of good red blood awy, and that one dy the old country would sort of collapse. It would sort of die, he said, like a body with no blood in it. And that's coming true. Isn't it?" he said fiercely to Lydgate. "Isn't that true? You talk about the British Commonwealth, but what does it mean, eh? Is America in the British Commonwealth, eh?"

"No," said Lydgate. "Not any more."

"Too true it isn't. And that's where all your arguments fall down," said Collie in triumph. "So we'll all have one more." He ordered. "The old country got rid of its best men," he repeated.

"Thank you," said Lydgate gravely. He drank his last brandy and felt able to tackle Mudd. At the same time he felt an alcoholic twinge of exile's self-pity. The old country got rid of its best men. Too true it did. He signed his bill and began to leave, throwing to the other drinkers a sour smile and a shy wave. At the door of the Kool Kaffi the manager stood, a smart negro with hexagonal glasses and collar and tie. He was reasonably sober and spoke Spanish to Lydgate.

"Buenos tardes, señor. Muchísimas gracias."

Tardes. Lydgate looked at his watch and saw that it was indeed afternoon. Twelve-forty. Mudd would have left his office and gone up to his house on the hill for lunch. He would be eating a cold-storage steak and tinned potatoes, gazing at a fair prospect from his dining-room window. The thought of the polished floor and the vista of trees and distant bay made Lydgate grind his teeth. There was over an hour to go before the necktied administrators returned to the Government Building. Grinding his teeth, Lydgate felt an exiguous flow of saliva. He too had better eat.

On Sir William Sidebotham Road there was a small Chinese shop where, for one buck, one could eat one's fill of a speciality of the house with no precise name: a kind of greasy spaghetti coiled and writhed in soya sauce; there gleamed through the coils small prawns in full armour, shreds of meat, bits of chilli, diced sweet potato and the odd wheel of cucumber. It did not take long to eat one's fill. Lydgate entered the shop, passing through a wall of radio music, and found it full of workmen who, just over an hour before, had been stuffing themselves with elevenses. But one mess of workmen he had not seen before on his morning's quest. These were a mixed league of marble-workers engaged on filling the Mosque with marble—a rushed job involving many strikes and much overtime, for the Mosque was—with many sacred visitors in attendance —to open in less than two months. With them sat a young Italian called Paolo Tasca. He was a hungry-looking Tuscan with a beardless goat's face and a boxer's body. He and his father had been sent by a Franco-Italian firm of marble specialists in Tripoli. They fitted into the community well, and three times the U.N. Adviser had talked of sending them packing and requesting two marble experts of more tractable race. They were a puzzle to the U.N. Adviser, for they did not fit into any known category of his colonial experience of races. To him a European was an Englishman or a Scot, possibly a Welshman, probably not an Irishman. Australians could be reduced to terms of the homeland—with a little twisting— and Eurasians, Chadis, Syrians, Sudus, Potoks, Chinese and the rest he felt he could handle. But Italians just would not fit. He could not talk to them of their duty to the community (that is, their duty to honour the flag, wear a tie in the evenings, do their drinking in the Club, treat white women with respect) for the father, who spoke some English, would say, "My duty to a the Mosque. What a I do outside a the Mosque not a nobody's business." Or, "I not see a my flag. Here is a no Italian a Consulate." Or, "It a custom in a my country to pinch a bottom of woman who is a *bella*. It not a disrespect." The father's name was Nando Tasca, but most people called him Tony. His English, self-taught in the British-administered territories of Africa, was of an extinct type. It had disappeared from England with the organ-grinders when Mussolini, for the sake of his empire's dignity, had recalled them. Here it was prized and relished, a rare antique. Paolo Tasca was learning English at his father's behest. It was a filial duty. "When e come a ome from a the Mosque e can a sit down write a the letters. I bring im a out a ere from a Italy. I give im good a job. I an old a man. I ave a oliday ere a in Dunia. E work for is old a father. When e knew a English good a like me I get a im job on a coconut estate in a Shurga. There I ave a friends." Nando Tasca saw dispassionately the time when he could be rid of his son for good and all. He would be killed by the local terrorists quite quickly. He was fairly sure of that, for Paolo was an unlucky boy. Always had been. He made no secret of his enmity towards his son. There had been a quarrel over their pursuit of the same girl in Tripoli. There had been many quarrels about Nando Tasca's dilatoriness in sending money home to his wife in Tuscany. Paolo was devoted to his mother. But Nando Tasca, according to his son (many times, and in public), was devoted to two things only. *"Lei ama,"* he would state, *"due cose. Due cose solamente."* He would hold up two thick worker's fingers. *"La birra."* He would make a beer-swiller's guzzling noise, flexing his strong arm in a pot-drainer's motion. *"E questa putana Tripolitana."* He would then say "Aaaaah" without satisfaction, and give an obscene mime of his father at work with the Tripoli whore. This was usually followed by rapid operatic recitative with orchestral punctuations of fist on table or a smack on Paolo's ear or a most unfilial feint with a prize-fighter's ham-hand. All this, reported by spies, worried the U.N. Adviser. But these two, sturdy peasants as they were, grew browner and browner, and could be passed off to distinguished visitors as Asians who knew no better.

What Lydgate did not know was that, with today's move, he had become their neighbour.

Now, as he sucked in his Chinese spaghetti and cracked his prawns, Lydgate listened to threats of another strike. Paolo Tasca supported the motion with vigour. He spoke a rough kind of Sudu, using, at fortissimo points, words of Italian and even English: *"Mio padre"* came frequently and, as if Chaucer were translating Dante, "My fader". That was the great evil image, filling the marble-dusty Mosque like a real presence, the more so because of his real, and daily, absence. The workmen pitied Paolo. One man, his uncut hair tortured into a rat-tail, comforted him with a hand on his shoulder. It was known, he said, that Paolo received no wages. They would strike over that. Then, when Paolo received some wage as inadequate as their own, they would be able to strike again.

"And all day," affirmed Paolo, "he drink beer or sleep like a pig. Aaaaah. *Come,*" he emphasised, *"un porco."* You could see he had mistaken the meaning of 'strike'. His dictionary was an old one, all his father would give him, published in Turin, 1839. He spoke of arranging for a marble block to fall on his father. It was objected by an Indian with glasses that his father never came near enough to the Mosque for that to happen. But, Paolo thought, that too could be arranged. His father could be enticed with talk of a young Sudu girl haunting the Mosque and the workmen. Especially, suggested Paolo with no false modesty, himself. That would bring his father. Beer or a woman would always bring his father. *"Farabutto,"* he said. It was Renaissance melodrama, with all the Senecan trimmings. Lydgate felt heartened with all this talk of striking and smashing. He would now go and see Mudd.

3

Two flags drooped over the Government Building. The rains would lash them to life, revealing not the triple crucifixion which is Britain's pride, but the U.N.O. banner and the more arrogant standard of Dunia—the moon of Islam in custard, and surrounding it, a symbolic armoury of traditional weapons, everything of curved, serrated, triple-spiked that could conceivably sophisticate the boring act of just execution. Under the flags was a sculptured frieze denoting the dignity of labour: men watching the grain grow, placid buffaloes unyoked. Below was the super-cinema entrance. A wide colonnade surrounded the building, and in the pillared shade clerks strolled, hand in hand, or workless men crouched sullenly.

The corridors of all three storeys were full of wandering spies. There were no closed doors, only saloon swingers, so that every office was like a small and dark Kool Kaffi. State secrets, reprimands, dismissals could be picked up with ease. On the second floor, to which Lydgate had laboriously climbed, there was a wide range of information to be gained, for here were nearly all the departments —Agriculture, Drainage, Education, Propaganda, Religious Affairs, Forestry, Law, Customs and Traditions, Modernisation of the National Language, Heraldry and Official Symbols, the Treasury. Here also was the State Council Chamber. Here too the offices, outer and inner, of the U.N. Adviser and his staff. And here Mr. Mudd.

25

In Mr. Mudd's office there was irritability—the strain of digesting a heavy lunch, the effect of too many fore-noon cigarettes, ill-advised lunch-time cans of beer. A blonde girl in a flowered frock, carrying files, came out, peevishly swinging the swing-door. Mudd's snarl could be heard clearly. Lydgate caught the door on its return swing and walked into the cave-like half-dark. Mudd sat under the fan, snarling.

Mudd looked like a retired jockey. This was because he *was* a retired jockey, though of amateur status only. He now wore a stock and a horseshoe pin only on Sunday mornings; on working days he wore the badge of the Inner Circle—a bow tie. A bow-tie on duty was worn also by the U.N. Adviser, the State Irrigation Officer and the State Architect. Lydgate now fixed Mudd's bow-tie with a stern and angry gaze. Then he spoke.

"It's about this house I've been allocated."

"Oh, yes? Everything all right? No trouble about keys and so on?" It was a voice fit for a bookmaker's clerk, thought Lydgate. Lydgate, with the miasma of the brandy fuming above the coils of spaghetti, felt in control of the situation and said:

"You know bloody well everything's all wrong. You know bloody well because you're bloody well responsible for it."

Mudd made various tic-tac movements. Then he said, "I don't like your tone, Frank. I'd resent that tone if I didn't know you better. I don't know anything about the house. It was available when you made your application, that's all I know. Allocations are made by the whole housing board. I'm chairman, and the chairman has no vote. If you don't like the house you can go back to your old one."

"Look here, Harry," said Lydgate. "You know as well

26

as I do that these meetings of the housing board are a mere formality. You make all the decisions. You never were much of a man for listening to the views of committees, anyway. You knew damn well what you were giving me. It's a sheer bloody insult, that's what it is. The whole thing's rotting. A slum landlord would be ashamed of it. What I want to know is, why did you give it me?"

"It's Class F quarters," said Mudd. "That's what you're entitled to. You're classed as a single man, you know."

"There's nothing about being single or married in the circular about points for housing. It says five points for each child. It doesn't mention wives. Well, that gives me ten points before we go any further. And I've been seven months in the territory. That gives me three points for each month of waiting. And I know damn well that that single New Zealand woman has just walked into a three-bedroomed house, and she's only been here a fortnight."

"It was in her contract," said Mudd. "She wouldn't sign it otherwise."

"All I ask for," said Lydgate, "is my rights."

"Rights?" said Mudd. "You've got no rights. Let's have a look at your confidential file."

"What's my confidential file got to do with it?"

"It always helps. I like to have all the information."

"I think," said Lydgate, "we know all there is to know about each other. I know I wasn't a government officer in Shurga. Perhaps that gave me certain advantages. Perhaps that gave me a clearer view of what was going on. I know you bitched every contract I tried for. I know that you as good as ruined me."

"That's a bit melodramatic."

"Life in the colonies *is* a bit melodramatic. Except that there are no pure-minded girls and no heroes. But there are plenty of villains. You, for instance."

27

"You failed because you were no damned good as a business-man. You were too soft."

"Yes, too soft. That's right. I honestly thought you could make money through fair means. I honestly thought that tenders were considered on their merits. You know why I failed. I failed because I couldn't give big enough bribes."

"Bribes?" Mudd twitched his nose as though hearing a dirty word. "Bribes?"

"Oh, stop playing the innocent, Harry. Who bought you that house in Wiltshire? I seem to remember a little Syrian called Amin. He did very well for himself in Shurga. He was properly grateful. But he was grateful in a very subtle way. Your bank account has always been above suspicion."

"Hup!" called Mudd. "Hup! Hup!" Lydgate stared. Mudd seemed to be having a passionate attack of hiccups. And then Sebastian Hup came in, crouched, obsequious, but his face twisted in tragic agony.

"Ah, there you are. Fetch Mr. Lydgate's confidential file."

"Yes, sir. E oblique C oblique L oblique seven two eight." Sebastian Hup nodded seriously at Lydgate and then smiled tortuously. Apparently he knew the book well and was appreciative of its contents. "At once, sir."

While they waited Mudd whistled four bars of the Post Horn Gallop. Then he said pleasantly, "And how is your little what's-her-name?"

"My little—?"

"Oh, your servant, your friend, your whatever-you-like-to-call-her."

"I don't know. Well, I suppose. But I can tell you how she's going to be when she sees the bloody rat-hole you've put us into. She's going to be bloodthirsty. And I don't think I mean that metaphorically."

Mudd laughed. "She was a nice little thing. One of the cleaner street-girls of Shurga, as I remember."

Lydgate smiled. "You don't remember. I know for a fact you don't. Nor does anybody. Strange, isn't it? But it's true. There are certain things that can't be faked, even in these days."

"Oh, well, she's made up for lost time, I gather. I gather that the child she's going to have isn't going to be your child."

"At least she's honest. Not like Mrs. Ali. Ali still, apparently, can't understand his good fortune in getting the cold storage import monopoly. And the child, so I hear, swears horribly when he's taken off his rocking-horse."

"Ah, here it is," said Mudd heartily, taking the confidential file from Sebastian Hup. Sebastian Hup decided to play a bird-boned midget yellow Christ-faced English butler. "Will there be anything further, sir?"

"No, no, that's all." Sebastian Hup bowed and returned to his pantry. "Now then," said Mudd, opening up the thick file. "Let's see, let's see. An interesting career, but a bit patchy. That was quite a respectable job in Madrid, wasn't it? Why ever did you leave?"

"I don't see what all this has to do with the Dunia senior officers' housing board."

"Three years in Nairobi, importing small machine tools. That didn't last long, either. Ah yes. That was the time of your first marriage. Was she a black girl?"

"Unfortunately, no."

"Anyway, it didn't last long. Then you were gold-prospecting in Malaya. You stuck it out a bit better there. I believe there was some talk of your marrying a Chinese girl."

"She died. Look here, Harry, what's all this got to do with anything?"

"Oh, nothing particularly. I just like to refresh my memory, that's all. If you *had* married her I don't suppose it would have lasted long. And then Changi during the Jap occupation. And then New Guinea in some capacity that doesn't seem at all clear. You soon chucked that. You don't seem to stick at anything very long, do you?"

"The trouble is, Harry, I always keep coming up against people like you."

"And then a year in Australia. And then Shurga. You seem to have liked Shurga. You stayed there nearly five years. Ah, yes. That's when you married Lydia. And you're still married to Lydia, aren't you?"

"Only because she won't divorce me."

"What I can't understand," said Mudd, "is where you got your money from. I mean, you started off as a contractor with about thirty thousand bucks in the bank. Oh, I know you lost it. But where did you get it from? Was it Lydia's money?"

"Mind your own bloody business."

"Well, you know, these things *are* my business. This state has to vet its contract officers very carefully, you know. On the whole, I think you were very lucky to get this job here. What are your qualifications? None. Oh, you know a few words of the local lingos, I admit, but that's not much really. You've no real administrative experience, and that's the thing that's needed."

"I can manage all right. A kid of two could manage. These government jobs don't take all that much managing. I'm only a sort of rubber stamp."

"Well, I still say you've been very lucky."

"Come off it again, Harry. You'd been trying to get a European Passport Officer for well over a year. What I want to know is, where is all this leading?"

"This, I suppose. You stay in the house we've given you. And if you don't like it you know what to do. That house is just about up your street. Literally, I suppose. It's a suitable house for a throw-out. Do you think we're going to have you and your Potok keep and a couple of illegitimate kids up on the hill? Don't be bloody silly. You're in your element there, man. You've got a nigger clerk with seven kids at one end and a couple of Sudu drunks at the other. Then you've got these two Eyeties who are putting the marble in the Mosque and soon you're going to have Forbes and his Chadi. They're a cut above you. They're married."

Lydgate could not speak. He had a pain over his heart, a click in his throat, blood in his eyes. "Why, you—" he tried. "You—" Mudd seemed well satisfied. "All right," he said. "You can run along now. Go and finish your unpacking. Though I don't suppose you have much."

"You—"

"Oh, yes," said Mudd. "I nearly forgot. There's one little item of news which may interest you. Lydia's coming back to Africa."

"What?"

"Yes. She wrote about a month ago. She says she's fed up with Sydney and hungers for African moons and palms and what-not. Silly girl. But a nice girl. And a useful girl, too. We're a bit short of typists who know how to spell. So she's going into the Police Department."

"I've been standing up a long time," said Lydgate. "It kills me to ask you, but may I sit down?"

"I wondered why you didn't sit down when you came in, old boy. I thought, well, it's up to you. I thought perhaps you had piles or something."

"I don't think I'd notice them if I had them," said

Lydgate, lowering himself on to a chair. "I seem to have everything else."

"Yes. Well, there it is. We're going to have Mrs. Lydgate and Mr. Lydgate in the same territory again. Just like the old days in Shurga. With certain obvious differences. But those needn't last long, need they?"

"What are you getting at?"

"It would be nice to see the Lydgates happy together again. In a nice little house on the hill. It would sort of clean things up. It's not nice to have government officers slinking about with Potok mistresses and what-not. The U.N.A. doesn't like it. It doesn't go down well with distinguished visitors."

"They don't have to know, do they?"

"They always find out. There are always people who are glad to tell them. And you're not exactly reticent about it."

"I," said Lydgate, standing up again, weary, an old man, "will do as I like. Which means that you'd better keep that bitch out of my way. Because I might do what I want to do. I might do what I should have done years ago. And you won't like that."

"Lydia a bitch? Dear little Lydia? She's a very nice girl. And a very attractive girl. Voluptuous—isn't that the word? And a very kind girl. We shall all be glad to see her again. Well, Frank, I think that's about all. I've got work to do, even if you haven't. Drop in again sometime. It's always pleasant to talk about the old days." Mudd made a great show of examining, with puzzled concentration, a random document from his in-tray.

"Oh, I'll be in again," said Lydgate. "By God, I will. I'll be in with a bloody big chopper. Or perhaps it won't be me. Perhaps it will be somebody with a family history of head-hunting. Good-bye, you jumped-up, short-arsed, big-headed little—"

"Hup!" hiccupped Mudd. "Hup! Hup!" Sebastian Hup, who had evidently been listening outside, came in as Uriah Heep. "Yes, sir," he said, rubbing his hands damply. "At your service, sir. What shall it be my humble pleasure to do for you, sir?" He bowed low, teeth showing in agony, moving his shoulders like one chilled by a Dickensian winter. "If Mr. Lydgate needs a cure for piles, sir," he began to say, "I can recommend—"

"Mr. Lydgate," said Mudd. "Yes, Mr. Lydgate. File Mr. Lydgate away," he ordered.

4

Lydgate sat lit by a lone candle. Terrible shadows moved around him as he ate sardines in olive oil with a tea-spoon. He had more or less dressed for dinner, having blindly found slacks and a shirt in a suit-case. It was too hot for a tie. Besides, he did not know whether Carruthers Chung would expect a tie. He would soon know when Carruthers Chung came to call for him. He had never played bridge at Carruthers Chung's house before.

The beds had dried up again. Electric fire and water had paid his house a brief shy visit at nightfall. Then he had been able to plug his bachelor's refrigerator into the light and been rewarded with a gnat's high buzz and the hope of a drink of cold water. He had also, during the half-hour wet season, been able to fill the square brick container called a *pong*. Unpacking his sheets and unrolling his mattress, fitting up his mosquito-net on the wire-hung wooden frame, he looked forward to lowering himself into that *pong* and washing his bad temper out. But, coming down from the one small bedroom, he found the *pong* less adequately plugged than he had thought, and the water singing into the drains in happy freedom. He had turned on the tap again to hear only a sort of empty-stomach rumble. So he had had to wash in one of his bottles of drinking water. And, during his washing, the light went out and the towel hid in the dark.

Lydgate finished his sardines but still felt hungry. He

crawled to the soap-box of provisions and found a round tin. Squinting at it from various angles of deep shadow, he saw that its name was *Mrs. Hobson's Tip-top Cherry Cake, Made in India*. He felt a sort of poor man's elation on remembering that he had remembered to pack the can-opener in an accessible place. It was, he knew, lying snugly in an angle of the provision-box, wedged in by a jar of salt. Unless that blasted ape had been rummaging round, looking for something destructive. But no, it was there. In his state of nerves, Lydgate whimpered softly with relief. Something had not let him down. Yet.

The tin was unbelievably difficult to open. Sweat glistened in candlelight on the tough metal top. A quarter open, he gave up. His right arm ached as if it had been rowing. He sat down on the termite colony which was a standard-pattern chair and slowly ate the cake with the still oily tea-spoon, digging it further and further in as Mrs. Hobson's creature waned. While he ate he listened to his right-hand neighbours. The walls were thin, and at picture-rail level they became a fret-work through which air and sound were free to leave or enter. The neighbours spoke Italian.

Lydgate could not remember ever having heard or heard of an Italian opera duet for two baritone voices. Wagner, of course, was different. But this, he thought, despite the obvious aesthetic drawback of lack of aggregate range, had a certain charm. There was dynamic differentiation, rhythmic counterpoint, and—that the medium might be exploited to the full—the frequent shuttling of theme from one to another of three languages.

"*Io*—uh? *Iki*—uh? *Me*—uh?" came the angry voice of the son. "*Lavoro*—uh? Work—uh? *Ogni giorno*—uh? Every day—uh? *poro-poro*—uh? And what you do? *Che fa?* Aaaaaah!" There followed a percussion of earthy

Tuscan which Lydgate, whose Spanish helped him only with very slow Italian, could make nothing of, except for *porco sporco*, which he took to mean "dirty pig".

"You speak a English," went the voice of the father. "It a good a practice."

"Aaaaaah! I speak you go to ell."

"You cannot a say that. You not a say 'speak'. You say a 'say'. You say, 'I say you go a to ell'."

"I say you go to ell."

"That a better. I say a you go a to ell. Now I say a you a this. It a right you a work all a day. You a young man. I a your father. Very old a man. I bring a you up. Send you a school a. Now it a right you pay a your father back. You a understand?"

"Non capito."

"Why a you not understand? I speak a very slow. Very clear. I say a you this. If you a want a go out a drink, it a not right. It right you a be a tired. You not a tired, you not a work a ard. And if a you say a want go out a drink, where you get a money? I not give a you a money. Maybe you steal a money. I not a know. I say you a stay in ere a slip. You ave a good a rest work a ard tomorrow."

"Non ancora mangiato."

"All right, you not yet a eat. I not yet a eat too. But you ave breakfast. Big a breakfast. I not ave a breakfast."

"You sleep till arf day."

"You mean a mid day. Mid day. *Mezzo giorno.* I slip till a mid day. That because I an old a man. I come a ome late must a slip late. You understand?"

"Non capito."

"All right. Now I a go a out. You slip a now like a good a boy."

At this moment there was the noise of a car approach-

36

ing, and the silver of headlights shone on Lydgate. Silver oil in a silver sardine-tin. Silver crumbs of Mrs. Hobson. The car stopped, brakes ground dryly, and Carruthers Chung knocked at the door, revealing himself at once as the door swung inward. He wore a tie. Suddenly, as if Carruthers Chung were a thaumaturge, there was a glory of yellow light. Carruthers Chung was wearing a Chinese brocade tie, willow-patterned. Lydgate began to search in his still unpacked suit-case. Carruthers Chung said, "Not velly adequate accommodation. Plobably it is better in the dark." Lydgate found a creased and spotty blue tie and wound it swiftly round his neck like a noose. "We are going to play," said Carruthers Chung. Then for some reason he chuckled.

As they went out they saw a fat squat form hovering round the car. "Ah," it said. "Who is a that? You a going to a town? You give a me a lift, eh?"

"We are going to my house," said Carruthers Chung. "To play," he chuckled. "To make a blidge."

"I go a to Dunia Hotel."

"I can dlop you there."

"*Bravo ragazzo.*" The fat squat man got in at the back. Lydgate sat next to Carruthers Chung.

Lydgate tried to take his mind off things, tried to talk bridge. He was a skilled player, lucky in cards. He wondered what the standard of play was like in Carruthers Chung's circle. He talked of a freak in Juan-les-Pins, of the proper defence to North's bid of seven hearts, of the ruffing by West of the conventional club lead. Carruthers Chung listened with great attention and said:

"West should not luff in case he is over-luffed and lose his tlump tlick."

Lydgate sighed with something like happiness. Tonight might be a good night. Brandy and ginger ale and a little intelligent bridge. There had been such parties in Shurga. His spirits fell as he remembered Lydia, the sweetly pretty smiling face, the plump slim-waisted body like a barrack-room dream. Lydia, too, had been good at bridge. And now the words of Mudd hit him out of the context of insult and cheap sneers. Lydia was coming back to Africa. Lydia Lydgate. What a silly name. Let her come back. They would never meet, even though the town was so small. Her world would be a clubby, partyish, swimming-pooly one. That was over for him. He had an African mistress and two half-breed children and a house appropriate to the status which this ménage conferred. But he felt disquiet, wondering why Lydia had chosen, in her nostalgia for palms and sweat and hot sauces, this particular territory: there were Shurga, Naraka, Kenya, Northern Rhodesia, Uganda crying out for shorthand-machine operatives and touch-typists. She had visited them all; they had been together. Did she honestly think Dunia could offer anything vastly different? They were all the same; all the African territories were the same—lazy villages and Syrian shop-houses and dry open drains and the fatiguing life of club and bar, a shortage of fresh vegetables and mascara and smart cotton frocks and conversation. With appalling clarity Lydgate saw that she wanted *him*. Either that (but after all he was grey and fifty; she thirty-six and with a clean chin-line still, unless the Australian years had started dragging her down, like Lawrence's kangaroo, towards the earth's centre); either that or she was to be used by Mudd as an instrument to torture and humiliate. Mudd still wanted to be a jockey. The horse's name was to be Lydgate—very long odds, no favourite. And, paradoxically, Mudd would pass the post when Lydgate had been well and truly nobbled.

"You a drop a me ere," said the garlic voice from behind.

They were at the public clock where the two main streets crossed. The clock, electrically run, the best that money could buy, had thrown up its hands in despair at the many cuts. It was now always midday or midnight, and that seemed somehow right for a state where there were no half-measures. Kill or be killed, eat or be eaten; high noon or the hour of ghosts and robbers. "From a ere I can a walk." The Dunia Hotel was a hundred yards away. Nando Tasca climbed out, panting. In the street lights he could be seen, in shorts and striped Manila shirt, as a one-time masher of village girls—sharp blue eyes, grey hair that waved, stubborn nose—now run to dancing bouncing blubber, a pregnant belly and woman's breasts, for men at length take on properties of the thing they prey on, and a chin of melting terraces. He waved now and, purposefully walking towards the beer that the British had taught him to relish above wine, presented to the two his broad stripe-clad moving back.

"A Loman Catholic," said Carruthers Chung, "and a velly flivolous man. For that leason I did not invite him to come and play with us."

Lydgate smiled. "You seem to take your bridge very seriously."

"Oh, yes. My blidge parties are a big thing in my life."

Carruthers Chung had an Educational Department house, for he taught in the English school, specialising in what he called 'inductive glamour'. Lydgate was surprised to see the house overspilling with guests. There were Syrians, Creoles, a few Potoks. Lydgate recognised Sebastian Hup on the veranda, talking in great agony to an exquisite young Chinese woman in swathed dragons and gold that flashed from the living-room lights behind. Lydgate had not known that Sebastian Hup was a bridge-player. Lydgate was led in, blinked in the brightness, saw candles ready for the next cut, massed tea-cups, no cards, no tables. Carruthers Chung introduced him to no one. Lydgate was puzzled. But almost at once the guests— some lovely girls among them—began to draw together, taking chairs all round the walls of the bare living-room, smiling at Lydgate encouragingly as they passed him. Lydgate smiled uneasily back. And then Carruthers Chung spoke He stood by the living-room door, his glasses filled with light, hands clasped easily before him, his voice amicable but strangely formal.

"We are all velly pleased to see a new fliend, a new comlade with us this evening. I lefer to Mr. Lydgate, who will be easily lecognised by evelybody plesent, for he is the only Eulopean." There were more smiles of encouragement for Lydgate, and some smiles of sweet pity as well, as for the only leper present. "Mr. Lydgate has been blought here tonight on false pletences. There was laughter, but it was obviously the laughter appropriate to an old joke. Lydgate looked furtively behind him but saw that the door on to the veranda was closed, was apparently guarded, moreover, by two seraphically happy negro youths. "He is a blidge player—" Very large laughter came now. "—and, as a blidge player, he will appleciate a velly blief lésumé of the oligin of our movement. It oliginated, as evelybody will lemember, in leal—or what Mr. Lydgate will, in his plesent stage of development, call leal—blidge parties. When I was a younger man I was addicted to blidge. Blidge was my opium. And, as some will lemember, I was for a long time blidge collespondent to a syndicate of African newspapers. But, one night, after a bid of five no tlumps, I thought I heard a voice saying: 'Play, not play. If you want a blidge, let it be a blidge flom earth to heaven. Let your blidge parties build leal blidges flom the tempolal to the eternal.' And that velly night I made a start. And, ever since that night, many of our new lecluits have come flom the blidge-players of this town, the thlowers-away of plecious time. Now they are ledeeming the time, now they are pontiffs or blidge-builders, and the blidge they help to build gets nealer and nealer to the Thlone of Glace." Lydgate began to sweat heavily.

"We believe not only in playing, but in pulification by confession. Mr. Lydgate must be assured that he is among fliends, not stlangers. Blothers and sisters in God, as we all are, cannot be stlangers. We will give Mr. Lydgate five minutes in which to think about his tlansglessions, and then we shall all give him a sympathetic healing. He will shed his sins in the plesence of his fliends and, by God's glace, be pulified. We will sing one hymn while our fliend and blother thinks about his sins." Everybody stood up, all except Lydgate to sing, Lydgate to cry out:

"No! This isn't fair! I've been brought here under false pretences." Everybody laughed in a friendly way. Carruthers Chung smiled and said:

"That is what I said. You have been blought here under false pletences."

"But I didn't come here to confess my sins. I came here for a night's bridge. It's not fair."

"Knightsbridge," whispered a charming girl near to him. "That is on the Piccadilly Line. I went to the London School of Economics."

"You accepted my invitation to come and play," said Carruthers Chung.

"Play, not pray," said Lydgate. "They're two different words."

Carruthers Chung made a delicate shrugging movement. "To me they sound velly much alike. They are almost the same word."

41

"Anyway, I'm going," said Lydgate, shaking. "This is not my idea of a jolly evening."

Everybody laughed again, and Lydgate began to feel a fool. Obviously, the jolliest evening imaginable was one devoted to sin in action, and, if action were not possible, reminiscence could be a good second-best. But not reminiscence in public. Although, thought Lydgate, by God, I could make them sit up, I could tell them a few things. Yet he was angry, his fingers disappointed of the feel of cards, his palate of the taste of accompanying cigarettes and brandy. The charming girl from the London School of Economics (Euro-African, guessed Lydgate) whispered:

"Don't go. Please don't go. You will spoil the evening."

"Oh, but look here," began Lydgate. Then all the lights went out.

"Oh," said the girl. "It's dark, I'm frightened of the dark."

"Where are you?" said Lydgate, the excitement of a fifty-year-old stirring in his arteries. But his groping hands encountered only the well-filled jacket of an aromatic male. The man giggled. Then candles were lighted and the room was full of shadows, huge, moving, like a procession of sins.

"Now," said Carruthers Chung, "let us laise our voices in a blief hymn."

"No, no!" called Lydgate. "I refuse to think about my sins. I haven't got any sins. It's the others who've sinned against me, not me against them. It's not fair, I tell you."

"More sinned against than sinning," nodded an intellectual-looking Potok.

"As a man sows," said Carruthers Chung, "so shall he leap. Now a hymn."

The congregation sang, in thin and thick voices:

"We will build a bridge to heaven,
Build in earnest, not in play;
Night and morning, noon and even,
We will watch and we will pray."

Carruthers Chung's voice, louder than the rest, insisted
on the homophonic nature of the even rhyming words.
Lydgate said, "I'm going. Thank you, thank you, everybody. It's been very pleasant. I hope we'll meet again."
He made for the veranda door. He felt, as he moved, that
there was a certain devotional quality about his valedic-
tion; it was even apt for a death-bed. He began to shake
again and he felt tears come into his eyes.

But already the hymn was over. Bright eyes in candle-
shine were expectant. "Sit down, please," said Carruthers
Chung. "Come forward, blother Lydgate. Come forward,
the Plompter." Lydgate stood impotent, blocked by the
two youths who, on examination, seemed to have sizeable
muscles inside their shirts. Sebastian Hup came forward
with Lydgate's confidential file.

"Look here," said Lydgate. "I'll say this. I don't want
to seem boorish. I think you're probably doing something
quite valuable in having these religious meetings. I'm not
a religious man myself, but I do believe in sin. I mean,
you can't live very long in a place like Africa without
coming to the conclusion that sin really exists. But I don't
think I've really anything to say about my own sins. I've
done my best all the way along, and I don't think I've
really let anybody down. It's always other people who've
let me down. I've been let down in my work, and I've been
let down in my private life. I've worked hard, but I've
never made any money——"

"That," said Carruthers Chung, "is the sulest sign of
sin."

43

"I've been let down by two wives. One after the other," he added. "And I never did them any harm."

"How do you know?" asked Carruthers Chung.

"In Nairobi," said Sebastian Hup, "you were married to a Miss Featherstone. She left you after six months. There must have been a good reason for that." He frowned in pain.

"Mind your own blasted business," said Lydgate. He began to shout. "What have my private affairs to do with any of you? I want to live my own life, that's all. People won't leave me alone. I want to be left alone. I want to be left to do what I want to do."

There was silence. Carruthers Chung said, "I think Mr. Lydgate has been velly flank. One of the flankest confessions we have ever heard. The question is, does he lepent? Does he see the light?"

At that moment, of course, the electric light should have flashed back to life. But it did not. The romantic sinful shadows still jostled hugely.

"I've nothing to repent of," said Lydgate. "Nothing at all. And now I'm going."

After the good-byes, which were cordial and sympathetic, Lydgate went out, standing on the veranda for an instant while he cooled down. He heard Carruthers Chung introduce the night's speaker—a Mr. Alfred, who was to talk about the Book of Revelations, the mark of the beast—666—and the curious fact that that was the number of the U.N. Adviser's car. Lydgate began to walk to the Kool Kaffi, angrily thirsty. Everybody and everything let him down.

5

The lamps of the town burst into song again (how long a song it would be, who yet could tell?) as Lydgate approached the Kool Kaffi. Its afternoon clientèle had long departed, leaving the fixed and comfortless bar-stools to a larger variety of accents, colours and beverages. The Australian road-men had taken their jolly swag of beer to their houses on the hill, an estate they called Little Australia. These houses had official unromantic names like PWD 157 and RSMQ 3, but the Australians had re-christened them straight out of Lawrence's *Kangaroo*: Knot-tu-wurri; Sleepitoff; The Homestead; Lyedown; Eezistreet. In their select colony, having inherited the pioneer tradition of early hours on week-nights, they would now be sleeping. Only one Australian, like an enharmonic chord, bridged the gap between noon and evening: Forbes of Marmion wore the same clothes, nursed the same children, drank at the same table as at lunch-time. His wife, however, had departed. He called over to Lydgate, eyes bright under the Aussie hat:

"Moving in tomorrow, old man. We're going to be nyebours, Lyddy." The golden-haired child cried loudly, trailer of forthcoming attractions.

The bar looked like the bar of Crewe station on a Sunday: the eccentric faces and talents of a low-grade touring company were ranged, the eternal wanderers, the nomads erecting nightly tents of drink—Fredericks, a thin and miniature stage colonel with a Liverpool voice, something to do with ships' stores, with a wife in Nairobi, medals for ballroom-dancing in Bootle, the desperate corn of the amateur entertainer on his lips, four thousand miles from home and wondering why; Crawshay-Davies and his wife—the wife half-Mongolian, half-German, over six feet tall, the exposure from foot to thigh in the cheongsam overfacing like an English Sunday dinner, Crawshay-Davies, plump, short, in schoolmaster's glasses, overborne and giggling; Frankie the Sudu epicene, between two worlds, growing his hair for a show for the Caliph's birthday, string-bag beside him, fingering a glass of mother's ruin; Patrick Ong, a straight cross of Irish and Chinese, on whisky, waiting to come up to the boil; Nando Tasca. Lydgate stood next to Nando Tasca. Nando Tasca said:

"I thought you a go a play a bridge."

"So did I. I thought you were going to the Dunia Hotel."

"I go a there. All beer become a very warm. No more a beer in a fridge. I come a ere."

Lydgate ordered brandy. "Tell me," he said, still irritated and disturbed, "are you what you might call a religious man?"

"What a you mean, a *religioso*? I a good a Catholic like all a Italian. Religion I a not think a much about. Not a need. God a take a care of all. I not a go a mass long time. I not a go a confession long time. God not a care. All that a not a matter to God. To be a good a man enough a for God." He drank his beer with a kind of panting complacency.

"What do you mean—to be a good man?" There was a sort of toothache-nagging in Lydgate's soul.

"Not a do a arm. Try a be good to a wife. Be good a to a son." He thought an instant and amended: "If a son a good to a you."

"I've had two wives," said Lydgate, "and both of them left me. Why?"

"Two wife not a possible in a Catholic a Church," said Nando Tasca. "One a wife a only. You ave a that one a wife for a always. Wife cannot a leave you." He drank a little, thinking. "Only thing is a leave a wife. I leave a Italy ten year ago, go to a Libya, to a Nigeria, many other a place in a Africa. In a Africa always a want good a man work a marble. I send a money ome when I ave a money. I still a good a usband." He thought further, drank further. "I not a think a much of a these things before," he confessed. "Ere I be a very good usband. Ere a no a girls. Ere *bordello* not a allowed. Very a strict. Ere I a not a slip one time even with a woman. True," he admitted, "I go a visit a village. Stay a night. In a village you *must* a slip with a woman. That a polite. *Scortese* a refuse. No good a say, 'I good a Catholic, I ave a wife in Italy, will not a slip.' They a very annoyed, bring a knife, cut off a ead. I go to a village many a times. But in a Benghazi, in a Tripoli very a different. In a Tripoli I ave a girl. She a arf Arab arf Chadi. I live a with a er. That all a right because I a there long time. It a wrong not ave a woman. It not a nature. I not commit a sin. *Non ho peccato*." He placed a fat peasant's hand across his sternum. "I cannot be a with a wife, so I ave a girl. I do a no a wrong. But," said Nando Tasca, "my son like a this girl. He thinks he very young, very a andsome. He think she will ave a im. But no, she know a best. She ave a me. I old man, but she ave a me. Now my son, e do a wrong. E do a wrong two times. E do a wrong because he want what a is father want. E do a wrong because e want a slip

47

with a woman and e not a married. E not a married, a not a know what e a miss. There a no need for im want a woman. It very dangerous me not a ave a woman, very bad for a ealth. So e do wrong two times, I do no a wrong at all. I do a right to a this a woman. I send money every month, one undred, one undred and fifty, two undred. What I a can afford. I bring a my son from Italy to work. E see strange a countries, very good education for a im. It not right e ave wages as a well. I draw is a wages from Tripoli, I send a some of is a wages to this a girl. I do a right all a time. So I a *religioso* man." He stopped, well satisfied. Lydgate thought that he deserved more beer, so he bought him a bottle. *"Tante grazie,"* said Nando Tasca. *"Salute."*

"The first one," said Lydgate, "left me after a few months. Mind you, I was glad to see her go. I hated the sight of her. And I hated the sight of the second one, too. But there might have been something wrong with me." He spoke now to the refrigerator behind the bar. "What is wrong with me?" he asked.

"Perhaps you not a slip with a them right," suggested Nando Tasca. "Sometimes a very *difficile*. Englishman not a always a very good in a bed."

"No, no, no," said Lydgate. "It wasn't that. It's tied up with everything, I think. I think it's a question of responsibility. Am I," he asked the refrigerator, "irresponsible?" The refrigerator, drinking its fill of temporary power, hummed loudly in answer.

"A man a get tired," said Nando Tasca. "A man a want a change. A man a want to live a own life. A woman *differente*."

"Lyddy, old man," said Forbes of Marmion; he stood behind Lydgate somewhat shyly, having left the children to crawl about under the table. "Old man, I've wanted to ask you one or two things for a long time. Come and sit down and I'll buy you a drink."

"If it's advice you want," said Lydgate, "advice about your marriage——"

"How did you know it was that, old man?" asked Forbes in wonder.

"—I can't give it. I can't give myself advice. I can't straighten out my own affairs."

"Come and sit down, old man, just for a minute," pleaded Forbes.

Lydgate, resigned, went with Forbes to the table. Its top was full of squashed cream-cake, peanut-shells, beer and lemonade slops, cigarette-butts that, lying in liquid, had opened up like flowers. Forbes's own child, golden and dirty, came to Lydgate as to Daddy, pounding with sticky fists on his knees. "What will you have, Lyddy, old man?" asked Forbes.

The Sino-Irishman or Hibernico-Chinese called Patrick Ong began to play the part of a drunken stage Mick, calling:

"Sure, and I'll murdher the spalpeens. Where are they till Oi get at them?" All around, as the drink warmed, the enemies were appearing, peering from behind curtains, leaning out from a limb of the turning ceiling-fan, making long noses, sneering. Lydgate's own enemy passed through from a side entrance to the inner dining-room, jockey-rolling to a collar-and-tied dinner with, Lydgate saw, the State Irrigation Officer and the State Architect and their wives. Fredericks, still by the bar, did a few steps of a soft-shoe shuffle. Sadly, with regret. Crawshay-Davies giggled.

"Now then, old man," said Forbes, "you know what it's about, because you've got the sime trouble yourself. The point is that I'm going back home in three months' time, and then what do I do with her? I mean, it's been all right

49

here, in a wy, but it's different back home. I mean, what would my mum and dad sy if I kime back with an abo wife and a couple of kids? I never told them, see, that I'd got married. But I want to do the right thing by the missis, you see, and I've been racking my blessed brine about it. I mean, what would you do, old man?"

"It depends how you feel about her, doesn't it? If you thought the world about her, you'd put up with anything, wouldn't you, just to have her with you all the time? And the kids, of course," added Lydgate, as he gently pulled a child's questing finger away from his fly.

"Yes, there's the kids too, old man. And the wife's not a bad kiddy, really. But I don't feel I can tike her back somehow, and the kids, you know. The Austrylian Government, anywy, is very sticky about passports. I mean, wife or no wife, it doesn't mike any difference to them. They're very sticky about letting niggers and Indians and suchlike into the country. It's a white country, you see, the wy thy see it."

"You could get another contract here, perhaps."

"Thy won't wear me, old man. The other Aussies are a bit crook about my getting married like I did, see, and getting another contract on road-work is right up to the Aussies."

"Well, you could leave the wife and the kids here and send them money from home."

Forbes writhed and bit his lip several times. "It's a bit of a wiste, isn't it?" he said. "I shan't be seeing them agyne, and I'm just sending money for nothing. And I don't know whether I'll be ible to earn enough, you see."

"Well." Lydgate was losing interest. "Well, you'll have to get a divorce somehow. If she starts going back to her old trade, for instance, you'll have plenty of grounds for a divorce."

"What do you mean, old man, by her old tride?"

Lydgate stared. "Surely you know? I thought you knew."

"If you mean what I think you mean, old man, I'd sy that mikes me go a bit crook. When she kime to me she was looking for a job, see. She'd had a good job, she said, witing on tibles in some plice or other, and this Hup treated her very bad, forcing her as you might sy, and this kid was no fault of hers. And she's never done anything that you might sy is bad. She sties in the house with the kids or comes out with me now and again, a real good kiddy."

"Where is she now, then?"

"She's gone to do a bit of shopping for herself. She always does when we come in, you see, because I only get the Land Rover twice a week, and our house is nine miles up the road. It's not easy for the poor kiddy. We can get rice and that from the village near the house, but she likes to look at a few frocks and buy a bit of lipstick. She works miracles, she does, with the housekeeping money. Never asks for an extra penny, that kiddy doesn't. A real siver, she is. You've no idea how much she's been ible to tuck awy."

"Perhaps she'll do even better when you're living nearer the town."

"Yes. A real good kiddy. It's a pity I can't tike her back to Austrylia."

Nando Tasca had started making trouble. "Somebody ere at a the bar take a my watch," he accused. "I come a out with a my watch on a my wrist. A watch a with a *luminoso* dial. Now I look at a the time, and my watch is a not there any more. Who take a it, I want a to know."

Frankie the Sudu protested as the sharp accusing eyes swivelled in his direction. "You horrible old man," he said. "I have a *perfectly* good watch of my own, thank you." He had learned excellent English from a Christian Brothers' school in Shurga. "I can get as many watches as I like." Patrick Ong said, "Who's he's saying's after taking it, then? He's nothing but an old rat-catcher and fornicator." Mrs. Crawshay-Davies boomed, and Mr. Crawshay-Davies simpered, that they knew nothing of his watch. Fredericks said, "Turn it up, Tony boy. Everybody's looking at you."

"It a present from a young lady in a Tripoli. She give it a me before I come ere. I wish now I never a come a ere. Too many thiefs. Mr. Lydagate, ave a you my watch?"

"No," said Lydgate.

"Everybody say they not a ave a my watch. Too many a thiefs and too many a liars. *Ladroni*," he said. *"Farabutti."*

"Perhaps Paolo's hocked it," suggested Lydgate.

"E not a dare. E not a dare a steal from a is father. Other thing e do, a yes. Steal e not a dare. I know a my son. You not a know a im."

A sudden black-out and a rush for candles. Nando Tasca said, "I ave a my fists a ready. Anybody want a come steal a anything more in a the dark, I a ready for im."

6

Paolo Tasca, left all alone in the house, marched about in the brief summer of electric light, his arms flexed like those of a stage strong man, marched about as to "The Entry of the Gladiators", saying "Aaaah" occasionally, occasionally deliberately colliding with a piece of furniture, then throwing the piece of furniture to one side, saying "Aaaah" as the orchestra orchestrated the effect with cymbals and Chinese blocks. He raised his muscled arms above his head, filled his chest to maximum, showed the audience his handsome Italian teeth. "Aaaah." He marched about on big feet, bending too much at his bare brown knees, hearing the circus brass in his head, Paolo Tasca, *il tigre Italiano*, who would take on all comers, five falls at all-in wrestling, bare-fist boxing or with the gloves. A man entered the ring, a fat man of fifty, with peasant's strength congealed to boozer's fat. The whispers went around: "It is his father. It is father and son. The father has done him great wrong. How? Yes, yes, great wrong. It is not to be talked about. What, you say unfair? Unfair for the son to strike his father? An unfilial act, you say? Never. Consider but the harm the fat one has done. He says he is an old man, but he is still young enough. You will see." Paolo Tasca, with a clenched tigerish "Aaaaah," squared up to the trembling fat. The trembling fat said, "I a sorry. I not a know you so a strong. I not a see your a muscle before. You a train every a

53

evening and I not a know. I not a see you with no shirt since you a little baby. I sorry I make a challenge. I make a public apology." Paolo led with his left, followed with a sharp uppercut with his right, peppered the bewildered gross body with an ammunition-belt full of blows, slammed the many chins with a crack of his left again, upped with his right, laid the body low on the canvas, which shook seismically. Then he changed to all-in wrestling, raising with ease the supine carcase by its stumps of legs, swinging it round and round by the ankles. Round and round and round. The side-drum throbbed in violent crescendo. In vertigo Paolo swung to his limit, and then: "Aaaaah." The carcase swung away into air, over the heads of the dumbfounded audience, hit and burst the canvas roof, went spinning off with a loud and terrified cry into the blue night. "He is avenged. The son is avenged. The father has got his deserts. But what strength. What virile beauty. Imagine"—(and now the audience was all female)—"imagine having that magnificent body to oneself. Such ecstasy." Paolo entertained smugly for five minutes or so a wealth of voluptuous images. He had once seen Gina Lollobrigida when on holiday in Rome. Anna Magnani had once sent him a signed photograph. "Aaaah." Paolo lay back in a chair for an instant with his eyes closed. Then he came to and began to cry very gently. He was an exile. He was unloved. He was hungry.

He began to pace the room again. There was nothing in the house but water, and that was in the tap, sun-hot, for there was no ice-box. Nay, there was not even tap-water at this hour. Paolo felt great self-pity. His tongue lolled and he panted. It was a desert march. mile after burning mile. Laughing cruelly, the gross cruel sergeant, his father, uncorked his water-bottle. "You swine," muttered

54

the ranks, "the selfish swine." "That," said Paolo thickly, "is my father. You watch. I am not afraid, even if you are. I will cut the swine's throat. Watch." He stuck him like a swine with his clasp-knife, blood stained the desert, the greasy hulk was left for the sand-drift to cover. "Give water to this man. He is dying. His need is very great." The dying man was now Paolo. Dying, unloved, friendless, hungry, tortured with thirst, in a strange place, thousands of miles from civilisation. There was a small cemetery by the tiny Catholic church here in Dunia Town. He would be buried there. Visitors would ask, "Who was this Italian who died so far from his native land?" Their hosts, handing round bottles of beer, would reply, "Ah, sad, very sad. He was a brilliant young man, *molto intelligente*, the most skilful marble-cutter in Africa. He died of starvation. Yes, starvation. It is incredible, in this year of Our Lord, but it is, God help us, true. His father, through jealousy of his youth, looks and superior potency, starved him to death. His father starved everybody to death. His son in Dunia, his wife and daughter in Viareggio, Italy. But he did not starve his Tripoli whore, oh no. Her he fattened with oily curries, plumped with Export Stout. Ah yes, in his unwholesome and unseasonable lust he did." And now it was the Sovereign Pontiff himself damning Nando Tasca, solemnly cutting him off from the body of the Church like a withered twig. No, not a withered twig. If there was anything that Nando Tasca did not resemble, it was a withered twig. *"Hic homo,"* said Pope Paolo, whose Latin was somewhat shaky, *"excommunicandus est. Aaaaaah. Hic homo est homo molto cattivo."* "Ere," said Pope Paolo in English as shaky, "is your passport. Your passport to Ell. Aaaaaah." Paolo became, in a rapid and irreverent transition, a devil from the *Inferno* he had had to read at school, darting here and there with a trident, pricking the swollen corpse of his father like a sausage. At the thought of one of the hot grilled sausages he had eaten (*il* breakfast *inglese*) on the Lloyd Triestino ship from Genoa, Paolo began to sob quietly again. He must eat. "*Io devo mangiare,*" he told a house lizard running up the wall. The lizard scuttled to safety. "Aaaaah," said Paolo, remembering that they had a new neighbour, remembering to have seen the swollen and unhinged door that would not shut. "*Il cibo.*" Food, food. Paolo tore, with his mind's teeth, at corned-beef tins, cracked the metal open like nut-shells. He lapped sardines and wallowed in butter, drank off pickle-jars and crammed loaves into his mouth. He marched off, howling like a cat, to Lydgate's house, left right, left right, left wheel, left right, left right, left wheel, door open, left right, left right, halt. Light on. Halted, he peered about him, smelling the smell of another man's house, though so like their own in its squalor, unlike only in the greater quantity of cases and boxes. And there, by the tiny humming ice-box, was a box of tins. "Aaaaah." First, he was athirst. He opened the refrigerator and drank cold water, eyes closed. Then he seized on a half-pound slab of butter and ate it like ice-cream. Then the light went out. In the dark, in the dark. A blinded Samson. His father was at the power-station, pulling, with fiendish laughter, at the huge extinguishing lever. *Farabutto.* Blind Paolo groped floorwards, met a slim round tin in the food-box, opened it eagerly and licked the smooth butter-like content. His father was at work troll-like, in the box. His father had put into his hand a tin of boot-polish.

In bitter agony Paolo polished his tongue against his hard palate, dancing in the dark house of another man. He took blind water from the blind refrigerator, drinking and moaning. Then, afraid, he crammed a dark square

shape from the box into his pocket and ran, falling over
things, out of the tiny black house. Right wheel. Double,
double, double. Right wheel. He was home. "Home," he
sobbed, "home, home." Ah, the irony. In the dark, so far
from home. In the distance a skull xylophone began to
play, over and over, a scale of six notes—D, C sharp, B flat,
A, G, E—over and over and over. He thought of the
mad scene of *Lucia di Lammermoor*. Then, in the black-
ness, he saw something small, a dim round glow-worm
mocking him. It was his father, his father as a mocking
glow-worm. But nay. He approached it on tip-toe. It had
numbers all round, which glow-worms did not have. It
had two tiny hands. It was his father's wrist-watch, which
his father, in haste to go out and booze, had forgotten
"Aaaaah." In the dark he felt a new voluptuousness enter
his wronged body. Break it, crack it, kill it, still its mean
little ticking heart, seize it by the strap and send it flying
against the wall, to fall in dwarfish slivers of glass and bits
of useless spring and wheel and ratchet. Do that thing,
Paolo, in revenge. But no, what is the use? His father does
not need to know the time. He has no appointments,
except for beer and sleep, and for these there are no fixed
seasons. Work he does not. Aaaaah. Sell it, Paolo, sell it
and see if you can buy—See if you can buy——

Very vividly in the dark the lost body of Francesca (yes,
yes, he knew, he was not ignorant, but her other name had
been Croce, not da Rimini) swam, very substantial, into
his boxer's arms. That day they had been reading together
a comic paper, listening to the *organo* Hammond on the
radio, and the words of the tune they both knew, full of
stretti, stretti, and kisses and perfume and love came into
their mouths, and then mouths came together, and then
bodies, *stretti, stretti.* Aaaah. The memory of the substantial furniture-maker's daughter's arms, the fine dark

57

moustache, the mingled spittles. The following nights of stolen love, *al fresco*, among the empty wine-bottles in the field by the *albergo*. And other memories: fat Anna, Bice with the squint, Maria, Isabella. And on the Lloyd Tries-tino boat the married woman. And once in Tripoli. But his father, aaaah, his father had in Benghazi and also in Shurga and Naraka and Asmara and other barbarous places done it. The libidinous one, the greedy, the gross and beer-stinking and lustful fat-dripping goat of a one.

Paolo, still with the dark square shape in his pocket, with the watch, wet from his father's sweat, ticking and glowing on his wrist, Paolo marched towards the town. Left right, left right. See me here now, in the dark, a poor Italian boy, walking lonely in a strange land. From certain houses came the blessed light of candles. Paolo the lacy altar-boy held a candle, innocent and undefiled. Now he was no longer innocent. His father had killed his trust, his innocence, violated his heart of piety. All his sins be on his father's fat goatish back, gross and strong for any such burden But he hoped that, in the town, he would not meet his father.

Suddenly all the lights went on for Paolo, the lights of streets and houses, the high sodium lights of the main road. He bowed from side to side, smiling with good Tuscan teeth. A rat-tailed Potok stared with suspicious eyes, and Paolo bowed more regally. Then he speeded his pace along the empty road. That was unfortunate; he had not noticed that lone man; that man would think him mad. Paolo, approaching the town, began to see more people. He made a grimace at three young Syrian girls who chattered near the Syrian Traders' Society's badmin-ton court, but they would have none of him. They giggled at his bare brown knees, from which he walked. He smiled soulfully at a black woman in a gold gown, noticing too late that her black man was with her. The black man made a fist, scowling, at Paolo. Paolo bowed and bowed, smiling, bowing, putting out finny hands in deprecation of his mistake. Arriving, in a mild mist of sweat, at the moon-face of the stopped town clock, he paused, wondering. Then, yes, yes, he remembered there were shops ever open on the street where he took his midday meal, the meal that was breakfast as well as lunch, so that his father could casuistically call one meal two and say that he, a growing boy, ate well. He could sell the watch at one of these shops full of of gold. He would get, perhaps, twenty bucks. A lot of money.

"*Buona sera,*" he said to the shopman. "This I will sell." The shopman looked at the watch with the twitched nose of a bad smell, shook it and wound it soundly. "Not good," he said. "Very cheap."

Paolo felt at first a kind of joy. He nearly said to the shopman, in some language to be decided on when his mouth opened, "Yes, it is cheap. I always knew it was cheap, but my father said it had cost many hundreds of bucks. Now we have expert confirmation of its real value. And also of the real value of the regard in which this Tripoli whore holds my father." But he said instead, "Cheap, uh? No, no, very expense. I know."

"How much you want?"

"Fifty." Paolo unclenched both hands five rapid times. The shopman laughed in Syrian scorn. "Ten."

"Thirty." Both races met on this—a bargaining zest which made the English blush to consider and their salaries go nowhere. "You try bloody rob me. Thirty I want." Paolo was not really trying to be offensive: he genuinely believed that, about certain English words, a red qualifier or modifier span like a·satellite.

"Ten I give. It is not worth ten. But ten I give."

"Twenty. I speak you bloody robber."

"Fifteen."

Paolo sighed like a busy man with little time to argue. "Fifteen I take. But I know you bloody rob." The shopman counted fifteen torn pictures of the Caliph and gave them to Paolo. Paolo nearly cried. He had never had so much money before. He said, *"Tante grazie."* The shopman did not say, *"Prego."* That was his Syrian ignorance. Paolo went out trembling, to look for a woman.

Now the State of Dunia was exceptional in possessing no professional body-sellers. This was because the Caliph did not allow polygamy and frowned on divorce. Hence there were no women to be thrown on the streets. The black and beautiful animists who lived out of the towns practised free love in their villages; the Europeans and Australians carried on their suburban week-end rites, based on a scheme of temporary marital exchange, in their distant bungalows; the Chinese and Syrians sold everything except the flesh of their daughters. Occasionally a foreign prostitute would find a sponsor in Dunia and creep in through a hole in the immigration laws. But Dunia on the whole was remarkably chaste, and waste male energy had to be used up in other vices. So the hungry Paolo, moaning through the back-streets like Stephen Dedalus, thinking in terms of a loose and human Catholic society, became further frustrated. His father had told him that, if he were not to suffer thus, he must throw all his strength into the marble-cutting machine, working like two men, but Paolo knew that his father, as well as being a pig, a hypocrite, a lecher, a tyrant, a drunkard, a wife-and-daughter-and-son starver and a bloody robber, was also a liar. But Paolo had never been taught that vicious-circle syllogism whose major premise quotes King Solomon as saying that all men are liars; whatever his father said, the

opposite must be true. So he went on, moaning, prize-
fighter's arms held out slightly at the sides, walking from
his knees, through the few streets of Dunia Town, wondering why hips did not wag at him in the cigarette-smoke
of lighted doorways, why perfumed bosoms did not sail out
at him from the dark.

At length, weary, he came to the Dunia Hotel, and
paused a moment outside its entrance. In the lighted
window of the restaurant he saw cakes and dried fish-strips.
He would buy himself a little cake: the butter he had eaten
would be glad of it. His father, having said that he was
going to meet a man in the Dunia Hotel, would undoubt-
edly be drinking with a woman in the Kool Kaffi. Where,
wondered Paolo bitterly, did he find these women? He need
not fear that he would meet his father. So Paolo went in
and bought his little cake, beating the man down automatically from two decems to one (ten decems to one
buck; to one buck two hundred lire). He stood and watched
the eaters sadly, sadly eating his little cake standing. Then,
being at rest, he felt his bladder full of Lydgate's cold
water, so he passed through to the hotel's vestibule. Behind the reception desk sat the under-manager, George
Lim, an intense studious thin man with glasses and
stretched parchment skin. Paolo said, pointing upstairs,
"My fader come?"

George Lim said, "Elsewhere he is drinking. He is sailing on a sea of drink in some other haven. You know the
line of your great poet Leopardi? 'E dolce naufragar in
questo mare.'" Paolo nodded, his goat's mouth open. "He
will be shipwrecked some day but he will find the ship-
wreck sweet," said George Lim. "Shipwrecked in a sea
of"—(he laughed at the paradox)—"Lighthouse Beer."
Paolo looked frightened and went upstairs.

At the bar upstairs nobody drank. At a table there were

61

some workmen teaching a large monkey how to take orange crush from a glass. The ape carried under its arm a picture, though now much mauled, of Lydgate and his New Guinea friends. Paolo passed on, turned left to the corridor where the lavatories were, and saw a thing which made his heart jump with excitement. A bedroom door was open, and an affectionate leave-taking was in progress between a man whose face was familiar to Paolo (a man whose name, he now remembered, was not unlike a hiccough) and a woman he knew to be the Chadi wife of an Australian. The woman wore an alphabet-patterned frock. She had the domed forehead of a milk-chocolate Mary Tudor, and her great pouting lips gave the man a kiss in which, on both sides, buck teeth were rattlingly involved. The man saw Paolo first. He broke off, lips moist in the corridor light, looked surprised, then fearful, then ingratiating. "My sister," he said, smiling falsely. "I kiss my sister good-bye." To Paolo, who understood the words, shock came to perch on excitement. Then the man went back into the room and shut the door. The Chadi woman stood looking at Paolo, holding in her right fist a small bunch of currency notes, her brown eyes doubtful. Paolo looked at her, not knowing what to say, not knowing what language to use to say what he had to say, when he knew what he would say, in. He knew one word of Chadi—*"Proh"*, meaning "hot". So he said, wiping his brow with his hand. *"Proh."*

She agreed, doubtfully. Then she stuffed the money in her handbag. Paolo pulled out his fistful of wealth, saying in Sudu, "I have money also." A picture of the Caliph floated down to the corridor linoleum. The tiny face looked disapprovingly up, between them, the head of the head of the faithful. Paolo picked him from the floor and said, "You come with me, uh?" to the Chadi faithless wife. She lifted her Tudor face in disdain and began to walk down the corridor towards the back exit of the hotel. Paolo began eagerly to follow. Then he remembered his bladder. "I come at once," he said. "Excuse." He rushed into the Gentlemen's, performed with difficulty—because of a certain ambiguity of organic function—the task of voiding Lydgate's water, and came out again. He ran down the corridor and met the Chadi lady at the foot of the stairs. He said again, breathlessly, "You come with me, uh?" She said, in fair Sudu with a sort of hot-potato accent:

"I go to meet my husband. I am late."

Peasant unscrupulousness scratched with dirty nails at the white shirt (his only white shirt) of chivalry. He said, "Perhaps I come too. I tell your husband what I see." Then, seeing the materials of shock and horror begin, with water, to be stirred in her face, he relented with haste, saying, "It is only a joke. I will say nothing." For people will occasionally do things out of gratitude, though less frequently than out of fear, if they will not do them for money. The Chadi lady, still in fair Sudu, gave Paolo a longer speech, most of which he understood. "It is Max Hup," she seemed to say. "I live with him before and have a child of him. Only him I see when he comes from Shurga where he works. Other men now never. I am a good wife to my husband. And," she added, "to Max Hup."

"Aaaah," said Paolo, nodding in approval. "Because you have a child by him. That is right. That is good. We should not," he moralised, and here the simple language nearly burst at the seams, "we should not ignore either the father or the mother of our children. If, of course, we can be sure they are our own. Too many take the pleasure but are unwilling to take the——" He cast round wildly for the Sudu word for responsibility but could not find it.

"Like my father," he said. His father was a gift for any moralist.

"And he is going away," said the Chadi lady. "He is going to Zanzibar. There he has wife and children. He has wife and children also in Jibuti." She began, very quietly, to cry. Paolo took from his left-hand pocket, where there was still also a square hard tin, a somewhat dirty handkerchief. Tonight he would have to wash it so that it might be ready for the morning. He gave this handkerchief to the crying lady. She wiped her eyes and then, looking at the handkerchief, said, "You have nobody to wash for you."

"I do the washing," said Paolo, "for me and my father. I do it on Sundays, when there is no work in the Mosque, and iron it on Monday night. My father bought me an iron," he added, grudgingly. "He also," he super-added, "buys me soap-powder. Little else he buys for me," he concluded.

"I must go now to my husband," said the Chadi lady, with fresh urgency. They were standing in the little dark vestibule at the foot of the furtive stairs. She fumbled in her bag for the lipstick and powder she should have bought but had instead been given by Maximilian Hup. "He is waiting for me in the Kool Kaffi Bar and Restaurant."

"What do I call you?" asked Paolo romantically. "For we must meet again."

"They call me Eileen," she said, "but my name is uncertain."

"Uncertain," said Paolo uncertainly. "That is a beautiful name."

"No, no," she said. "Nobody was ever very sure about names in our family. Sometimes I was called Seven and sometimes I was called Eight. They could not remember how many children there had been. And Max"—(she began to sniffle)—"Max called me Eileen because, he said, it was his mother's name. So now I am Eileen to the world."

Paolo was charmed by this little speech. He made a short chivalrous one of his own. "If ever," he said gallantly, "you go back to your former occupation, I should be happy to be one of your clients." He bowed slightly.

"My life is very dull," she said, "so far from the town. But tomorrow we shall be moving nearer. Now I must go to the Kool Kaffi Bar and Restaurant." Suddenly, as a sort of earnest of her forthcoming re-establishment of contact with a more sophisticated world, she broke into Australian. "My husband wite for me. He get not very pitient." And, with a sad smile, she ambled off. Paolo, left alone, said, "Aaaaah." A yellow-topped taxi came by, driving it a Chinese youth in sun-glasses against the mild sodium lighting, "You," he said.

"Taxi," said Paolo, feeling lordly. "You take me ome."

As they drove off, the Chinese youth broke into a clipped dry nocturne. "Night now. Light on here. Light on there. In street all lights. People walk in street. Some people go home. Some people not go home. Some go pictures. Some go eat. Some drink."

"My fader drink," said Paolo.

"In Kool Kaffi your father drink. I see. He angry. He say Sudu boy steal watch. He want fight Sudu boy. I see." They arrived at the mean row of throw-outs' quarters. "One buck," said the Chinese youth.

"Four centem."

"Eight centem I take."

"Five only I give. Bloody robber."

"Seven I take."

"I give six."

"No time argue," said the Chinese youth. "Six I take.

65

What use money anyway?" This was so unusual an apophthegm from a Chinese that Paolo grew frightened. "Here one buck," he said. "You give me change another time."

Paolo climbed upstairs, not displeased with the evening. He had robbed his father. His right pocket bulged with notes. He had met a woman. He had eaten half a pound of butter and a little cake. Taking off his trousers in the one squalid bedroom shared with his father (a naked light on tossed blankets, torn mosquito-nets, scurrying creatures of the night), he remembered the hard square tin in the left pocket. He took it out and lay on the bed to examine it. It had a picture of a pink healthy pig. Paolo laughed, saying, *"Mio padre."* There were English words, some of which Paolo understood. "PORKYBOY", it said. "Chopped pork with sodium nitrite. Delicious hot or cold, fried with eggs or chilled with salad. Made in Australia." "My fader," laughed Paolo, as he unrolled the metal with the key provided, seeing a pink band of Porkyboy appear. Soon he lay content, munching the salty and thinly spiced sponge-meat. As he reached the end, poking out the last pink gobs with his fingers, he heard the owner of this and other so whimsically named foods coming up to bed next door. Every sound was clearly audible—the rustle of shirt, tinkle of metal trouser-fasteners, the double clump of shoes. Paolo listened for sounds of a woman, but he heard none. But he heard words that he did not clearly understand, words, as it seemed to him, of Protestant prayer.

"God," went the words from next door. "God, let me sleep. Let me sleep and let me not wake up again. Make it easy. Make it as easy as that." Paolo stared at the wall, his long goat's face made longer with an open mouth of wonder, holding in his right hand the ravaged tin of Porkyboy.

66

7

Ah, Francis Burroughs Lydgate, why dost thou seek not temporary oblivion merely but a sempiternal quietus? Sleep is thy meed, thy due after the long rigours of the day, but why callest thou on thy Maker (with as little ceremony as thou wouldst call on some heathen boy from Cathay for a strong but well-watered potion) for a cessation of his great gift of existence? Existence, thou echoest? It is but that. What more dost thou want? Thou hast work, a wage, a board and a bed. Thou hast the benison of perpetual heat, an endless sojourn in a land where summer dieth not. Thou hast the sun in the morning and the moon, in her several quarters, at night, with often a jewelled canopy of stars that the dweller in cold lands knoweth not. Dost thou want everything? Thou has a dusky doxy who hath borne thee two children and, at this very instant of thy yielding up thy senses to the embrace of sleep, calleth on thy name in the sweet agony of bearing one child more, though, true, it is not thine. Thou hast known the joys of the wedded state, however briefly. Thou hast seen the world and eaten of its strange fruits. In this land of the cannibal didst thou not, from a youthful spirit of bravado, once eat a small roasted portion of human flesh, though thou vomitedst it up at once, and with it almost thy heart? What grumblest thou about? Many men, tied to the rack of pedestrian endeavour in those lands that but rarely see the sun, would envy thee, knew they how colourful an existence thou hadst enjoyed. Why seekest thou to put an end (though, true, it is rather that thou seekest an end to be put, lacking the ancient Roman virtues) to a life that the world would account most rich? Speak from thy soul while thou sleepest. Is it that tonight thou wast involuntarily nagged and pricked to an awareness of fault in thyself that formerly thou hadst thought not to be there? Thou answerest not, turning restless in the hot night. Sleep hath come to thee, and that, if not deep, sufficient for thee not to hear the homecoming of the Italian artisan, thy neighbour. He is not sad. He hath drunk deep and singeth. He waketh his son in the still watches and it shall be accounted no curse to him, save by his son, who lacketh (and let it be shame to him) the traditional filial virtues that first built his Empire. He would in no wise be willing to carry his ancient father (as Aeneas did Anchises) from blazing ruin. And, talking of still watches, he wisheth to know if his son hath seen his watch, gift of his own doxy, swarter than thine but less faithful, on the Middle Sea. His son affirmeth that he hath not seen it for many hours. The father singeth loud, old songs of Italy. He is happy. He hath little money. He is burdened with wife and daughter and with a son. He hath, as hath been said already, a mistress who is too well-favoured to be trusted in a land of flashing eyes and strong urges. He hath much to complain of, but he is happier than thou. Why canst thou not be like him?

Thou hast a sense of guilt, meseemeth, which thy neighbour lacketh. Thy neighbour is saved. He hath thrown his guilt on to the shoulders of One Who will bear the guilt of all mankind, and that gladly. And, indeed, thou feelest that thy failure in thy past ambitions, the enemies about thee, are not the random bestowings of a malign and potent destiny. Was there not something in thy past, some sin, which, like Cain, thou wanderest through distant lands to forget? We shall not know till thou speakest, and speak thou wilt not.

Thy Italian neighbours, having spent some of the night in loud and rapid altercation in their own musical tongue, are now most still in sleep. The father snoreth and the son at times calleth out from the prison of his slumber some Italian name or other, belike a woman's. But thou snorest not and no woman's name escapes thy open lips.

What of the night? The moon moveth over trees and plants of outlandish name, over the dwellings of Christian and Mussulman, over the lowly huts of paynims, fire-worshippers, adorers of wood-nymphs and water-goblin, them who worship nothing but their own fat, and those, like thee, who worship nothing at all. Dogs roam the empty streets, dogs that call no man master, that lick no boot and are collarless, answering to no name. They are not unlike thee, except that thou hast a name and art alone. For a moment thou thinkest thou art not alone, for thou huggest thy bolster, which men call a Dutch wife in some parts. And the night moveth on and soon in the black oven of the east, the fire will be lighted and the long cooking of the day begin.

But stay. Is it hope that cooleth? Is it sweet water coming to refresh your soul? For a wind shaketh the louvers and the trees are writhing in that wind. The parched grass looks up to be fed. Is it rain? Is it indeed rain, long looked-for? Shall the dried-up streams sing again and ride in high pride of water? It looks like it. How cool the air as dawn approaches. With a glory as of thunder and a loud, proud laughing, with a hiss and a roar, here is the rain. The dogs rush panting for shelter under the high-stilted houses. The gutters gurgle. Praised be God, on Whom thou so wantonly and, as it shall turn out, fruitlessly

69

calledst, for the dry land drinks. How wilt thou get to work? The taxis will be doing a roaring trade in the town itself, taking the little ones to school. None empty will pass down this road. The Italian father has no worry, for he will stay in bed. The son will walk, arriving drenched, but his shirt will dry off him for he worketh naked in the temple of the Mussulman. Only thou wilt arrive, collar-and-tied and creased-trousered, in unseemly wetness at thine office, unless some man will give thee a lift.

Do not worry about that now. Sleep. The dawn is rising in pain, like a man trying to get over a wall. The morning glory will be obscured. Sleep. Time enough to worry when you, like the dawn, rise. Painfully. Thou smokest too much.

Sleep recedes. He dreams that he is in hell and that Lazarus (though he is indeed no Dives) comes at regular intervals and drops water in his open mouth. He wakes to find the roof leaking. The cigarettes on his side-table are soaked. He has no others. Water is dripping on him with the regularity of a Roman water-clock that thinks the Empire will last for ever. God curse them all.

PART TWO

8

The rain punched the town till the town was drunk with rain, drunk as the river, which, having drunk more than its fill, now lurched and spewed and spoke dirty words. The rain entered the house of Lydgate (and various other ill-caulked dwellings) in laughing person; in mansions on the hill it was happy to wall in the heat, send emissaries of mould, and sit disguised as sweat on the skins of the white. But in the State Council Chamber it was as if there were no rain. The conditioned air purred like a doctored cat that never went out, licking itself endlessly clean of the Caliph's endless cigarette smoke.

The Caliph smoked so much that he was as good as a tobacco cure to the assembled councillors. Even the U.N. Adviser had a sour-lemon look as he sucked his empty pipe. Where his brothers of the Middle East had harems, the Caliph of Dunia had cigarette-tins. Smoking was his only vice. It was doubtful if his meagre body could have supported more substantial vices, but he affected virtue because of the sins of his ancestors. They had been Berber pirate-kings and had called themselves Sultans; he was a Sultan and called himself Caliph. There, of course, in the pretension to that title sang the braggart blood of the pirate, and, in the claim to be the only living spiritual successor to the Prophet, there was a sort of arrogance of black flag and cutlass. He was lucky to be able to indulge the dream of a pure primordial Islam (realisable in time, when his people had learned enough from the infidel) which should be a macrocosmic image of himself: uranium earned money for him while he thumbed the Koran. His ancestors, on the other hand, had had to work hard for their gold moidores, religion being as much a luxury as sleep. He spoke now to the hereditary chamber about the great Mosque which, when the marble inlays had been fitted, would be opened with prayer and trumpets in the presence of Islamic leaders from all over the world. He spoke quietly, so that all had to strain their ears and incline their bodies to hear: here again was a kind of arrogance. And the U.N. Adviser was a little deaf.

"I didn't quite get that, Your Highness," said The Honourable Mr Tomlin in the National Language. He spoke the National Language with a minor public school accent. "Would you mind——?"

Smoke came from the mouth of the Caliph and, with it, words. "I visited the Mosque. There seemed to be a sort of strike. The men were sitting around, smoking. There was a young man who looked like a European. He was doing a sort of dance, almost naked. The dance seemed to involve pretending to strike repeatedly at one of the pillars. It was perhaps more boxing than dancing. The young man alleged that the pillar was his father. The workmen clapped and cheered. Is the young man mad?"

"Oh, yes, Your Highness," said the U.N. Adviser. "I have every assurance that the work will be completed in time."

"The young man was almost naked except for his shoes. The Mosque is not yet completed but it is still holy ground. He should have taken his shoes off."

An ancient councillor spoke loudly. "Why does the work have to be entrusted to Christians? Are there no Moslem marble-workers? Moreover, I learn that the marble, like the

74

workers, comes from Italy, which is a Christian country. Is there no marble in Moslem countries? After all, a mosque is essentially an Islamic structure." He champed his bare gums, nodding vigorously.

The U.N. Adviser heard every word and spoke confidently. "There is no marble, as far as we know, exported from any Moslem country. The best marble seems to come from Italy. And the best marble-workers come from the marble-producing district of Italy." An illiterate councillor, scion of a noble house of illiterate river chiefs, said he did not know where Italy was. He was told by his neighbour, inaccurately. "And," smirked the U.N. Adviser uneasily, "presumably His Highness wants only the best for his new Mosque."

"If they are striking for more money," said the Caliph smokily, "let them be given more money. The terms of the contract are very wide. At this feast it is not seemly to count each rice-grain."

"That has already happened many times," said a councillor. "My brother-in-law was drinking the other night with the old Italian man——"

"Drinking?" said the Caliph, taking a fresh cigarette.

"Orange crush, O Father of the Faithful. But the old Italian was not drinking orange crush. He seemed to say that more money had been three times requested and three times granted. But he, the old Italian, said that the money was rightly his, and not the workmen's, for his responsibilities daily grew greater and greater. And so the workmen still strike."

"We should have workmen of our own people," said another councillor. "Good Moslems, aware of the holiness of the work. They would not strike."

"They would not do a stroke," amended the Caliph realistically. "Besides, the time is not yet come for my people to work. The time will be when the infidel is no longer with us." He bowed slightly to the U.N. Adviser. "When the Australians have built their roads they will go back to Australia. When the Europeans have shown our people how to do their office jobs the Europeans too can go. Then there will be no need of the Chinese with their drinking-shops and pork-markets. The lesser breeds of the State will be given an opportunity to enter Islam. If they do not wish to, they too may go. Then our people will have the State to themselves. But in the meantime it is not seemly for them to work. It is seemly for them to think on their immortal souls. Work can come later."

The U.N. Adviser cupped his deaf ear but could hear little of this speech. He nodded, as in sage agreement, and fiddled with his silver pencil. It had been given to him by his office staff when he had retired from the post of District Officer, Number Four Division, Shurga. It was not solid silver. Much of the plating had come off.

"All right," said a councillor. "We have foreign workers. Right. We let them into the State. Right. They do their work. Very well. But when they have done their work, what then? Eh? Can they do what they like? They are our guests. Is it right for them to abuse our hospitality? Eh? Answer me that."

"Who is to answer that?" asked the Caliph.

"Anybody can answer it for all I care. Let him——" The councillor pointed rudely at the U.N. Adviser. "Let him answer it. That's what he's paid for. To give us a bit of advice. That's why he's called the U.N. Adviser."

"What exactly is meant?" asked the U.N. Adviser.

"Getting drunk instead of spending the night in prayer. The Mosque is holy. Right. They don't consider it holy. They get drunk and go out after women. Is that right? Eh?"

76

"What women?" asked a young rather gangster-looking councillor. "Our women?"

"Any women they can find. If they have not found any yet it is not for want of looking. But the old man pinched the bottom of one, a good Moslem mother. And the young one has winked at our young women in the streets. He has also made signs at them. They must remember they are not in France now."

"Italy," amended the U.N. Adviser.

"It is all one. Frankistan. That is the old name of the faithful for the barbarous countries outside the pale. It is all one. Right. What are you going to do about it?"

"It does not come within my jurisdiction," said the U.N. Adviser. "What expatriates do in their spare time is not my affair. Not officially. They could be warned, of course," he said unhappily. "But they have already been warned several times. At least, the old man has been warned."

"Islam," smoked the Caliph, "is one and indivisible. No distinction can be made between the secular and the divine. No distinction can be made between the morality of work and the morality of leisure. In the true Islam there is no leisure. The soul is constantly at war with evil. The essence of Islam is the doctrine of unity." This speech was, save for its structural words, pure Arabic. The U.N. Adviser had to guess at its drift. He said:

"As U.N. Adviser I must point out that it is not in my province to help uphold Islamic law or custom. Islamic law and custom do not apply to everybody in this State. There are some Christians, for instance. I am one myself. Church of England."

"What has England to do with it?" asked a councillor. "This is Dunia, not England."

"That is the name of the Christian sect to which I belong," said the U.N. Adviser. "If Christians want to be immoral that is entirely their own affair. I mean, it's something they have to sort out with their own consciences. Nobody can stop a Christian committing adultery or getting drunk. Unless, of course, he interferes with law and order when he does these things."

"So Christianity condones immorality?" asked a bright-eyed young councillor.

"No, no, no. He must settle everything with God. I mean——" The U.N. Adviser was embarrassed. He had used the name of God, or rather of Allah. He felt he was getting into deep water.

"Allah?" said a councillor. "And is there not also the question of Allah's representative?" Allah's representative took another cigarette. He blew numinous smoke.

"But it's not the same Allah," faltered the U.N. Adviser. "What I mean is——"

"There is only one Allah," pronounced the Caliph. "Moreover, I must remind the U.N. Adviser that according to the Treaty of 1951 no U.N. Adviser has any authority to interfere in matters of religion. It is not seemly for the U.N. Adviser to make heretical pronouncements of that nature."

The U.N. Adviser did not hear correctly. "Thank you, Your Highness," he said. "As long as we keep the idea of a division of function or authority in mind we've nothing to worry about. I'm glad we all agree on that. Perhaps we'd better get on to the next business."

"Perhaps," said the young gangster-looking councillor, "if these two Italians had women of their own they wouldn't want to interfere with our women. The Mosque must be finished on time. They must be kept out of mischief until it's finished. Then, of course, they can be booted out."

"Are you suggesting," asked the Caliph, "that we import immoral women to make a kind of harem for these two infidels?"

"No, O Father of the Faithful, not quite that. I merely meant——"

"I do not think," said the Caliph, "that our immigration laws are tight enough. We had the instance, a month or so ago, of some kind of Japanese stage show coming into the State from Naraka. It was not a stage show at all. At least, I understand that none of the members of the company, which was all female, had much talent for singing or dancing and did not pretend to have much. It was a kind of travelling brothel. What would happen if such a thing occurred again when our visitors were here for the opening of the Mosque? Our morality is in grave danger if we allow people of easy virtue into the State. Nobody should be allowed into the State at all unless they have a definite position to take up, sponsored by a person of high authority and proved morality."

The U.N. Adviser heard a great deal of this speech. A sort of indignation had swelled the volume of the Caliph's words to very nearly the level of normal conversation. "The immigration laws of Dunia," he said, "are, Your Highness, the strictest in the whole of Africa. I don't see how they can be made any stricter."

"Too many loop-holes," said the Caliph. He lighted the thirtieth cigarette of the forenoon. "Too many people creeping in, without jobs. And, when they've gone, creeping back again. Women especially. There are Australian road-foremen with imported mistresses. That lets down the State very badly."

"Only one," said the U.N. Adviser. "And she came from Naraka as an ayah. And he married her. It's perfectly above-board."

"Yes," said the Caliph. "Married in the eyes of the Registrar. But not in the eyes of God. Now, what is the name of the Passport Officer?"

"Lydgate, Your Highness."

"Ah, yes. He is living with a Potok woman. He has two children by her. Is that seemly? Is it seemly for a man whose task it is to control immigration to bring in wanton women from Shurga? Will not people say that he is taking advantage of his office?"

"I understand that they were together for a long time before he came to Dunia, Your Highness. And she came with him as his ayah."

"And one of the tasks of an ayah is to bear children for her employer? This is a strange world the Europeans are helping us to make."

"They cannot marry," said the U.N. Adviser. "He is married already."

"Has he never heard of divorce? Does a Christian state forbid divorce so that it might the better encourage concubinage?"

"You have to have grounds, Your Highness." The U.N. Adviser felt miserable. He could have throttled Lydgate. He could have knifed the two Italians. Cheerfully. Why couldn't people live normal decent lives—a little tennis, a couple of pink gins before dinner, a little very mild flirtation? Why did they have to cause trouble?

"The Senior Establishment Officer," said the Caliph, "Mr. Mudd. He ought to have more control over immigrants who come ostensibly to work in the State. Especially now. Especially when we shall soon be having so many distinguished visitors. Holy men," he added. "Men of virtue and piety. Are they to take back to their countries stories of my allowing this State to be run as a brothel? Things must be tightened up." He put the lid on his tin of cigarettes. The councillors began to rise. The U.N. Adviser said, "There is more business, Your Highness. There is the question of the water supply. There is the question of building the new catchments."

"Ah, yes, catchments," said the Caliph. "Next time, I think. There seems to be plenty of water at the moment. Plenty." He looked incuriously at the streaming windows. "Some things are more important than water." He closed his eyes for a moment, though none could see him do this. This was because he always wore sun-glasses, even indoors, as though in pain of perpetual hangover. Here, presented binocularly, were the black patches of his piratical ancestors. His council stood about him, small black men whose race was Moslem and whose language was the National Language, not without cunning, some not without brains, waiting to hear what he would say. He said, " *'And thou, Mohammed, seest the earth barren, but when We send down water thereon, it doth thrill and swell and put forth every beautiful kind of growth. That is because Allah, He is the Truth. Lo! He quickeneth the dead, and lo! He is able to do all things.'* " He turned to The Honourable Mr. Tomlin saying, "Catchments." Then he went out into the unconditioned air and the eager fingers of the rain on the open veranda. The State Umbrella-Bearer appeared from nowhere.

9

The U.N. Adviser liked to drive his own small car (D666) to and from work, leaving the flagged and chauffeur-driven official monster to his wife, one of whose few pleasures, poor woman, was to queen it. He splashed through his dismal realm (how sordid the shop-houses, the box-like offices of the trading companies, the stucco police station) towards the river-road and the hill, the swishing wiper swabbing in vain, himself hot and headachy in the airless rain-beseiged car, home to luncheon. There would be guests; nearly every day there were guests—American travel-book writers, Gauguin-style painters, missionaries, district officers making reports, wild-life-protection cranks, birth control propagandists, members of the town community pricked off from a roster. The U.N. Adviser would have preferred bread and cheese and bottled beer in his office, but he had a strong sense of duty and was adept at the false welcoming smile and the hearty handshake. He tried out the false smile now like a pocket torch as he passed the Sailing Club and climbed to the wide-spaced suburb whose crown was the Residency. On his right was the rising river, opening out to the estuary, and beyond the river the river village, stilts of the houses on the river-fringe already thigh-deep in water. There was really nothing to smile at, even falsely. Yet what was there in life? You looked forward to leave and Piccadilly Circus and the shows whose tunes your daughter played on the

Residency gramophone, and at home you were called "mate" by jostling workmen and your wife was insulted by teddy-boys, and you wanted to be back out here again, sweating and longing for Regent Street and the shows whose tunes your daughter played on the Residency gramophone. The U.N. Adviser, as the car climbed, uttered a strange word: "Reality". This term was to be his last; his application for a further term, a postponement of retirement and Piccadilly Circus always only a two hours' drive away, had been inexplicably refused. He was going to face reality at last, and he had nothing to face it with. Nothing, except his pension and the small house on the South Coast, his wife and his unmarriageable daughter. He was going to become a stock type of the stage, a cut above the blistered Anglo-Indian colonel who already belonged to the past, but fit only for the justices' bench and the rose-garden and the band-performance on the pier. And he would become really deaf, not just hard of hearing, and the band on the pier would mean little, and he would have to ask police witnesses to speak up. He would have to live inside his own head, a head furnished with monotonous jungle and river, and listen to voices half-remembered speaking languages despised by the humanists of the West.

The Residency had a vast hilly garden full of hibiscus, orchids, canna lilies, flame of the forest, and other gaudy but scentless blooms of Africa. It had a swimming pool, a private jetty at the foot of a stone stairway, two small guest-houses. In the porch of this house (built for the Colonial Resident in 1911, vaster but much shabbier than the dwellings of his subordinates) the official car was parked, and clustered about were the cars of some of the luncheon guests. The U.N. Adviser was obliged to park some yards from the house, and, getting out, he plunged into the vertical river of the rain, which soaked his head and his shirt and his bow-tie and his trousers, while he trod deep water in a rut of the drive. He cursed a word: "Reality." Entering, he saw himself in the cheval-glass in the hall: tall, with all his hair, not yet paunched, a school prefect grown up. To his right was the open sitting-room, closed in today from the rain with striped blinds, and in it people were drinking weak cocktails (this was a working day). His wife presided, speaking loudly as befitted a U.N. Adviser's lady. Her vowels were patrician enough, but odd lapses of grammar (the U.N. Adviser heard distinctly "Between you and I") betrayed her lower middle-class origins. He had met her in Harrod's, when she was a salesgirl of gramophone records, he still a cadet in the Shurga Civil Service. And now she said, "Ah, here is Mr. Tomlin," though she was not speaking to servants, was not an American, was not a Jane Austen wife. Mr. Tomlin hesitated, wondering whether to change his clothes, but his wife called brightly, "Come on in, dear. Ahmad is getting you a pink gin."

The U.N. Adviser looked at his guests with a sinking heart. They had risen, holding their shallow cocktail glasses with care, fingering their ties, trying to smile. One of the guests was black, bearded, long-haired, true to the party vow not to shave till the day of independence. But he was no mere party member; he *was* the party—Patu, author of *The Coming Day of Power* (not yet published; manuscript in the hands of the State police) and of a sheaf of inflammatory pamphlets printed in Nairobi. He grinned viciously as the U.N. Adviser gave him his hand, spilling, in the force of the shake, some of his tomato juice on the carpet (he was a Moslem), where it lay like blood. The U.N. Adviser's head, which all the morning had toyed with the prospect of aching, now tossed a coin and settled stoically to a megrim. For here, next to Patu, was Nando

Tasca ("Just think, Jim," said Mrs. Tomlin, "he actually knows the manager of that little *albergo* in Piombino where we stayed.") and Nando Tasca, over a flabby hand, said, "A please a to meet a you." There were two other guests: a District Adviser with incipient D.T.s, called Rowlandson; a Czech painter from Asmara who was going to hold an exhibition in Dunia Town. Everybody sat down again, and Nando Tasca said, "This a very nice a ouse. I not be in your a ouse before. When you tell me I not a do a right you a tell a me in your office. I think you not a like a me. But now a I know you a like a me because you ave a me ere in your a ouse. We a friends a now. That a very good." Rowlandson's cocktail glass clattered against his teeth; he looked furtively behind him and at the curtains, as though fearful that enemies might lurk beyond. But from behind the curtains came only Penelope, the daughter of the U.N. Adviser. Eighteen, weedy from an African upbringing, she danced in in a mauve cotton dress that was fussy with frills; her yellow hair, clawed at by the damp heat, was growing piebald; the mauve of her garment did nothing for her complexion; her nose was long, her spectacles had tortoise-shell rims. But Nando Tasca was gallant. "You a daughter," he said, "a very a beautiful. Like a mother." The mother simpered, rocking her bulk on the rattan chair. She showed dimples, saying, "Oh, Mr. Tasca." Penelope sat down next to her father, ruffled his hair and said, "Dear Daddy," and leaned forward, hands on her shins, face shining, with a young girl's eagerness to hear more compliments.

"I ave a daughter," said Nando Tasca. "Back a in a Italy. She a good a girl. Elp a mother in a ouse. Not like a son. E a no good. E a bad a boy a to is a father."

' And when is your er," said the U.N. Adviser. "That is to say, when are you showing your er? Mr. er?"

The Czech painter rose, said "Smetana" fiercely, sat down again. "I shall hold my exhibition in the Rest House on Tuesday and Wednesday," he said. He had fiery hair and bad teeth. His suit had been made by an Aden tailor. His hands on his knees were tense, knuckle-bones gleaming in the rainy light. "I hope you will buy. It is the duty of those in authority to encourage art." He looked at the one wall (the other three sides of the big room were veranda) and said, "These pictures you have do not set a good artistic example. That, for example." He nodded fiercely at a washed-out English landscape, boarding-house greens. "Inept in composition, insipid in colour. That is not good artistic taste. It does no credit to you and the ruling class." He fiercely flicked his head as if to spit at the picture.

"My daughter," said the U.N. Adviser. "That is to say, my daughter painted it."

"Oh, Daddy," said Penelope, "you shouldn't have. I mean, I was only just learning when I did that." She blushed and squirmed. Her mother smiled uncertainly.

"It not a right," said Nando Tasca to Mr. Smetana, "to say a thing like a that in other people's ouse. It a rude."

"An artistic judgment is an artistic judgment," said Mr. Smetana. "That vase over there is also in bad taste. I would say the same if you had that vase in your house, and, if I should turn so moronic as to have such a vase in my house and you developed, which is perhaps not likely, sufficiently sound artistic judgment to be able to assess the artistic qualities of that vase correctly, I should not be offended if you said it was in bad taste, as I have just said."

Nando Tasca understood little of this. He said, "I not a ave a you in a my ouse. In a the war we ave a foreign men in Italy. I not ave a one in my ouse. They not a ave good a

86

manners. I not a ave a you in a my ouse so you not a say what you a say just a now."

"I think," said Mrs. Tomlin, "that lunch is ready. And Mr. Tomlin has to go back to the office at two. Ah," she smiled as a white-coated servant hovered at the dining-room door, "is lunch ready yet, Ahmad?"

"Five more minute. Electric cut off." The servant showed neither regret nor satisfaction.

"Please," said Rowlandson. He held up his shaking glass pleadingly. He was youngish, colourless, lank-moustached. He had had a bad time in his district where, according to his report, cannibalism and head-hunting had recently been revived. "Please, could I have another? In a bigger glass, so I can have more water?"

"Ahmad's gone," said Mrs. Tomlin. "It hardly seems worth while to call him. After all, lunch is nearly ready."

"I'll help myself," said Rowlandson. Unshakily he made for the bar and the glint of bottles.

"Rowlandson," said the U.N. Adviser, "I don't think it advisable, if you want my advice. You'd be better off with some food in your stomach."

"I've wanted this opportunity," said Patu with sudden urgency. "You never seem available when I come to your office." The U.N. Adviser watched uneasily while Rowlandson, whimpering with relief, slopped gin into a beer-glass. His first job that afternoon, he thought grimly, would be to chastise his secretary, one of whose duties it was to issue luncheon invitations.

"I could a do with a one glass a beer," said Nando Tasca. "This weather make a very a thirsty. You tell me where a ice-box and I a get."

"I'm afraid I don't know where it is," said Mrs. Tomlin queenlily. "I leave all that to the servants."

"If you a my a wife," said Nando Tasca roguishly, his

87

piggy blue eyes wrinkling up, "you a not ave a no servants. We a live in a little ouse and you a cook a for me. Every morning you go to a market and all a the men they a whistle to a see you. They say a Nando Tasca very a lucky man a ave a wife so a beautiful. But not a possible," he sighed. "You already ave a usband. Very good a man. Very beautiful a daughter. Nando Tasca ave a no luck."

"It's this question," said Patu, his beard wagging fast, "of an entry permit for Bastians. Why won't you let him in? He's been to our party conferences before. It's only right that our own movement here should keep in touch with what's happening in other places. Bastians is a very good man, a very fine speaker, he has a fine revolutionary record. I can tell you, my own party is going to take this very hard. This is undemocratic, repressive, tyrannical."

"You really ought," said the U.N. Adviser, with almost no voice, "to come and see me officially." Rowlandson was drinking on his own at the bar, a gin bottle in his left hand. "Although it won't do any good, you know."

"I've tried five, six times," said Patu. "They won't let me in. Is that justice? Is that democratic?"

"He's politically undesirable," said the U.N. Adviser. "He nearly caused a riot in Colombo. We're not having him. I'm not really prepared to discuss the matter further."

"He's only coming for one day," said Patu. "Is this Western justice?"

"You not a worry," said Nando Tasca. "It a no trouble. Ice-box must a be in a kitchen. Kitchen must a be through a there." He pointed to the dining-room. "Nando Tasca can a not ave a beautiful a wife. Nando Tasca ave instead a one bottle a cold a beer." He marched off sturdily. He paused at the dining-room door to wave his hand at Mrs. Tomlin. Then he did a little dance-step and, with a stage tenor's wide gestures, sang one or two bars of *"Celeste Aida"*. Then, with a bow, he was gone. The servant came through to announce lunch, but a far voice said, "You wait a one a minute. Not a urry. One bottle cold a beer." The servant looked at Mrs. Tomlin, mouth open, undecided.

"Two more minutes," said Mrs. Tomlin. "This Italian charm," she said to her daughter. Smetana was gloomily wandering the room, picking up *objets d'art* and sneering at them.

"I have to get back, you know," said the U.N. Adviser, looking at his watch. "Shouldn't we eat now?"

The Czech turned, frowned, said, "Eat, yes, eat. You invited me here to eat. Even artists must eat, though the world thinks not." In the U.N. Adviser's head, megrim-racked, great express trains began to approach in thunder. "Oh," he said, "you must eat, must you? Put that thing down," he added. Mrs. Tomlin, Miss Tomlin turned startled eyes on their man.

The Czech looked with a world of scorn at the sentimental painted china Harlequin he held. "This," he said. "Art, eh?" He put it down on the small polished table, clanging it against a cloisonné vase, Harlequin's chessboard backside facing the audience. A fresh rain-gust agitated the striped veranda blinds. The U.N. Adviser said, "Reality. What do any of you know about reality?" He stood up, shaking as Rowlandson had done. It was to Rowlandson he went. "Give me that bottle," he said. "If I'm not to eat I might as well drink."

"Jim," said Mrs. Tomlin. "What have you been doing this morning?" She spoke sharply. His daughter breathed, "Daddy." The U.N. Adviser could not hear. Nando Tasca returned with a bottle, singing from Rodolfo's aria, *"Per sogni e per chimere e per castelli in aria, l'anima ho milionaria.*" The U.N. Adviser could hear. He turned, saying harshly, "Reality. What are we all doing? What do you all want?"

"I want to eat," said Mr. Smetana. "And I want this man to stop singing. He cannot sing. He has not one ounce of beauty in his body. He has no voice. He has no appreciation of anything artistic. The Italians are a superficial race."

Rodolfo Tasca sang to Mimi Tomlin, *"V'entrar con voi pur ora, ed i miei sogni . . ."*

"I feel," said Patu, "that it is perhaps the Government that knows nothing of reality. The movement towards the realisation of self-government for this State cannot be halted. 'The gradualness of inevitability', as your Lord Passmore put it, showing that an aristocrat could, if he wished, be democratic. You cannot hold us back. We march steadily on to the end."

"What is this about reality?" asked Mr. Smetana, pricking up his ears at the rustle of an abstraction. *"Wirklichkeit? Realität?* Is an Englishman asking about reality?"

Nando Tasca happily caught up the word in the twindling broth of his song. *"Realtá,"* he sang to Mrs. Tomlin, and again, in a cadenza, *"Realtá."*

"What I say is this," said the U.N. Adviser in a prefectly voice. He used the base of the gin bottle as a gavel. "What I say is that this is no way to behave. This is my house. My wife and my daughter and I are being very patient, very tolerant. And I've been patient and tolerant all morning. And I come home for a bit of rest and a quiet drink and a meal, and all I get is this. It is not good manners," he said primly.

Nando Tasca agreed heartily. "That a what I a say," he said, "to this a man. E a very rude. But all a German very a rude." ("Czech," said Mr. Smetana, as in chess.)

"After all," said the U.N. Adviser, "I *am* the U.N. Adviser." The stress on the 'am' sent the tail of the statement too far into the air, making it a querulous question, almost a prayer for confirmation.

Nando Tasca confirmed with a nod of shaking chins that the U.N. Adviser was the U.N. Adviser. "You," he said, "a the U.N. Adviser."

Rowlandson, hearing authority invoke itself, sat down with a full glass. The U.N. Adviser said, "All I say is that this is no way to go on. Why can't everybody learn to behave properly? I mean, it's easy enough, isn't it? We just try to behave decently to the other fellow and have a bit of a joke now and again with his wife, nothing more than that. And just a couple of drinks now and again, and the odd game of tennis when the sun's on its way down, and perhaps a trip to the Sailing Club to have a bit of a yarn with some of the chaps. And a game of bridge. Decent behaviour, a decent life, everything in moderation. That's right, isn't it? That's what we Anglo-Saxons have tried to teach the world, isn't that right? Isn't it?" he repeated, with little hope.

Mr. Smetana said, "Your people are not really equipped for answering questions about the nature of reality. They have never had any need to probe into the nature of what lies behind phenomenon, the *Ding an sich*. Metaphysics to them was always a game. Now they have nothing to hide behind, now they have to face the great emptiness without tea-cups and cricket and trade expansion and ruling subject races. It is the *Untergang*."

"Mummy," said young Penelope, "shall I hurry them up? I'm sure lunch must be ready."

"There remains beauty," said the Czech. "That is real enough. To capture the transient on canvas and make it eternal. That is what we must try to do." Penelope, running towards the kitchen, was met by Ahmad announcing lunch. "I think," said Mr. Smetana, "I have succeeded in capturing something and making it worthy of contemplation." Then, rising, he said, "Thank God we can now eat."

"Shall we go in?" smiled Mrs. Tomlin, the hostess once more in her depth. Now a pattern could be imposed, conversation could be led into the right channels from the head and tail of the table.

"I bring a my a beer with a me," said Nando Tasca. He gallantly offered Mrs. Tomlin his marble-worker's left arm, the beer-glass in his right hand. Mrs. Tomlin's right hand gently rode on the tide of decayed muscle. Patu (black flesh, black mop and whiskers) took in washed-out white and yellow Penelope. Rowlandson went in somnambulistically, Smetana fiercely and hungrily, the U.N. Adviser wanly, jerkily, worries pushing his shoulder-blades.

The girl and the woman steered into place the artist, the hedonist, the dipsomaniac, the politician, the U.N. Adviser. Water sang chillily into their glasses, water still raged hotly outside. Soup was already on the table. It was intended to be *bouillon frappé*, but the power-cut (now, as the fan above the table proclaimed, restored) had sent it on a journey back to hot broth. At the first tepid mile-stone it had halted. It was spooned in now without much conviction, though Nando Tasca smacked his lips politely and kissed his fingers. Patu said:

"You will forgive me if I do not eat. I am a very orthodox Moslem. One cannot be sure whether the food one eats outside a Moslem house is *halal*."

"Oh," said Mrs. Tomlin, unkissing her spoon, "really, I can assure you——"

"If he doesn't want to eat, don't force him," said the U.N. Adviser somewhat sourly. The headache still sat there, now watching him take his soup.

"How," asked the Czech, "can you reconcile your advanced political views with a blind acceptance of primitive food taboos?" He had already finished his soup and a slice of bread. He leaned across the table hungrily at Patu.

"I am a Moslem, that is all," said Patu. "I see nothing illogical about wishing to practise my religion in a democratic state that shall grant freedom of worship to all its citizens. I claim that freedom for everybody. Including myself."

"Then how," said the U.N. Adviser nastily, "do you reconcile being a good Moslem with having a non-Moslem state?"

"I don't quite see that," said Patu. "Would you mind——?"

"You talk it over with H.H.," said the U.N. Adviser. "He says it's all one and indivisible. If you want a democratic state you can't have a Caliph. If you don't have a Caliph you can't have Islam. You can take it or leave it." He almost snarled over his last tepid spoonful. His wife and daughter looked at him anxiously: they had never seen him like this before in company. What was the matter? Was it the rain? Was it something that had happened that morning? Was it because this was their last term? Nando Tasca said:

"It like a not eat a meat a Friday. What difference it a make? God a not care eat a meat or not eat a meat. God not care whether it a Friday or not a Friday. God not know it a Friday. If a man a good a man it a all a right." The soup-bowls (blue, Chinese, crawling with dragons) were removed, and a dish of Chinese spaghetti endragoned with prawns was brought. Cold damp plates were placed before the guests. "This look a very nice," said Nando Tasca bravely.

93

"I think," said the U.N. Adviser, "I'll join Mr. Patu in not eating anything. I've got rather a bad headache."

"Oh, you poor dear," said Mrs. Tomlin. "Oh, poor Daddy," said Penelope. "Have a couple of aspirins and lie down," said Mrs. Tomlin. "Don't go back to work," said Penelope. "Take an afternoon off, Daddy. I'll ring up."

"You might as well," said Patu with fresh viciousness. "The work of repression can go on equally efficiently in your absence."

Suddenly Rowlandson lifted his head and bayed at the ceiling-fan. The waiting servant opened his mouth in fear and dashed to the kitchen. "Now then, Rowlandson," said the U.N. Adviser sharply. "Pull yourself together."

"Oh, Mr. Rowlandson," said Mrs. Tomlin. "Oh, please, Mr. Rowlandson."

"Shut up," said Rowlandson, "Shut up up up." His accent was revealed as basically North Country. "What do you know about it? Eh? The U.N.A.'s right. We try to do our bloody best." ("Oh," blushed Penelope.) "We won the war, didn't we? Try to give 'em peace and show 'em how to behave? Isn't that right? No good German but a dead un," he said. "Hitler was a bloody painter. A bad un like you," he said to Smetana. ("Czech," chessed Smetana.) "Race of bloody organ-grinders," he said to Nando Tasca. "Black bastards," he said to Patu. "You'll have your own bloody way, but what do we get out of it? Sitting there smug on your arses, having a crack at the poor bloody British. Income tax fifteen bob in the pound. Fags five bob for twenty. Purchase tax on every bloody thing. Can't afford whisky. So that all you smug bastards can sit comfortable on your arses and have a smack at the British."

"That's enough, Rowlandson," said the U.N. Adviser. "You've said enough. More than enough."

"*Es ist genug*," said Mr. Smetana, the four syllables

rising in whole tones firmly, the opening of the Bach chorale. He ate his lunch imperturbably.

"Everybody having a go at the British," said Rowlandson. "Look at the Middle East."

"That is enough," said the U.N. Adviser, percussing an accompaniment with his fork-handle. "I shall send you away from the table," he threatened. "I know you've had a bad time, but that's what you were sent here for. The British are supposed to have a bad time. That is their destiny."

"Please, dear," said Mrs. Tomlin, "don't you start. Please."

"All right," said the U.N. Adviser. "Bring on the next course. Let's get this lunch over."

"I understand what a e say," said Nando Tasca. "E say thing a not a so good about a Italian people. I not on a side a Mussolini. I against a Mussolini. I against a German people. And," he added, leaning forward with sharp blue eyes, "if a Italian people not a good why you a bring a Italian people a ere put a marble in a Mosque? If a British a people a good why they not a do it? I not ask a come a ere. I better in a Tripoli. I ave a girl a there. There nobody insult a me. I not a finish a work in a Mosque," he said. "I ave a strike. Mosque a not ready when they want a it a be ready."

"Do what the hell you like," said the U.N. Adviser. The rain teemed down, his head was near cracking. He got up. "I'm going to bed," he announced. "I'm ill. I'm sick. Send a message through to the office," he said to Penelope. "Good afternoon, everybody."

"You cannot evade your responsibilities so easily," said Patu.

"I don't feel at all well," said Rowlandson. "I think I'll go back to the Rest House. I'll have a rest there. I don't want anything more to eat. I'm sorry for what I said. I don't know what came over me. It's not like me at all."

The U.N. Adviser, head and shoulders bowed, went out. His wife still tried to fly the flag that was now much mud-spattered. She rang the little silver bell. A servant called Haroun, braver than his colleague, changed the plates for dishes of melted ice cream. Nobody fancied it. Smetana had expected at least a steak. Nando Tasca breathed heavily, but soon, when Penelope returned from the telephone, he returned to his Latin gallantry. "It a very nice a lunch," he said. "Now I return a ospitality. You two a ladies," he said, "must a come to my a ouse. I arrange. We ave a pasta. And a bottle a Chianti. Ere very expensive, but I a buy. My son a cook for us. E sometimes cook a good. Sometimes e a good a boy. When e *told* be a good a boy e sometimes good a boy to is father." He kissed the hands of the glum ladies who, ice cream left to liquefy, had risen to escort their guests out. Smetana bowed stiffly and hungrily. Rowlandson tottered to his feet. Patu grinned maliciously: the luncheon party had been a great success. They went out to their cars—Smetana's hired, Rowlandson's junior government officer's Morris, Patu's opulently new, ready for The Coming Day of Power. Nando Tasca had no car, he had come in a taxi. "You take me ome," he said to Patu. "You not a drunk and you not a Czech. He say a Czech, really he a German. I go with you."

The afternoon, a time of oblivion for the U.N. Adviser (today most exceptionally), Rowlandson (during this brief season of rest), Nando Tasca (habitually), was a time of activity for others. And the rain, of course, having shut out the sun, needed no siesta. Darting like the rain, Patu leapt from his car outside the Government Building, leapt up stairs and along corridors, flattening himself at intervals in niches and round corners as listless clerks and secretaries passed along with papers, emerging into the safe clear by the U.N. Adviser's office. The U.N. Adviser's office door was ever-open, signifying that the U.N. Adviser was always available to all classes of men except revolutionary leaders. Patu peered inside and saw a small thin birdlike man, face twisted in agony, rummaging in the desk drawers of the absent U.N. Adviser. Patu whispered, "Ah!" and Sebastian Hup looked up in agonised guilt.

"He is not here this afternoon," said Sebastian Hup. "He phoned through about something in his drawer. It has to be sent up to the Residency."

"That is not true," said Patu. He grinned through his beard. "I know. I was just now with him."

Sebastian Hup gave a grin of pain. Confused, he fumbled for a language, and Spanish came out. *"Pero es verdad. Yo——"* The head of hair and the beard, against a window vista of relentless rain, frightened him somewhat. But then, boldly, he said, "You should not be here. You are not a government officer."

"There is not much time," said Patu urgently. "I want the 'approved' stamp and the facsimile signature. They must be there." He pointed a black finger at a kind of small metal Christmas tree from which rubber chops hung by handles fitted into grooves.

"What do you want them for?" asked Sebastian Hup, swiftly revolving prices in his mind.

"A friend of mine wants to come from Colombo. The U.N.A., because this man is a friend of mine, wants to keep him out. It is as simple as that."

"It can't be done."

"I shall want also a piece of U.N. Adviser's notepaper. How much will that be altogether? But we'll have to be quick."

"You can't take them away," said Sebastian Hup. "Much too risky." At that moment a woman's footsteps and a woman's humming could be heard coming along the corridor. "Miss Fanshawe," breathed Sebastian Hup. "Behind the desk, quick." It was a big desk. Lightly the two hid behind, crouching low. Miss Fanshawe looked in, humming, an ugly ginger woman, saw nobody there, hummed off. "A near thing," breathed Sebastian Hup, a tight vice of agony gripping his face and body. The two straightened, still fearful the one, alert the other.

"Five hundred bucks," said Patu.

"What? Five hundred? And I may lose my job. It's very, very risky."

"And supposing I say that I saw you in here looking in his desk?"

"That's different. I work for the Government. One thousand bucks. You've got plenty in the party funds."

"Seven fifty."

"Eight."

"All right, eight."

"When do I get it?"

"I've got my cheque book," said Patu. "Quick, some paper."

Sebastian Hup hopped about like a bird. The middle drawer, long and shallow, contained paper embossed with the arms of the State, the legend "U.N. Adviser". "Stamp several sheets with his signature," said Patu. "It will be useful for other occasions."

"That puts the price up," said Sebastian Hup. "Very, very dangerous. Why, you might try and bring *anybody* into the State. This man Bastians, for instance. Quick," he added urgently. "Down." Two men, bulky and loud-mouthed, arrived at the threshold the instant the other two ducked. They were Mr. Covendry, the State Irrigation Officer, and Mr. Brethren, the State Architect.

"Wonder what's the matter with him," said Mr. Covendry. "Not like him at all. Between you and I, I think he's got something on his mind, Jack."

"Could have sworn I heard voices," said Mr. Brethren. "But there's nobody here."

"You and your hearing voices," laughed Mr. Covendry. "Bad as bloody Joan of Arc." It was considered appropriate for a State Officer to lard his talk with literary allusions. "And I thought you was on the wagon, too."

"Am till the next Lodge meeting," said Mr. Brethren. "Come on, we'll have to see him tomorrow." They went away bulkily and loudly. Sebastian Hup knifed up again and began furiously stamping pieces of official paper.

"A couple of flimsies, too," requested Patu. "For copies, you know."

Sebastian Hup stamped madly. "Here you are," he said, holding out the sheets. "Take the lot for one five."

99

"A thousand."

"Done. Let's see the colour of your cheque book." Soundlessly a man in a white suit and dark glasses had arrived at the door. He knocked politely at air, his mouth open. "Have I," he said, "the honour of addressing the U.N. Adviser?" He inclined slightly towards Patu.

"Can I do anything for you?" asked Patu in a fair minor public school accent. But he looked round furtively for other exits. Sebastian Hup grinned, hands clasped tight before him, nodding and nodding and bowing slightly. "The U.N. Adviser is rather busy now," he said. "He has an appointment at the barber's."

"I see," said the stranger. "The stress of work. So little time." He was vague-coloured, his accent unplaceable. He had a walking-stick. "Perhaps I can make an appointment for tomorrow. I represent the International Herbal Health Association. You will have received a letter about me. I am to lecture here. Under the auspices of your Information Department." He started to fumble in an inner pocket.

Patu spied danger. "Yes," he said. "That's right. You're to go up-river. The villagers are anxious to hear about it. Everything's laid on. There's a boat going to Preku at three o'clock. Get a taxi down to the quay. We're a bit short of official transport, I'm afraid." It was true about the boat: there was one taking some headmen back: they were taking to their village-folk, along with Government orders, some pamphlets in Sudu written by Patu: these, designed to inflame simple hearts, were to be read out to the village-folk: the boat came and went once a month: not for nothing was Patu accounted a leader of men.

"I had thought," said the stranger, "that, perhaps for tonight——"

"The matter is urgent," said Patu. "There is no time to

be lost. Taxis are difficult to find in this weather."

"So I noticed. The hotel had some difficulty. Perhaps I could telephone from here?"

"The telephone is out of order," said Patu promptly; "it is best to stand out in the rain and wave. But lose no time. The villagers are waiting to hear about Herbal Health."

"Thank you, thank you," said the stranger vaguely. "But I had thought——" He wavered, swung his stick, turned, hesitated, turned back, looked at the grim hair and beard and the agonised obsequious grin, and said, "Thank you, thank you," and was gone.

"Herbal Health," said Patu. He sat for an instant in the U.N. Adviser's chair, like Satan in the Book of Job usurping the throne of God. Then he got up briskly. "That cheque," he said. "You shall have it now. I am a man of honour. I have the signed sheets in my pocket. There is no proof of anything. But I will pay you. We'd better go into the lavatory to fix that up. Too many people about here."

II

Mr. Smetana sat in the empty living-room of the Rest
House all through that rainy desert of time between
luncheon and tea. He bridged the gap with work and a
prolonged beaver, calling the sleeping boy at intervals to
renew his plate of corned-beef sandwiches and replenish
his lager glass. How dim the Rest House was. Old maga-
zines flapped and flapped in the wind of the fan. The three-
year-old *Illustrated London News* lay on a table near
Smetana: the fan-wind flicked it open, page by page,
and at the last page clouted it in boredom and sent it flop-
ping its wings to the floor. The telephone rang twice but
nobody came to answer. It rang yet again and Smetana,
putting down his drawing-block with a Czech oath,
strode to it, lifted the receiver and said loudly, "He is not
here." Then he returned to his work. He was not painting
today; he was practising his subsidiary gift of caricature.
He was trying to fix in hard pencil his memories of the
luncheon-party at the Residency, and he was helped here
by certain photographs on the walls—photographs of the
U.N. Adviser and his lady and his daughter, taken at
various minor functions over the last few years: a farewell
dinner for the Caliph's brother-in-law, off for further study
in Cairo; the opening of a new Bata shoe shop; a gala
performance of an Arab film in aid of the Junior Koran
Reading Society. To these Smetana occasionally strode,
humming Siegfried's horn-call. Then he would go back

to work with new vigour, hearing over the rain the odd groan from Rowlandson asleep in his room.

Smetana completed several deft drawings before the noises of rising and tea-making came from the servants' quarters. There was a cruel one of Penelope, the washed-out colonial miss, writhing at a Latin compliment; there was Mrs. Tomlin, surreptitiously picking her teeth with a little-finger-nail; there were two of The Honourable Mr. Tomlin himself, one petulantly assuming the god, the other blubbing like a fag after a prefect's beating. Smetana felt sure he could sell these for a very good price. But he would not sell them before his exhibition. How dare they insult him and half-starve him. He called for more corned-beef sandwiches and lager, well-satisfied.

At four-thirty Rowlandson came out in bedroom sandals, hardly better for his sleep. He had dreamt of seeing his own head, shrunken but still recognisably his, held up before him by grinning black people in a kraal besieged by rain. The dream had been detailed and vivid: behind his held-up head had been a wet vista of date palms and ducks splashing in puddles. He had been told that he could have the head, suitably mounted, for the sum of three thousand bucks. In the dream this had seemed an exorbitant price: he would have to sell his car. But, he had dream-reflected, a car was not much use in a land where the roads were rivers: yet, seeing his car disappear from the porch of his bungalow, it had seemed somehow worse than losing his head. He had awakened very thirsty.

He saw Smetana tying the tapes of his portfolio, humming something aggressive and Slavonic. He would not speak to him. Then, to his relief, a taxi appeared, a man he knew got out of it, paid the driver who said merely, "You", and began to climb the wooden steps, stiff as though with age.

"Hallo, Frank," said Rowlandson, shaking towards the head of the steps. "It's you, isn't it?"

"Oh, yes," said Lydgate, "it's me all right. How are you, Rowley?"

"Thirsty."

"And how long are you here for?"

"I'm not going back," said Rowlandson with passion. "Not there. I've been there long enough, haven't I? Wouldn't you say so? They'll have to give me somewhere else. Or send me home. Let's have a drink."

To reach the armchairs they had to pass a big varnished map of Dunia. Civilisation of a kind had nibbled at the coastline, leaving tooth-marks of names, but the hinterland remained uneaten save by rivers. Rowlandson shivered and pointed shakily. "There it is," he said. "They should never have sent me there in the first place."

"It used to be all right," said Lydgate. "The women were well-known for——"

"It's not all right now. I don't know what's come over them lately. I mean, they've got plenty to occupy their time. Schools and what-not. Maize-planting. We've given some of them battery-radios. Some of them have got portable gramophones. We're trying to civilise them."

"Perhaps they're bored," said Lydgate. "That's what's wrong with civilisation. It's boring."

"We got a bit of football going. And then one day I found they weren't using a ball. They were using——" Rowlandson began to shake furiously.

"Take it easy," said Lydgate. "Have a drink."

"Boy!" called Rowlandson. "Where are you, boy?" The aged negro came out at once with a bottle of lager for Mr. Smetana. "I was first," called Rowlandson. "You've got to serve me first. This isn't German territory. They wanted to be boss but they're not boss. I'm boss, do you hear? Me, me, me!" ("Czech," said Mr. Smetana.)

"Two cold beers," ordered Lydgate quietly. Rowlandson subsided. He looked again at the map. So did Lydgate. Rowlandson had an awkward territory. It was on the very fringe of Dunia; across a river hardly wide enough for a natural frontier lay the jungles of Shurga; south lay Trognika, marked off from United-Nations-protected land by the third parallel of latitude. Across Rowlandson's river lay the village where Lydgate's mistress should now, if computation had not erred, either be about to give birth or already have just given it. Lydgate said:

"Have you heard anything about Wajak?"

"Who's Wajak? Oh, I know, that one of yours. Yes, she's going to have a baby. Wait," said Rowlandson. "I knew there was something. I've had so much on my mind, you see, what with one thing and another. I've got it here somewhere. Wait." From his trouser pockets Rowlandson pulled out a schoolboy collection of string, pencils, nails. At length he found a mildewed wallet and began to fumble with it.

"I'll open that if you like," said Lydgate.

"No, no, I can manage." Rowlandson disclosed crumpled money and bits of paper. "A bloke came over the river with this. It's a sort of letter. They've got a kind of letter-writer somewhere down-river."

Lydgate opened the sort of letter. It said, in pencil: "My dear husband I very good but not yet been born I hope be born very soon then if you send ticket to Mister Ali in town he come fetch in boat I come in flying ship I hope see you soon both child very good now have three child we be very happy letter writer say five buck for write letter I tell him you send soon I no money love." It was as satisfactory a letter as he had ever received from a woman. He folded it up, put it away and felt happier than he had felt for a long time. The beer came and he drank contentedly, Rowlandson desperately.

"I wouldn't worry," said Rowlandson, "if they'd stick to their own heads." The drink had made him calmer. "But they keep looking hungrily at mine, you see. Oh, I know you can say it's only imagination, but that's the way it gets you up there. Anyway, they're not so friendly as they used to be. It's only my car that keeps me going."

"But I don't see what good a car is where you are."

"It occupies my time, you see. I keep it clean and rev it up and drive a few yards with it. And I think of the time I'll be able to use it. I had it sent in advance to meet me here. But it's not going back with me. Oh, no. Because I'm not going back myself."

"You might feel better after a few days' rest," soothed Lydgate. "It might not be as bad as you think it is."

"Are you saying that I'm a bloody liar?" said Rowlandson fiercely. "Are you like the rest of them?" He glowered round the room, ready for the rest of them, but there was only Mr. Smetana placidly eating a tea of corned-beef sandwiches: a regular meal had caught up his long snack. Mr. Smetana was also placidly drawing. Rowlandson said, "There are things going on, you know. There's that blasted man Patu and his revolution. He's probably telling everybody to kill off the white oppressors. And how do we know what's coming up over the border? There's a lot of trouble in the Congo just now. And I know for a fact that there's a bit of head-hunting across the river. They've been digging up some of the old ones, too, hanging them up after giving them a dusting. There's a Belgian one, complete with horn-rimmed glasses. And they've even put Brylcreem on his hair."

"That's civilisation for you," said Lydgate. But he added,

"Across the river, you say?"

"Yes. You want to watch out for your kids. There's one that's very white, golden-haired, so they say. You've got one like that, haven't you? I wouldn't trust any of them. If they can't get a two-bob piece they'll take a tanner."

Lydgate now knew that Rowlandson was suffering from mid-term nerves. But he felt a curiously strong desire to have his love-children about him, irradiating his dim hovel. And he saw Wajak's black body lying across the bed. That reminded him; he must ask P.W.D. for a double-bed. And he also, in an unbidden vision, saw a line of shrunken heads, some of them recognisable, most of them of senior government officers. Mudd's shone out clearly, topped by a smart jockey-cap. And there was one he never expected. But no, no, no. That was impossible. "More beer," he said. "Boy!" he called.

"What's that bastard drawing?" asked Rowlandson. He got up from his armchair. "He keeps looking over here all the time. If he's drawing me——" He went to Smetana who, with bold sweeps of pencil, was finishing things off. "Let's have a look," said Rowlandson.

"You can have it if you wish," said Smetana. "Fifty bucks only."

"It's not too bad," said Rowlandson, with the first smirk of pleasure he had shown since coming to Dunia Town. He held up the sheet to the light. "I'll say that for the bloody Germans. They're clever all right. Sometimes a damn sight too clever. He's got me all right, hasn't he?" he said to Lydgate. "Expression and everything, eh?"

"Your face is a bit fatter than that," said Lydgate. "And he ought to give you a neck."

"But it's all right, isn't it?" said Rowlandson. "He's not made too bad a job of it at all. But I can't give three thousand bucks for it," he said to Smetana in a sudden passion. "That's too much. I'd have to sell my car."

"Fifty," said Smetana, his mouth full of bread and corned beef.

"Fifty?" said Rowlandson. "For a few minutes' work like that? We U.N. officers aren't made of money, you know."

"Fifty," said Smetana, eating. "Even artists must eat, though the world and your U.N. Adviser think not."

"All right," said Rowlandson. He began shakily to count out notes. Near-broken, he was still an Englishman; he would not bargain. "I'd hang it up in that bungalow of mine," he said, "if I was going back there. But I'm not going back," he said, "whatever they say. You can be quite sure of that." The rain began to ease a little.

12

Lydgate got home while it was still light. A green and terrifying sunset sky glowered over the Mosque and was kicked and ridden over in the puddles. The fickle electricity supply, cut only twice that day, would fail with the dark because then it was needed most. It was necessary that Lydgate should see what areas of his house were flooded, necessary that, having cursed the plethora of water, he should, blessing the plethora of water, take a bath in the *pong*. Water was one thing that would not let him down tonight; that was certain. The taxi-driver said, as the wheels hissed up spume from the road, "Today rain. In morning it rain. Afternoon it rain. Now it not rain. But tomorrow it rain. Rain," he said sagely, "water. Water from sky."

The house or *casa* stage-right of Lydgate's was most still: the father slept, the son had not come home. The son had money to spend; the sole of his left foot had known it all day, folded notes snug in his canvas shoe. But the house stage-left was busy with moving-in. Lydgate remembered, paying off the taxi-youth, that this was the flitting-day of Forbes of Marmion. The unloading from the Roads Department truck went fast; fast flowed in the tide of the evening. A workman carried in a child's chamber-pot, another a pathetically small gramophone. "Quick about it," called Forbes in shorts and Aussie hat from the doorstep. And, "Hallo, Lyddy," he said. "We're nyebours, Lyddy." All about his front door there were plants like strong weeds in pots and sawn-in-half kerosene tins, many of them, unbelievably squalid. "You can have as many of these as you like, Lyddy," said Forbes of Marmion, "'cause you're my cobber as well as my nyebour." His two children, quite naked, crawled about the tiny front area very slowly, like small arthritic ghosts in the dying light. "Thanks," said Lydgate, thinking how hopeless was man's condition. "And where," asked Lydgate, "is the wife?"

"She's leaving it all to me, Lyddy," said Forbes. "But I don't mind. The poor little kiddy's real excited at being near town. She couldn't wite to put her new frock on and do herself up a bit and go into town, poor little kiddy. She said she'd have a look at some stuff for curtains. But she wouldn't tike any money, says she's got plenty. Real little siver she is. Anywy, by the time she comes back I'll have everything shipshipe. Kids in bed and pictures on the wall and everything. She'll be real pleased. Oh, my word," he said as a workman languidly brought a jam-jar flower-vase. "They'll tike all night at this rite." Forbes's pictures stood about the front step, like the work of a pavement artist: dimly Lydgate could descry a coloured print of kittens in sweet blue ribbons, a photograph of a battleship firing its guns and, strangely, a steel engraving of 'The Last Watch of Hero'.

"I'll leave you to it," said Lydgate. "If you want to borrow anything——"

"Thanks, Lyddy, old man. I could do with a hammer, some niles, a mop to mop up the rine from the floor, a bucket, and some spice in your fridge to put a pound of butter in. And a couple of cold bottles of beer, if you've got it. That'll help to mike room for the pound of butter."

"I'm going out again," said Lydgate. "The front door's open anyway. Just walk in and take——"

"Thanks, Lyddy, dear old man. You're my cobber."

Dark came completely, but there was electric light. This was proved not only by the sudden flowering of the street lamps but by Forbes's reaching indoors for the switch and finding that the switch responded. Forbes was delighted as the front room became a box in raw yellow, damp-gleaming, a small river on the floor rippling the reflection of the crude bulbs, bundles wrapped in old curtains lying everywhere. "This mikes a chinge," said Forbes. "We had nothing like this in the other plice. No more oil-lamps, no more candles," he said, with pathetic optimism. He switched the light off and on, off and on, a signal of his pleasure.

Lydgate entered his own house eagerly as, on past occasions, in other torrid countries, he had left his house eagerly to catch on his bare body the rare shower, to catch now the rare shower of light. He tidied up a little, took his box of foodstuffs to the kitchen, swabbed at the worst patches of wet. He plugged the outlet of the *pong* securely, turned on the tap confidently. But there was no water. Amazement swamped annoyance. Why was there no water? The river was bubbling over, the tanks must be full. Perhaps, at the water-works, they were gloating over their hoard, unwilling to spend those ducats. Lydgate noticed that water was flowing in a steady trickle from upstairs, falling to the floor from between two banister-rails. He stripped hastily, offered soap to the thin cataract, foamed his body and let it languidly be sluiced. Mudd, he decided calmly, must definitely die. The people on the hill had water, that was well known; they were fed by a different system. As for the commonalty in the valley—they have no water: let them use beer. In Lydgate's washed belly the tumbrils grumbled. Meanwhile the pool that had gathered all day in the bedroom gathered dust as it marched over the uneven floor upstairs, finally baptising soapy Lydgate as it trickled between the fingers of the banisters. Soon he felt cleaner. He put on a clean shirt and trousers and shoes, combed his grey hair, made a bundle of his dirty linen and set out for the Dunia Hotel, whose laundry service he used. He also wished to eat: a greasy mutton curry rich as red earth, or crackling suckling-pig, or duck so tender it yielded to the chopsticks while basking whole on the dish. But, he knew, there would only be spaghetti, prawns, equivocal meat, specious gravy, wherever he went. Life in Dunia was stripped down to essentials.

But not, tonight, for Paolo Tasca. For him tonight the luxury of quantity: more spaghetti than he could eat, a second helping of sweet-sour prawns, a fish-head in curry gravy, minced liver on a bed of cucumber bleeding with tomato sauce. He said "Aaaaah" occasionally as he ate, looking up to see whether others were envying him. He drank beer with louder smacks than his father. He grinned at the women of the loud dark shop, congratulating them in Italian on their pregnancies, whether but newly evident, newly completed or soon about to be completed. A dog came up to him, cowardly and villainous-looking, its tail thumping like the Anvil Chorus on the spittoon under the table. But Paolo did not shoo it away; instead he addressed it as his father, offering it fish-bones and prawn-armour and a single worm of spaghetti. Paolo was ignorant of Oriental lore, honestly believing that the Chinese had stolen spaghetti from the Italians, for instance, but he had a cloudy notion that some Indians believed that a man's soul could pass into an animal or insect, even into a tree or a stone. His father metempsychosed into a dog: that pleased him. "Come, Nando," he said, "sit up and eat this piece of liver, blast you. It is dipped in a highly poisonous sauce. Eat it all up: it is good for you." The Anvil Chorus came faster.

Paolo paid, left a tip of one decem, and left the shop (unshaven, unwashed since morning, in dirty shirt and shorts, walking from the knees.) The night was all before him, but he was not sure what to do. He stood on the pavement, a tooth-pick wedged between a pre-molar and a canine; he flicked the tooth-pick up and down with his tongue, so that it signalled tinnily; nobody responded. A woman? Where would he find one? Had he not tried hard last night? Nobody could say of him that he did not try hard. Trying hard was one of his great virtues. True, he had met the married Chadi woman whose name was uncertain, and she had seemed to hold out the offer of a promise, but not yet. No, not till her paramour was gone. Paolo stood on the five-foot way, looking out on to the wet road with its drowned lights, tonguing his tooth-pick. Across the road was a cinema hoarding. That was it! He would go to the cinema! There would be some little adventure in the dark, perhaps, some married woman bored with her husband but faithful to him on the side adjoining him, deliciously and wantonly—if but manually —unfaithful on the side next to a handsome Italian boy, exotically irresistible. Or some single girl whose dark shyness would only in the dark allow her to make her urgent needs known, and even then very discreetly. Aaaaah.

Paolo did not know the time. Next to the eating-house was the goldsmith's shop where he had sold his father's watch. He peered round its door and called, "Eh, what time?" The Syrian replied, "Here many times. Right time is seven ten." Paolo said, "Watch I sell have good time, yes?" The Syrian replied, "Have sold." Paolo said, "Who?" The Syrian replied, "To man and woman. Woman give man present." "Good," said Paolo. Paolo walked through back streets full of hens and refuse to the

Chin Chin Cinema. It was hard to tell from the posters what film was on. Cloudy glass cases full of stills (titles in many alphabets, but all heroes and heroines trying to approximate, through barriers of pigmentation, to the Hebraico-Caucasian norm of Hollywood), pasted banners, bill-boards seemed to give a whole year's prospectus of attractions. The vestibule disdained the soft lights and carpets and flunkeys of Europe: there was a pay-desk, a concrete floor, an open lavatory smelling unashamedly of its function. Paolo paid his buck and three decems and went in. A European who had paid for a European seat at the back, he fumbled his way along a row and found himself seated next to a woman. Good. If here there were no prospects he could at least survey with ease other, more promising, rows. Blinded to the audience for the moment, he could see only the screen. But the torch of the attendant had shown definitely a woman next to him, though of what age or degree of attraction he could not tell. He settled to the film. Of peasant stock, brought up to have frugal habits, he did not believe in waste. One did not, after all, pay for dark and possible dalliance; one paid for a film. The chance of dalliance was a divine proffer, like grace.

But Paolo could understand little of the film. It was a Hindustani costume-drama, played in a kind of perpetual twilight in a sort of medieval royal court. Plump dark girls ambled round in a ring. A woman with a fat midriff sang. Bearded potentates bellowed and shook scimitars. There was a long tepid love-scene under a cardboard moon. In the middle of this scene the electricity failed, and there were heartening female giggles in the complete dark. Paolo took a boxer's deep breath and turned to his neighbour. "Not be frighten," he said.

"I am not frightened," said the woman indignantly.

Paolo could not judge of the woman's social status: to him English was just English.

"It is dark," said Paolo, "but I am a good boy." This was meant to be encouraging. The woman did not reply. Paolo was aware in the dark of a stiffening, of a sitting bolt upright, of an outraged indrawing of breath. Poor woman, she was obviously afraid of the dark. But the dark now was shot with struck matches and the glow of cigarettes deeply inhaled, and cheerful comments from row to benighted row.

"I have cigarettes," said Paolo. He had, in fact, a packet of Camels, his first cigarettes for so long, the virgin cellophane unravished. "You feel less frighten if you smoke."

"Really," said the woman. At this moment a youth in the front seats let out a jocular scream as of one who is being robbed or raped. The woman responded with a tremor and a cry. So, now Paolo noticed, did another woman next to this one. He saw, in transitory match-light, the glint of glasses and the sheen of fair hair. And then darkness, and the woman next to him was still unassessed as to age or beauty. But Paolo gallantly sought to soothe, to take the woman's hand and say again, "Not be frighten."

"I don't think," said the woman, "you realise who I am."

"I not understand," said Paolo. "But I am a good boy."

"Boy!" called the woman. "Boy, boy!"

"Good man, I mean," said Paolo. "Not boy, man." But an attendant had come.

"This man is annoying me," said the woman. She was agitated and her words came breathily. Paolo was unperturbed. He was only twenty-six but he knew all about these gambits, the conventional coyness of the woman when first accosted. "I want the manager," said the woman. The voice came from above Paolo. She and her companion were on their feet. It was hard to see, but in the odd in-

curious flickers of the attendant's torch the row was disclosed as empty save for these two women and Paolo, and
a way out for the women on the farther side was made impossible by the presence of a structural pillar. "I want the
manager," said the woman again. "Please let me pass. I,"
she said, "am Mrs. Tomlin."

"Oh, you married," said Paolo. "Your husband not
here?"

"My husband," said the woman, "will have plenty to say
to you about this, whoever you are. An African," she said,
"an African daring, daring to——"

"I said we shouldn't have come, Mummy," said a
younger woman's voice. "I told you it wasn't the right film.
Oh dear," she added, and seemed as if about to cry.

"You be quiet, Penelope," said Mrs. Tomlin. "I want to
see the manager," she said to the attendant. "Kindly let
me pass," she said to Paolo.

"Daddy will be angry, I know he will. Oh dear." By
now many members of the audience were interested. The
nearest rows were calling encouragement in various
tongues. Mrs. Tomlin gave Paolo a smack on the head, a
head lit briefly by the attendant's torch. Paolo said, "Why?
I am a good boy." But he stood up and Mrs. Tomlin and
her daughter pushed violently past. "Why you hit?" asked
Paolo, bewildered. The electricity cut was rudely restored,
and the screen became dimly alive with unagile dancing
girls; the sound-track with loud and barbarous instruments
ground into gear. The exit-curtain was open, and Mrs.
and Miss Tomlin made for the lighted vestibule. Paolo
followed, saying, "Why are you angry?" (One of the
evidently useful phrases in the phrase-book which his
father, with rare generosity, had given him.) "What I do
wrong?"

"I'll show you," said Mrs. Tomlin. "The manager will

send for the police. How dare you, an African——" But now she saw Paolo—a goat's face unshaven, minimal working clothes, disreputable but no African. "You're the son," said Mrs. Tomlin, "of that man. Oh, it's a disgrace." Paolo saw a well-fleshed woman in her late forties and was abashed. "I not know," he said abjectly, "you are an old woman. I am sorry." Now the manager appeared, a nondescript Chinese with chopsticks in one hand and a paper napkin in the other, rushed by the attendant from a leisurely meal. "Get the police," said Mrs. Tomlin. "This man insulted me."

Paolo looked around, his tongue between his teeth. His boyhood had been protracted; he had few of the inhibitions of the adult. How many times had he and his boyhood companions—having broken a window or thrown stones at one of the village greybeards—run gleefully when the cry was raised! Now Paolo, suitably shod in canvas, flat-handing the manager out of the way, was off with a loud halloo, leaping the three concrete steps, landing with a splash, then down the main street, past the monstrous car with the official flag, the staring astonished aimless strollers, the shopmen picking their teeth and scratching their armpits, round the corner into the blaze of light of the Dunia Hotel, a blaze whose reflection on the wet pavement he made dance and shimmer with his running feet. But here he paused, looked round. Would he be followed? Would a police car come screaming for him? Would he be apprehended by some ebony vizier, to be clapped in a cell crawling with vipers? The ways of this land were strange. He, a poor Italian boy, had meant no harm, but he had read about Caliphs and carpets of execution, the unjust summary decapitations by barbarous rulers. He would hide till all had blown over. But, wait. Enter the hotel as if nothing is amiss, pass the reception desk with a smile and a wave, then dash up the stairs and hide in the lavatory. Paolo recomposed his breathing and walked in. George Lim sat behind the desk talking to a man with a portfolio under his arm. "*Na, Herr Smetana,*" said George Lim, "*wenn Sie mit der Suppe nicht zufrieden sind, so müssen Sie den Teller nicht werfen.*" The man addressed said, "Everywhere they try to starve me. The world will not let the artist eat." Paolo waved, gave a goat's smile, and ran softly up the stairs. Aaaaah. On the first floor he took in with satisfaction the deserted bar. He squelched in canvas swiftly to the lavatories, opened the main door that led to closets, stones and showers, and met, to his astonishment, his father.

But not his father alone. There was the man of the night before, Maximilian Something-like-a-hiccupp, and, though at first he did not recognise her, the woman too. She was clothed no longer in the alphabet but in flowers. Her milk-chocolate Mary-Tudor-domed face wore lipstick and powder. She was near to tears. Maximilian Hup (that was it) looked frightened. Nando Tasca turned on his son, saying, "What a you a do a ere? Why you not a go ome? But now you a ere you be a witness. I come in a ere *per pisciare* and a find im kiss a er."

"I was kissing her good-bye," said Maximilian Hup. "I am away tomorrow morning. She is my sister."

"You not a kiss a sister like a that," said Nando Tasca. "I a see a you. And why a you come ere to kiss er?"

"There was nowhere else," said Maximilian Hup. "It was only for a minute."

"All right, we forget a that. This a much a more worse. *Guardia,*" he said severely to his son. He pointed at Maximilian Hup's left wrist (thin, sinewy, brown). "He wear a my watch. I know it a my watch. I know it because it ave a paint a missing from a and. I know it a my watch

118

from a strap. Like a my own child I know it a my watch. You a thief," he said.

"She gave it me," said Maximilian Hup, treacherous as his first ancestor. "As a farewell present."

"That a true?" asked Nando Tasca. Paolo translated. Nando Tasca turned on him suspiciously. "Ow a you know what language she a speak? You meet er before?"

"She bought it in a shop," translated Paolo. "As a farewell present for her brother."

"E not a er brother," said Nando Tasca, concerned with justice and hence clinging to English. "But that not a point a now. Point a now is this. She not a buy, she a steal from me when in Kool a Kaffi."

"She says she bought it," said Paolo.

"I was there when she bought it," said Maximilian Hup. "We were together, brother and sister."

"You a liar too," said Nando Tasca. "You I not see a before. I see a man with a face like a you, but you I not a see. You not a thief," he said, "but you a liar. You a liar two times. You not er a brother."

Eileen cried. "I not tike your watch," she said in Australian. "I py for it. I py one hundred buck."

"One hundred," cried Paolo. "He is the bloody robber." Then he, just in time, clamped tight.

"That a good a watch," said Nando Tasca. "It a worth a many undred a bucks. It a present from a very old a friend." Paolo snorted. "Why a you a laugh?" glowered Nando Tasca. "You tell er she a thief. Better you elp a father not a laugh at what a e a say."

"She did not steal it," said Paolo. "I am certain."

"Ow you a so a sure? I know a er, I know a er usband. I tell er usband. Ow she a like a that?" The automatic time-flush of the urinals flushed the urinals. It was an ominous sound. "She understand," said Nando Tasca grimly. "She know a what I a say. She a crying."

"She did not steal it," said Paolo in the most manly Tuscan. "That I know. I know because it was I who stole it." By rights angelic trumpets should have sounded through the privies, cherubim should be sailing about him Botticellianly, trailing endless festoons of medicated paper. "It was I," said Paolo.

Nando Tasca was calm. "You," he said to Maximilian Hup. "Give a me a my a watch."

"It was a present," said Maximilian Hup gamely, "from my sister."

"Give it a back to a er," said Nando Tasca. Maximilian Hup hesitated, but he caught an image of himself in the mirror above the wash-basin, small and bird-like as his brother, threatened by marble-worker's bulk, formidable though decayed. He obeyed. Eileen tried to press it on him again, but he would not have it. It was charming mime, hand-movements graceful, eyes melting. "Now," said Nando Tasca, "you a tell a er a give it a me." Maximilian Hup coughed some Chadi.

"One hundred buck I py," said Eileen. She was pathetic in her flowered frock and smudged lipstick, her powder the wrong shade. Paolo's heart liquefied. Eileen handed over the watch. Nando Tasca said gravely, "Thank a you." And then, to Maximilian Hup, "Ow a much she really pay?"

"Fifty," said Maximilian Hup promptly. "I gave her the money to buy it. After all, she is my sister."

"I a tired you a keep a say a sister," said Nando Tasca with loud and sincere weariness. "My son steal a watch and sell a watch. E very very bad a boy. But e ave a money if e not a spend it. Money e give a to er."

"But I gave her the money to buy the present," protested Maximilian Hup. "It is not fair."

"She buy a other present for a you," said Nando Tasca. "If you a gone she a send a present. Now," he said formidably. "You a go, she a go. You trust a me. My son give a you a back what a e a owe. I a talk a to im now. It a very very serious. But I a talk a im *alone. Noi due soli,*" he said. The words had a final sound, as of a liturgical dismissal. Eileen cast soft but troubled eyes on Paolo, Maximilian Hup looked like a man who was thankful soon to be leaving Dunia. They went.

"Now," said Nando Tasca. It was a signal.

From ancient drains and sewers of the language (maritime inns and brothels, soldiers' tents of the days of the Empire's decline), from scrawls in the catacombs, graffiti dug up from beneath the preservative lava, from parodies of religious ritual, whoremasters' chapbooks, with slang of the craft, low terms of the byre and stable, the vocabulary of tavern brawls, with a richness of precise gesture and rudimentary dance they tore into each other. The automatic flush of the urinals stopped, obeying the lever at the water-works, the lights went out and came on again, and still it continued—the recapitulations of past crimes, the threats, the feints, the pursuits, in the narrow home of visceral relief. Until at length a man walked in—Fredericks, the miniature stage colonel from Bootle—to say, "Let the dog see the rabbit." Nando Tasca came away from the step of the urinal, whither his son had pushed him, to say, "I a beg a pardon." To his son he said, "It a not right a talk a like that to a your a father in a ere. You come ome."

Paolo Tasca danced on swift feet. *"Al inferno,"* he said.

"It not a right a go on like a this in a *gabinetto*."

Fredericks looked round from his slow task. "What's he been doing now, Tony boy?"

"You not a worry what e a do. I take a im ome. I arf kill a im in the ouse."

Suddenly Paolo stood deflated. His goat's face made longer by a jaw dropped in distress, his eyes growing misty, his arms falling limp, he saw himself in the mirror and felt sorry for that unkempt and ragged image. What had he done wrong, he, who had always tried to be a good boy? Why was the world against him? He only wanted his rights. The wave of the stress of the evening broke. He began to cry. Nando Tasca said, "Ah, now a e a cry. E a cry more worse when I a finish with a im."

13

It was downstairs, in the grim restaurant where the counterfeit presentment of the Caliph watched, from all angles, every mouthful, that Lydgate saw Eileen. Lydgate had handed his laundry in and eaten in the small Islamic restaurant run, cynically, by Chinese Taoists. The curry had been like fiery liquid mud. He had drunk a liqueur or two in the Kool Kaffi, spoken with simpering Crawshay-Davies and his tower of a Mongol wife, rejected the advances of the Sudu Frankie, and walked back to the Dunia Hotel, weary, aimless, yet unwilling to go home and sleep. The restaurant was near-empty. Only a party of Chinese clerks and small traders poking their chopsticks into a central cauldron, only Eileen alone at a table, orange crush growing warmer before her. It was purely in a neighbourly spirit that Lydgate joined the wife of his cobber.

"Have," he said, in her language, "a proper drink. Orange crush is bad for the stomach." She gave a conventional brave-smile-through-her-tears and shook her head. She was not, thought Lydgate, a bad-looking woman—big lips, splay nose: the ungenerous noses of Europeans, shrinking at cold air, had long seemed unlovely to Lydgate; thin tight lips held no more for him any osculatory allure. But the body below would, flayed by the dark, announce no race but that of woman. Lydgate looked at her with only vicarious desire: to Wajak, who had been unfaithful to him, he had been faithful. Yet Wajak did not know what fidelity was and certainly would not prize it in him. Was it because of this that he had been faithful? Were there some seeds of virtue? Had he, in some way, achieved a slight sense of responsibility simply because responsibility had not been asked of him? The loss of a tooth reveals to the living tongue the presence of an area of the body formerly only known from anatomy books. Like a small patch of sore gum Lydgate's soul made itself felt. That ludicrous prayer-meeting had yanked a tooth out.

"Did you," asked Lydgate, "buy cloth for curtains?"

She frowned, puzzled. "Cloth? Curtains?" And then, timing the tears perfectly with Paolo's on the floor above, she wept quietly for the departure of Maximilian Hup (who, however, had not yet departed, being engaged in other damp farewells in other places).

"You shouldn't cry," he comforted. "You've got a nice new house near the town, and two lovely children and a husband. Have something to drink."

"Husband," she said, in her hot-potato voice. "I do not care now. There is no need to have a husband now. It was only to see Max that I had a husband. I kept myself for Max. 'A husband didn't count,' he said. But he would have killed me if I had gone with other men. And he couldn't marry me. And he couldn't give me much money. So he said I had to marry this one."

Lydgate found this hard to follow, but he thought he saw a way out for Forbes of Marmion. "You mean," he said, "that you'd go back to your old trade?" One of the pleasures of talking to a Dunia light woman was the complete candour possible—no simpering coyness, no European whore's mock-respectability. You could discuss clinically every detail of the act, strip away the cheap moral curtains that immorally pretended to hide the nakedness but, being raggedly translucent, turned nakedness into nudity.

"I shall do that," she said. "There's nothing left but

that. Not now." Love, so little known on this continent, had given this woman a soul, a capacity for choice.

"But you can't, you know," said Lydgate. "Not in Dunia. You'd have to go away."

"I can't go away," she said. "I have to look after Max's child." She bowed her head in tears again at the name. Lydgate looked round for a waiter. He could hear them quarrelling in the kitchen. He called a loud word, was answered by derisive Chinese noises. But, hoisting his underpants, a chewing waiter appeared, taking his time. The Chinese eaters had reached the succulent coda of their meal: their dish was 'steamboat'—water kept bubbling over charcoal; slivers of meat and fish-gut and vegetable pincered in, pincered out when cooked; the residue of suspended matter and water making a rich and sustaining soup. The waiter belched at Lydgate; Lydgate ordered whisky and water for two. Lydgate said, "You could go to Shurga or Naraka. You could take the child with you."

"And who would look after him in the evenings? And what would he think, having no father? But here I am still a married woman. And that makes me safe, too. It makes it easier for me to go back to what I used to do." She had clearly worked it all out.

"But," asked Lydgate, "do you want to go back to Australia with—" (he did not know Forbes's first name)— "with your husband?"

"Oh, no," she said. "I have heard all about Austrylia." (This carrying-over of the natives' pronunciation of the name of their continent to her own tongue sounded strangely pedantic to Lydgate—like an Englishman's calling Paris by its French name.) "It sounds not very good," she said. "It is very big and the people are very noisy."

"Oh, well," he said. "That's all right, then." Forbes's problem was solved. Lydgate raised his glass as in a toast.

125

"Drink that," he said. "It will cheer you up." Should he tell Forbes that his problem was solved? *She* probably wouldn't.

"Will it?" she said. "I have never drunk whisky before." She drank it all off and twisted her face in nausea, hand at her sternum. "Oh," she said, "it's very hot. I don't like it."

"The second one always tastes better," encouraged Lydgate. "One more, and then I'll take you home."

"In a taxi?"

"In a taxi."

"I don't want to go home," she said. "I want to stay out."

"But the children will be expecting you. And your husband will, too."

"I don't feel so bad as I did," she said. "That tasted bad, but it's very good medicine."

"One more, and then we'll go."

Her eyes looked brighter already. She even took out her lipstick and mirror. She examined professionally the Chinese eaters, now spooning in the last of the soup. "They would not have very much money," she said. "Five bucks a time. That is not very much."

"It's money you want, is it?" asked Lydgate. "Doesn't your husband give you enough?"

"Oh, no, it's not really the money. I like to meet different people. Sometimes they give you presents. And if they give you a lot of money that means they like you. It's nice when a lot of people like you. You said I was to have more whisky." She seemed to be looking at Lydgate with reborn professional interest, the odd ultra-feminine tricks peeping out, like house-lizards at nightfall. Lydgate gave her, and himself, more whisky. She took it as quickly as before, this time with no grimace. "Like fire," she said, as other neophytes had said before her.

126

"And now we ought to go," said Lydgate.

"Oh, not just yet. Somebody nice might come in. Perhaps," she said, beginning to droop once more, "Max might come in again. To say good-bye again." She sniffed, rubbing her rubbery nose with the side of her hand. "I feel sad again," she said. "I'll have one more of those."

"I think," said Lydgate, "you've had enough." One never knew whether one was doing the right thing: how frightful was responsibility.

"One more. To stop me feeling sad. I'll drink it very quickly."

"I don't think you ought really. Two's enough if you're not used to it."

"Oh, it doesn't matter," said Eileen, "if you don't want to." She looked round, head proudly high. "Perhaps one of those men will buy me one. Don't worry about me. You go on home if you want to."

One must try to do one's best for others. Let it not be said that he, Lydgate, ever threw a wife and mother, with a nail-hammering singing husband innocent at home, into the opportunity of sin. Sin? What the hell was that, anyway? "All right," said Lydgate. "One for the road."

After the third it became evident that they would have to go. Material for a temperance tract, thought grim Lydgate. The monster in the dram. "Come on," he said. She threw off drops of her womanhood all round, shaking herself as from an aromatic bath, so that perfumed spray hit the tooth-pickers at the next table and made them turn to look at her. She advertised dentifrice, eye-drops, the cut of her brassière. She giggled, spoke loud, crossed her legs. Warily the Chinese replete sucked their tooth-picks, watching, assessing. "Home," said Lydgate firmly. It was almost like an amateur stage performance of drunkenness—too swift in its onset to be true, like falling in love in a film.

Lydgate had to put his arm round her to get her from the chair. She laughed delightedly as she nearly fell. Outside, the yellow-headed taxi waited. The youth said, "She drunk. Drink too much get drunk. I know."

"I don't want," said Lydgate, "any more of your bloody profundities. Home, quick."

Eileen tried to make a sort of bed of Lydgate in the back of the car, giggling, snaking her arms about his neck, flipping through the English vocabulary of her trade: "Darling. I love you. You like? You want?" But Lydgate knew that this was a mere limbering-up, a running-through of lines before a revival. Forbes, he thought, was a fool and ought to have known better at his age, but he did not feel like dropping a drunken wife on her husband's doorstep, saying, "This is what you married. Sort it out for yourself." To Eileen he said, very slowly, "We must walk round for a little while before you go home. You'll feel better then."

"But I feel well," she said. "I don't feel sad any more." To prove it, she giggled.

"What would Max say?" said Lydgate. "You giggling like a girl and calling another man darling the night before he goes. He wouldn't like it, would he?"

The mere name was as good as a swig of vinegar. Eileen jammed herself in the corner and cried without tears. "That's better," said Lydgate. "You think of Max and we'll have no trouble with your husband. Here," he said to the driver. "Stop here. We'll walk the rest of the way."

The youth turned round to flash from gold teeth in the lamplight the grin of one to whom life, like language, is simple. "I wait," he said. "Good place there. Workmen hut."

"You," said Lydgate tolerantly, "are a dirty-minded little boy. Here is one buck. Now go."

Eileen's legs, unmoved by the mention of Maximilian Hup, went their own way, asking for a great deal of the road. Lydgate's arm scooped Eileen's body sternly in to his side. "I won't go home," she said. "I'm going back. To see Max. Max," she told the moon, boss of a round misty shield that spoke of more rain to come. The taxi reversed and made for town, the youth giving Lydgate a good-hunting wave.

"Just a little walk round," said Lydgate. "Then home. See, there it is, over there. Your new house. We mustn't have you spoiling your first night in your nice new house." It seemed then that Eileen began to recite violently and intermittently the surname of her departing lover. Lydgate banged her on the back, but the noise went on. It was the only noise of the night, except for the sound of hammering in the distance, Forbes still at work.

"Water," said Eileen swiftly between hups.

"Round the other side," said Lydgate. "We mustn't pass your place. I'll give you some water." They walked, she still unsteady, a regular co-ordinated rhythm reserved for the passionate glottal strokes, on the side of the road opposite the tiny houses, near to Patu's small mansion. They crossed, went round the back of the end house, loud with its two drunken Sudus, and found themselves among the dust-bins. They trod mean sandy grass, seeing on their left a slag-tip made romantic by compassionate moonlight. Lydgate counted the dust-bins. Eileen's noise was swallowed by Sudu song, a recrudescence of the Italian quarrel, her hammering husband's anvil chorus, one of her children crying. This was a night of light; the humdrum bulbs in the houses seemed almost festive. Lydgate's back door was open. He switched on the kitchen light, thought it best to leave the living-room in penumbra. "Sit on this chair," he ordered Eileen. It was a rickety structure by the

kitchen sink, one of many knocked out by an Indian contractor at fifty bucks apiece (twenty to the contractor,
representing a profit of nineteen hundred per cent; thirty
split on a sliding scale among various interested parties).
The chair could hold Eileen but hardly her hiccupps.
She nearly hupped on to the floor, clawing at the sink just
in time. Lydgate felt inside his refrigerator, crowned by
Forbes's butter, and gripped the neck of a bottle. It was a
pint Gordon's, emptied of gin, filled with water. He took
it to the kitchen, where Eileen sat on the floor, head against
the food-cupboard, hiccupping against hammering song
and a Tuscan duet (*stringendo molto*, but already *fff*), and
slopped the water swiftly into a tea-cup. "Hold your
breath," he said softly. "Drink it in ten big sips." He knelt
on the floor beside her. She sobbed in breath like an
asthmatic while he held the cup to her paint-smeared lips
with one hand, steadying her small head with the other.
At the first swallow she protested loudly, spitting it out.
"Come on, more," said Lydgate. "It's the only way." She
took half the tea-cup bravely, moaning, twisting her face.
"That's better," said Lydgate. She panted desperately, but
the hiccups had gone. "That's much better," said Lydgate.
   "Like fire," she said. "Like that whisky."
   "Nonsense," said Lydgate. He finished the cup himself
and, with his dry mouth, could taste no no-taste of water.
Came the last trickle. Even though he was a gin-drinker,
even though he had had his share of American martinis,
he spluttered and coughed. Some bloody fool had put a
fighting-cock in among the capons. Forbes perhaps, doing
a good turn, had swigged a couple of bottles of water in his
worker's thirst, found no water in the tap, seen the Gordon's
bottle, thought, with his limited knowledge of civilised
drinks, that such bottles were made, label and all, only for
chilling water, and put it in to cool for his cobber. Lydgate

looked fearfully at Eileen. She drooled, lolled her head, but seemed happy. Lydgate tried to lift her, but tropical heat and a low diet had taken away his youthful strength. 'But,' he thought, 'I can't be blamed for this. It's Forbes's own bloody fault. He can help to carry her in.' Eileen tried to get up, failed, laughed loudly. "Wait," warned Lydgate. "Just a minute."

Next door Forbes had laid down shining oil-cloth on floor and table. His pictures were on the walls. An old horse-hair sofa snarled at the bright, cheap P.W.D. furniture. In one corner there was already a sand-pit for the children. Blue crockery in the book-case clattered at the final hammer-strokes. Forbes stood back to admire the coat-rack he had fixed on the wall—ornamental, Lydgate had time to suppose, for Forbes possessed no coat. "Hallo, Lyddy, old man," said Forbes. "Looking ship-shape at last, eh?"

"Your wife," said Lydgate, "is in my house. I gave her a lift home. She wasn't feeling well. She wanted a glass of cold water. You haven't got a fridge, so——"

"Poor little kiddy," said Forbes. "She's been pretty ill some mornings. Sick and all. I shouldn't have let her go out."

"But this is the trouble," said Lydgate. "She drank out of the wrong bottle, you see, and——"

"Not poison?" said Forbes, hushed. "Don't sy she's tiken poison."

"No, no, gin. She's all right, but she can't get up from the floor. I need your help. Or perhaps you can do it yourself." 'Women,' he thought, 'women.'

"Gin?" said Forbes. "Gin? That little kiddy never touches a drop. Oh, my word, she will be in a stite. I'd better go and get her." His hand on the door-knob, he turned to Lydgate. "I don't quite get all this, Lyddy, old man," he said. "You've not been trying to get her tight, have you? Because if you have I'll get a bit crook, you know."

"Oh, don't be silly," said Lydgate with irritation. "Why on earth should I——?"

"But I don't like it," said Forbes. "The first night she wears her new frock and goes down into the town. How do I know what's been going on? You're not an Aussie, either, see. You're a Pommy, aren't you? You're not like us."

"Oh, let's get on with it," said Lydgate. "If you want to know, it was all your fault. You've been into my house, haven't you, drinking water?"

"I had a couple of beers, and perhaps I'm a bit sorry I had them now," said Forbes. "And I'll bring round my pound of butter home along with the missis."

"You put a bottle of gin in with the water bottles."

"Are you saying now that I've been tiking your gin along with your beer? That mikes me get a little bit crook, that does. Gin's a woman's drink, anyway."

"That takes us back to where we started," said Lydgate. "Bring your wife home."

"After you've been gallivanting round with her," said Forbes. "That's it, eh? Throwing her to one side when you've done with her, eh? Getting that poor little kiddy drunk, eh?"

"You know what she's like," said Lydgate, nettled. "Or, if you don't, you ought to. She can look after herself. But I've not been touching her. I wouldn't if she paid me instead of me paying her."

"I don't quite like the sound of that," said Forbes. "Sy that again."

"What do you want? You're always saying you don't want to take her back. She'll never change. Women of that sort never do. Now please come along and carry her home."

"That little kiddy's a good little kiddy. And you know it," said Forbes. "Pure and innocent she was till that bastard got hold of her. And now you're trying his gyme, just because your bit's gone and left you. I know. The other Aussies know all about it."

"Don't be a bloody fool," said Lydgate. "I've got witnesses, if you're going to make an issue of it. Now try and be sensible and come and get her home."

Forbes had the door half-open. Even if it had been closed they would have heard the great cry of Paolo going out into the night. "What's he sying?" asked Forbes. "What's he doing? If he's been in on this too I'll get him. Have you been miking everybody tight?" he said fiercely to Lydgate. Paolo stood in the middle of the road, shouting loud, conducting a *brio* passage. *"Io dormiro,"* he yelled, *"nel minaretto!"*

"He's going to sleep in the minaret," said Lydgate.

"How do you know his language?" asked Forbes suspiciously. "I don't like this one little bit. What's everybody plying at?"

"Come and get your wife," said Lydgate wearily. "Never mind about him."

They went through Lydgate's living-room to the back, where the light still burned. Even from there they could hear Paolo going off shouting down the road. The kitchen was empty.

"Where is she?" said Forbes. "You've got her upstairs in bed, haven't you? With no frock on. And it was a new frock, too. Bloody shimeless," he said. "I'll kill you, old man, that I will."

"She's not upstairs," said Lydgate. "Look if you don't believe me. She doesn't seem to be anywhere," he added, coming back from the lavatory next to the kitchen.

"What have you done with her, eh? Just tell me that,"

said Forbes. "Tell me what you've bloody well done with her."

"Nothing, nothing, nothing," cried Lydgate. "Have some blasted sense, man. Let's start looking. Perhaps she's being sick on the slag-heap."

"Poor little kiddy," said Forbes. They went out and looked round in the rainy moonlight. Eileen was not by the dust-bins, not by the slag-heap, not by the abandoned tractor on the waste land, not in the thicket of scrub among the tin-cans. "Where are you?" called Forbes. "Where've you got to, my little kiddy?" There was no answer, except from a distant pie-dog. "Gone," said Forbes. "Gone out of my life. I didn't want it to be this wy."

"Take it easy," said Lydgate. "She's probably on her way to town. You'll soon catch her up."

"You're coming too," said Forbes. "You started all this."

"I've finished," said Lydgate with passion. "I've finished with women. She's your wife, not mine. I," he said, "have wives of my own. I've finished with wives."

"Except other people's, eh?" said Forbes. "Come on, you're coming with me. Anything might have happened to the poor little kiddy. Anybody might have got hold of her. That foreign bastard," he added, immediately loping off in long Aussie strides. "That one who was shouting just now. I don't trust him," he said to Lydgate by his side. "I don't trust any of you. And if I catch him at it I'll kill both of you, because it'll be your fault as well as his. Getting that poor innocent little kiddy drunk on gin," he added. "The more I see of you Europeans the more glad I am I'm an Austrylian." They marched down the road, one out of step with the other, Lydgate impelled, as he had to admit to himself, by guilt, but by a guilt older than anything Forbes could possibly suspect.

14

Ah, young Signore, stride in anger, dost thou, back that
way that but lately thou didst come? The anger thou
quelledst in tears thou badest revive in thy father's house.
The sin of anger is in all truth bad enough, but anger
toward thy father, who gave thee thy being, who main-
tained and schooled thee, who is now the means to en-
lighten thy mind further through travel in outlandish
parts, this is of all sins perhaps the most reprehensible,
being the most unnatural. Filial piety was ever accounted
by the ancients the most goodly of virtues in the young
and the crime of parricide was of all crimes punished
with the most ingenious severity. Here in truth there are
monkeys, parrots and snakes enough to be thy uncomfort-
able partners in a sealed sack to be thrown in the sea,
though parricide, thou wouldst say in thy rustic and barbarous dialect, thou hast as yet only committed in thy
heart. But the Almighty, in matter of sin as of virtue,
taketh the will for the deed. Remember that. Add to
this sin the sin of theft and, occasioned by that, the sin of
gluttony, also the sin of lecherous intent toward an
honourable and high-placed matron, and all this in but
two days, and thou hast a fair bag. But more sin is to
come, and that sin a double one, namely of both lechery
in act, perhaps venial in the young but by no means to be
condoned, and of adultery, which Saint John saith shall
be punished by fire for the act and brimstone for the stink
of the ordure of the partners in that sin. One partner this

night may in no wise be eternally punished, for she knoweth not the enormity of the commission nor, in her invincible ignorance, hath she heard the Word and seen the truth of it. She is but a heathen, thou hast been schooled in the right way and didst once even kiss the toe of the Sovereign Pontiff. But what grace remaineth in thee? Thou wilt like some young bull go to it, slaking thy parricidal anger in its relief but by no means quenching it finally.

Thou walkest but a little way and then hearest a voice as of one calling. It is a woman calling from a safe covert, a hut for day-labourers long neglected, the home of spider, scorpion, lizard and human lust. With the instinct of her kind she knoweth the best and most secret places for lechery. Thou hearest, attentively thou listenest, thy head on one side in manner of a hound, thou followest that voice. Outside the hut are palm-trees, but these call not to thy mind stories of the Holy Land. Holiness thou dost not desire; thou art bent on sin, the act of darkness.

On her breath is no honey but the smell of strong drink, the potent mingling of barley and juniper in deadly ferment. That smell thou recallest not from early days when thou wast but young in sin; then it was the smell of the grape. But no matter: the grape, the barleycorn, the juniper berry, given by God to gladden man's heart but not too much, can be the fuel to unlawful passion, more, they can be its excuse. For thee no extenuation stands. If thou art drunken, it is with anger. It maketh a bull, a goat, a stallion of thee; in awful joy thou goest to it.

But, stay, who are these? One man is from the Antipodes but, contrary to the superstition of the vulgar, he is like other men. His companion is the eternal wanderer; he acknowledgeth neither kin nor birthplace. He approacheth eld, he hath experience. It is he who seeth the cabin where thy lust worketh itself out, he remembereth lewd advice of the charioteer of Cathay. He beckoneth his fellow closer to it, he heareth, approacheth on tiptoe the sound of beastly gratification. With somewhat of envy he heareth, but with somewhat more of loathing.

In flagrante thou hast it, but the shameful detail hid by the dark, that hell-born abettor of sin. What followeth but a Babel, a confusion of unholy cries, kicks and blows, screams of woman in fear. Lust croucheth now above in the rooftree, his wings fearfully foldeth. The watch cannot be called, for the watch is ever distant from crime, keeping away, in terror of what they should prevent or, following their duty, arrest. But this is a heathen land and the law is but a scrawl on old sheepskin, meet only for derision. It sufficeth to seek revenge in place of justice, though the wronged husband, doubt it not, will speak angry words in the chambers of the high. Thee he blameth bitterly, seeing in thy person and thy acts all that he most loathes in thy race the which, in his antipodean way, he allegeth to be most vile and corrupt. The other man he blameth for being the witting cause of the weakening of his wife's hitherto, so he insisteth, inviolate virtue. But in his rage he spareth not her, calling her Jezebel and harlot, asking heaven where now is that small and tender one of the goat's flock that, in this land at least, had all his heart. Thou, trained in the art, hittest shrewdly, dancing on swift feet. Thou hittest too hard and layest him low. Out for the count. Over his corse sobs the woman.

Wilt thou never be out of trouble? Wilt thou never learn to avoid the occasions of sin? What will thy father say? A chariot, with roof of royal yellow, halteth by the carnage. Sacklike the seeming corse must be lugged aboard. The charioteer asketh double fare for transporting of a corse to the laying-out. Other care hath he not. But much care hast thou, young Signore.

PART THREE

15

The passionate rain returned. Slumped in the back-seat of the official monster, The Honourable Mr. Tomlin saw the vegetable and mineral parts of the kingdom he was supposed to rule, on his way, behind a forlorn little flag, to the Astana, residence of the Caliph. He saw failed cocoa, half-hearted maize, scooped rock, mud, sleeping bulldozers, abandoned native houses. Under these sheltered pie-dogs, his visible animal kingdom. The Astana was a long way out of town. In their corral the royal elephants raised rods of sugar-cane, like primitive elephant flutes, to the sour-milk sky. The Honourable Mr. Tomlin passed the houses of court officials with pretentious and unpronounceable titles, their washing on the line swilled by the great taps of the air. He passed the *surau* or private mosque and entered the palace grounds. Here the driver was challenged, as in a charade, by black sentries. Driver and sentries knew each other and, with golden jaws ajar, exchanged banter. The U.N. Adviser was then saluted in American fashion and allowed to pass.

The Astana was a very comfortable-looking Edwardian mansion. Here was nothing of the Alhambran super-cinema or the provincial Turkish baths. With its imported red brick, its gable-ends, its weathercock, it was easily the most exotic building in the State of Dunia. But no venerable butler came to the door. Instead a pert young flunkey in silk, a red sash, a tarboosh with the royal badge in silver, with a mouthful of good teeth, jauntily swung open the heavy oak and greeted the driver cordially. The Honourable Mr. Tomlin tapped on the glass to stem the long discussion of debts and family. Big lips came down like funeral blinds over shining teeth. The U.N. Adviser was bowed from his car and admitted to the Astana. There was a long smoke-room with club chairs and pictures of shipwrecks. A fresh flunkey led him to deep plush, another brought him warm orange-squash, another offered cigarettes and a Queen Anne silver table-lighter. Like any other visitor, he was being looked after. He sat in gloom, waiting, seeing in the long wall of windows wet greenery slobbering, rain rushing from ornamental pipes, the terrible sky of Africa over an English park. At length an official of the palace came, a fat healthy-looking young man in a well-cut lounge suit and a tarboosh, educated at Achimoto and Magdalen, welcoming but not deferential. The U.N. Adviser was led towards the Presence, through corridors loud with royal children in wet-day play (nephews and nieces mainly, but sufficiently intimidating to the new arrival. The Honourable Mr. Tomlin knew them all well, hated them, showed his teeth at them in a horror-film smile). Soon they came to the tabernacle. The U.N. Adviser entered, his breathing shallow, his heart faster than usual. Had he been of the faith of Nando Tasca he would have recognised the feeling of entering the confessional ("twelve months since my last . . . missed Easter duty . . . drunk . . . adultery . . .").

The first thing the U.N. Adviser saw was himself. Like the Magis Zoroaster, my dead child, he met his own image, but twice, pinioned in Mr. Smetana's art. And his all too live child. And his tooth-picking lady. He stood amazed, his mouth open. The Caliph was seated and drew down the eyes of his visitor with a formal Arabic greeting. The Caliph was in white silk shirt, black wide trousers, dagger in belt, cigarette smoking away, dark glasses.

"And may the peace of God be with you," responded the U.N. Adviser. "Where did you get these things?"

"Do be seated. A young foreigner gave an exhibition of his pictures in the Rest House. Tuesday and Wednesday. I was invited to open it. It was generally regretted that you were not able to be present."

"You can't hang those up there," protested the U.N. Adviser. "You just can't."

"You really should have been present," said the Caliph. "A very clever young man. A most interesting exhibition, much appreciated by all."

"I had to work," said the U.N. Adviser. "Somebody has to work." He kept his eyes still on the cruel likeness.

"I?" said the Caliph. "I?" There was reproach in the flood of cigarette-smoke. The U.N. Adviser remembered he was in private audience with the ruler of Dunia. It was meet for him to use the special terminology, survival of ancient days, happy days, days before the West had brought in the whisper of democracy. "Dog had to work," emended the U.N. Adviser sullenly. "Dog could not go to the exhibition. If Dog had been there Dog would have bought up those pictures. Dog would like to buy them now off Your Highness."

"No can do," said the Caliph in crisp National Language. "May it please the U.N. Adviser to be seated."

"Your Highness can't do it," said the seated Honourable Mr. Tomlin. "Your Highness is making a laughing-stock of Dog to all Your Highness's visitors. Dog is, after all, representative of the United Nations Organisation."

"I have worked out reform of the currency," said the Caliph. "Or rather, I should say, of the nomenclature of the currency. That is why I summoned you. You are entitled to give me your U.N. Advice about secular matters."

"But Your Highness did not summon Dog. Dog arranged this interview with Your Highness through Your Highness's private secretary. Dog has more urgent matters than currency to talk about." The U.N. Adviser's eyes could not leave the wall.

"Oh?" smoked the Caliph. "The messages must have crossed. We will take it that you are here at my summons. You will give me your advice about the currency. 'Buck', I have discovered, is a vulgar Americanism. Why was I not told before? It seemed formerly a reasonable Anglicisation of the National Language *bukh* which, as you know, means anything folded. Now, I have had a dream, or, rather, a vision. In this vision an angel appeared and said that our unit of currency should be divided into eight and called a piece of eight. Eight seems a more satisfactory division than ten. It means we can have quarters. Now, as to the names——"

"But, Your Highness," said the U.N. Adviser, "this is frivolous, if Your Highness will permit Dog to say so. Dog comes on a matter of morality, of religion."

"Frivolous?" puffed the Caliph sharply. "An angelic vision frivolous?"

"The Mosque," said the U.N. Adviser. "The marble. The Italian workers. Does Your Highness realise that one of these attempted to rape my wife, then my daughter, then succeeded in seducing the wife of one of the Australian road engineers, then half-killed the husband?" In the urgency of his words The Honourable Mr. Tomlin had forgotten to inflect "Dog" to the possessive form. The Caliph was indulgent and let that pass. He looked up, instead, at the pictures on the wall, the blind dark glasses seeming to assess the seducibility of the U.N. Adviser's wife and daughter. He said:

"Surely this is a criminal matter. I am not the Chief of Police. He has his office, I mine. We will return to the currency."

"Dog is not going to the police," said the U.N. Adviser. "The wife of Dog is making no charge. The wife of Dog has no intention of making an exhibition of herself."

"That," said the Caliph, gazing still through smoke and dark lenses at Mr. Smetana's art, "has been done already for her."

"Dog begs Your Highness's pardon?" The two sat as close as in a cabin of a children's joy-wheel, black knees almost touching grey. The U.N. Adviser had so far had little difficulty in hearing. But now the Caliph had decided to start mumbling. Now, as they neared the crux.

"If it is not a matter for the police," said the Caliph firmly, "it is not a matter for anybody. I would say only this: it is hardly seemly for the wife and daughter of the U.N. Adviser to render themselves so easily accessible to repressed Italian workmen. Unless, of course, the Italian workman broke into the Residency."

"Dog's wife and daughter were at the cinema, Your Highness."

"Without escort?"

"Dog had a headache."

"You see," said the Caliph, "what happens when you relax the ancient rules. When my womenfolk pine for the cinema, the cinema is brought to them. This excessive licence you grant to women—it is that that is bringing Europe to ruin."

"We will forget that," said the U.N. Adviser. "The other matter is a matter which calls at once for action.

The husband saw his wife assaulted and was then assaulted himself."

"Look," said the Caliph, "Allah knows that the time for living the good life is short. There is this question of the currency. Let the wronged man seek redress of his wrongs through the channels that you, the United Nations, have appointed. This is no concern of mine."

"Oh, but it is, Your Highness. There is the question of the Mosque. The internal decorations of the Mosque are by no means completed. The day of its consecration and opening approaches. I—" (in his sense of power and authority he instinctively dropped the "Dog") "I am forced to give the two Italians notice to leave the State. They are undesirable elements. The question of police action is neither here nor there. I think, Dog thinks, that it was Your Highness himself who declared, in full State Council, that there is no room for immorality here."

"It was you," said the Caliph, in sharp blue smoke, "who seemed to imply that there was."

"There was, Dog said, a difference between private and public morality."

"That I cannot see."

"Dog and Your Highness will not argue about that now. Dog, as Your Highness will admit, is responsible for the expatriate community. The two Italian expatriates must go."

"Very well. Let them go. How quickly can replacements be found for them?"

"Replacements cannot be found, Your Highness." The Honourable Mr. Tomlin sat back and looked up at the spinning fan in hidden triumph. The tail of his right eye caught his blubbering image on the wall and, framed in the window near it, the blubbering sky. 'Reality,' he thought.

"Replacements must be found."

"The firm in Tripoli has a virtual monopoly of this kind of work, Your Highness. There are, it would seem, other skilled workers in marble, also Italian. They have just completed some work in Cairo and have now been sent to Zanzibar to decorate the offices of a Turf Commission Agency. But there are no others. Only the Tascas are now available, and there is no possibility of recruiting other skilled workers. Not in the time. A cable was sent to Tripoli and that was the reply. So that is the position, Your Highness."

The Caliph poked blind fingers into his cigarette tin. It was empty. He rang a bell, made a silent victory sign at his lips to the entering flunkey. The flunkey brought a tin, feverishly rotating the lid with its attached metal-cutter. In the silence, to which the perpetual fan-whirr was assimilated, the two seated men, Head of the Faithful, Head of the Infidel, heard air rush into the air-tight vault of the stacked white tubes, heard the thin clatter of the circumcised tin top as the flunkey detached it clumsily. The full tin was placed on the Caliph's smoking table; two full ash-trays were removed; two empty ones set down. The Caliph smoked. The smokeless interval had been like a cessation of breathing. The Caliph breathed smoke. "I see," he said. "You can go," he said to the flunkey, who, with open mouth, wondered at the pictures on the wall, wondered where he had seen that face before. "Him," he suddenly, happily said. He smiled at the Caliph. "You can go," said the Caliph, not unkindly.

"So perhaps the opening of the Mosque will have to be postponed," said The Honourable Mr. Tomlin. "Unless, of course, it is opened in its unfinished state."

"It's quite true," the Caliph mumbled. "The white men are clever. One oughtn't to underrate them."

"Dog begs Your Highness's pardon?"

"Now," said the Caliph, with new vigour, "I think we shall have to overlook the viciousness of these Italians for a time. I think they will have to be allowed to stay till their work is completed. Don't you think so?"

"But Your Highness cannot possibly condone vice, even where a great and holy occasion is at stake. The holiness would, surely, be impaired? Wouldn't it?" asked the U.N. Adviser.

"Oh, fool," said the Caliph impatiently. "I beg your pardon," he said. But The Honourable Mr. Tomlin had not clearly caught the word. "Oh, don't you see that virtue can use sin? You people don't know enough theology, that's your trouble. Coming here with your police stations and your water-closets and your expurgated copies of *Macbeth*." (The Caliph had once taken Senior Cambridge.) "You know nothing of the real things."

"What was that word, Your Highness?"

"Reality, reality. God can use sin. God clearly wants to use sin now. Can't you see it?"

"Religion is not the province of Dog, Your Highness. Your Highness told Dog that the other day."

"How much notice have you given these Italians?" asked the Caliph. "Twenty-four hours?"

"A week, Your Highness. The father says that the son gave his passport away. He didn't realise its value. A new one's being rushed through."

"Well," said the Caliph. He took comfortably a fresh cigarette. "You realise, of course, that nobody may leave the State without requesting the Caliph's permission?"

"But nobody may stay in the State without sponsorship. That's laid down in the Immigration Enactment. And Your Highness and the entire State Council have expressed a desire for greater stringency in the application of the Enactment."

"Well?"

"These two Italians have no sponsor," said the U.N. Adviser. "The sponsorship of the appropriate department has been withdrawn."

"Oh." Blue smoke rose to the ceiling-fan. The arms of the fan danced with the veil of smoke and then tore it into shreds. "They have a sponsor," said the Caliph. "There is no difficulty. I shall sponsor them myself."

Both men sat back, a new image dancing between them, under the fan: two ragged infidels, drunk or immoral, certainly irresponsible, tucked under the mothering wings of an Islamic potentate. The U.N. Adviser almost saw it projected on to the wall, limned by the sharp pencil of a Czech from Asmara. "By God," said The Honourable Mr. Tomlin, "to think that that man accepted my hospitality."

"I beg your pardon?" The U.N. Adviser had spoken English. "Perhaps you didn't quite hear," said the Caliph. "I sometimes forget your infirmity. I shall sponsor them myself."

"Yes, Your Highness. That seems to be the best thing to do." He saw a new image, jerkily replacing the last one as in a lantern lecture—a gunboat steaming up the river. "And then Forbes can charge young Tasca and young Tasca can go to jail. So the Mosque still won't be finished."

"Oh, if a charge *is* preferred, the trial can always be postponed. There would be difficulty in getting an Italian interpreter, for instance. I don't see anything to worry about. Now shall we return to this question of the currency?"

"Those pictures there," said the U.N. Adviser very sharply. "Those insulting and libellous pictures. In the name of the United Nations, I protest. I, I, I," he repeated. "Not Dog. I. I protest." He stood up, the better to protest.

"You see," said the Caliph, "why you can't possibly come back for another term. You see, don't you? You've probably been out in the tropics too long. It affects one's nervous control, after a time. One must be born to this climate." He waved his cigarette in a proprietary way at the endless energy of the rain outside, at the fan above whose cool draught was an emblem of the heat. "But, when you have gone, I shall have something to remember you by." He conducted a bar of common time at the art of Mr. Smetana. "And Mrs. Tomlin. And Miss Tomlin. The Potoks used to hang shrunken heads at their waists. We are more civilised than that. And he tried to rape them, did he? Remarkable."

16

Mr. Smetana managed to get out of the State of Dunia without being assaulted by Lydgate. Sitting in the aircraft Mr. Smetana was able to munch sandwiches and reflect that, on the whole, he had not done too badly out of the trip. He had sold all his drawings and half his canvases and cleared something like two thousand bucks (or pieces of eight). There had been things to annoy him —the weather, the food and lack of food, the inevitable colonial philistinism. Also the demand on the part of the State Board of Literary and Film Censors that he give its members a pre-view in the Chin Chin Cinema on the Monday morning. It was all a mistake, of course: the Board had understood that a Frenchman (Frankistani) was bringing in blue films of his own making, and there had been many *ad hoc* co-options to the Board. The large audience of purehearted Moslems that filled the cinema was naturally disappointed when the pictures were found to be static and, moreover, harmless; some members of the Board had become captious and grumbled about naked Sudu bosoms in some of Mr. Smetana's village scenes; Mr. Smetana had shouted back and the morning had become lively. However, a palace officer had, as a member of the Censorship Board, been able to report back to the Caliph that the exhibition would not be without interest, and Mr. Smetana had been paid, for four little drawings, more than he had ever expected to be paid. So everything had gone well.

Now for Tanganyika and more black beauties and dripping date palms, more rest-houses and bad food and philistines. Still, one had to suffer for one's art. Then back to Asmara and little golden-skinned Paul, very good Christian boy, waiting shyly in the two-roomed flat, and to the State of Dunia no *auf Wiedersehen*.

The U.N. Adviser snarled at Lydgate for letting Mr. Smetana into the State. Lydgate had had to point out that, as Controller of Passports, he had a right to exercise his own discretion as far as temporary visitors were concerned. The U.N. Adviser snarled that there must be no more visiting painters, especially Czech ones. Before closing-time on the second day of the exhibition Lydgate went to see what were left of Mr. Smetana's paintings and saw a portrait of a Potok girl nursing a golden-haired boy, price eighty bucks. The Potok girl was, all that was visible of her, naked, and there was a pleasant counterpoint of floating wavy gold and firm round black breasts. Lydgate asked Mr. Smetana where he had met Wajak and Mr. Smetana said that she was a little whore whom he had met in a cabaret in Shurga four months previously, pregnant but ready for superfetation. Lydgate had not been able to hit Mr. Smetana there and then, for the State Education Officer and his wife were present and also the State Marine Officer and three New Zealand stenographers. The next morning Mr. Smetana had gone.

The trouble was, thought Lydgate, sitting in depression in his office, that it might be true. Wajak had left for Shurga ridiculously early, only five months gone, as far as he could reckon, on the plea of a premonition that the child would be born about six months after conception. She argued that this must be so because his, Lydgate's, children had been born after nine months and he, Lydgate, had been about fifty; this new father was only about

thirty-five and one had to make a proportionate adjust-
ment in calculating the time for gestation. Lydgate's
counter-arguments had made no impression: Wajak was a
primitive person, and primitive people take a long time
to learn to observe; Wajak was also, though sweet and
pleasant to cuddle in bed, not very bright. Still, Wajak
ought to learn to tell the truth and not pretend she was
living quietly in her native village when in fact she was
earning pin-money in a dance-hall. 'Women,' thought
Lydgate, 'women.'

Lydgate prepared to look at the mass of official cor-
respondence on his desk, ready for strange syntax, weird
spelling, atrocious typing, ambiguity, nonsense—work of
ill-trained administrators, executives, clerks of the new
post-war breed. But first he comforted himself with looking
out of the window at his car, but newly arrived by coastal
steamer—parked shining in the sunlight that had returned
to the town. He was mobile again, independent of yellow-
headed taxis. Then he looked at the opposite wall of his
office, whereon a patch of damp was hidden by a Syrian
calendar, and thought that the portrait of Wajak and his
son George would have graced it. But you can't buy a
man's picture and threaten to hit him at the same time.
Besides, the real Wajak would be back soon, together with
three children. Work for them. Through the glass wall that
was an eye on the general office Lydgate could see his subordinates of many races, not working much. Humble folk
of the town sought passport renewals, travel permits, identity cards; the black and brown clerks were lordly behind
the desks, making the human right to stasis or mobility a
costly privilege. Lydgate, incorrupt, looked at his letters.

The first one was not ill-spelled, not ill-typed, and this
was unusual for a letter from the U.N. Adviser's office.
Under a glory of crest and embossed titles the rubber-

stamp U.N. Adviser informed the Controller of Passports that the decision to refuse entry to Mr. M. Bastians had been revoked: he would be allowed to remain in Dunia for twenty-four hours. At the bottom of the curt but literate page was typed "Copy to Chief Police Officer". Lydgate was surprised but approved the wisdom of the U.N. Adviser's change of mind: Patu, sponsoring Bastians, had a fair and dangerous following. Or perhaps the U.N. Adviser had decided that politicians were less dangerous than artists. The second letter was from Mudd's office: it gave a list of quasi-permanent immigrants who would be working in government departments, together with expected dates of arrival. Lydgate reached in a desk drawer for a small flask of brandy he kept for stomach upsets: prominent was the name of Mrs. Lydia Lydgate. She would be arriving by air in, Lydgate checked by the calendar, less than a week. He swigged some brandy shakily. Taking a hold on himself, he reflected that he was mobile, had a fast car, never went to the Club, was rarely invited out, need never meet her, could always flee her. But what a damnable thing. His body and nerves seemed to tauten under the blow of the brandy; he seemed to foresee an annihilation of the space that would separate them, the full bulk of her hip pressing against his through a mile of air, her un-Australian actress's voice striking an ear that had become a radio receiver incapable of being switched off—"He's living with one of the abo women. How many bastards has he got? Whisky ginger ale, please." He threw her full body, her clear voice, her ridiculous name into the in-tray.

The next letter was again from the U.N. Adviser's office but, unlike the first, so clumsy in diction and orthography that Lydgate doubted for a moment if it were genuine. It stressed the need, especially during the period preceding the opening of the Mosque, for strict observance of the Immigration Enactment. The regulation concerning sponsorship of intending immigrants applied, Lydgate was reminded, to re-entrants as much as to original applicants for entry into the State. Sponsorship for previous entry was not automatically valid for re-entry. The time-quota for immigrants who were not employed by the Government was two years, but, even if unexpired, it was deemed to have expired if a period of intended temporary absence from the State were prolonged beyond three months, no matter what the cause. In view of the impending shortage of accommodation which would be occasioned by the arrival of the visitors who were to assist at the opening of the Mosque, along with their entourages, it was obviously necessary to limit the number of temporary entrants coming even on *bona fide* business. As for intending entrants whose business was not *bona fide*— let it be remembered that the State would soon be crawling with holy men who would be informed—in a hand-out prepared by the Information Department—that Dunia's secondary title (conventional Arabic epistolary) was *Daru'r-ridzwan*—the Abode of Grace. What grace could there be (the letter clumsily implied) where the reek of opium, of pork-seller's stalls, of whore's perfumes rose to choke the calling muezzin?

Lydgate smoked and thought. He saw, and did not see, through the glass wall by the tail of his right eye, urgent bargaining proceeding over the right of identity. Clearly on the wall opposite he saw Wajak, in full black, projected, along with a golden-haired child, a gold-bodied child, and a child whose colour he had yet to see. So she was not to be allowed to return. Status? Not wife. Occupation? Mistress, not to be found in the schedule of government posts. Or perhaps servant, keeper of his house, suckler of one child he must call his, groundnut-boiler for the two perhaps certainly his. "Madam I may not call you, mistress I am ashamed to call you." So Queen Elizabeth I had greeted the wife of the Archbishop. But, whatever she was, she was heartily welcome. For Wajak, however, there was no welcome.

In a flash, in the lighting of a fresh match, Lydgate betrayed Wajak. If she could not enter Dunia, was that his fault? The Controller of Passports, of all officials, should be above suspicion. It would be the foulest sort of corruption to take advantage of his position, would it not? Besides, was his house really big enough for a mistress and three children?

Sex. Did he really need that now? He thought, tested his reactions to various images, tried to be honest with his glands. Yes, he did need it. Occasionally. He again saw Paolo Tasca and the wife of Forbes of Marmion in the street lighting that shot thin shafts through the cracks of the workmen's hut. Disgusting, ridiculous, when other people did it. Still, it was there, if he wanted. Next door too, everything laid on. Forbes of Marmion had learned nothing: the poor little kiddy had been taken advantage of by men who should have known better. Nightly she was allowed to go to town while he nursed the children at home. And nursed the back of his skull, still sore.

Lydgate felt, for some reason, virtuous. He was being faithful to something, if only the Immigration Enactment. And, before he sank into the sleep of his routine work, he caught an image of Lydia Lydgate, the barrack-room beauty, dream of home, not now able to sneer at abo keeps and chocolate-coloured bastards.

17

Forbes of Marmion came of stock that had no love of police
actions; he sought wild justice several times after, and once
during, the working hours of Paolo Tasca. Attempting to
bring anger and violence into the holy coolness of the
Mosque, he was met by tough Sudus with marble-workers'
tools. Hammering for revenge at the door of the *Casa
Tasca*, determined to "have it out", he himself was had out,
and speedily, by the father as well as the son. But, he
promised, one night he would bring his road labourers
along, tougher than men of marble. Let the two Eyetie
bastards beware.

Nando Tasca's attitude to his son changed somewhat
now. He was determined to finish the marbling of the
Mosque on time, for (and this Paolo did not know, nor did
the labourers) he had been promised a bonus of so many
bucks per marble block should the time-limit of the contract not be exceeded. It was important that Paolo not
be beaten up and rendered incapable of working the
cutting-machine. Though he deplored his son's incon-
tinence and, more, his foolishness in letting himself be
caught in the act, he had to admit to a faint admiration
(faint as angostura colouring gin and water) for Paolo's
enterprise and achievement: the boy was a chip off the
old marble. And Nando Tasca felt, too, a certain awe that
the Caliph himself should seem to condone the act, along

with an itch of approval for a religion whose morality was so elastic. But Nando Tasca had a new annoyance. He had to watch over Paolo now, take him around in the evenings or sit in with him in the hot little house, and this at a time when some small sexual adventure, its intensity tempered to his fifty-odd years, could be his for the asking: nightly Eileen Forbes went down to town to consider, and reject, the curtaining materials on sale there. Still, soon Nando Tasca would be in Tripoli or Zanzibar on a new job, and he felt he was not yet too old for patience.

Tonight father and son lay at home. Paolo stretched near-naked on the grey sheet of his bed, hands joined on his shaggy nape, showing to the light-bulb two dark beards of under-arm hair. His father drank from pint beer-bottles on his own bed, decently clad in striped shirt and shark's skin trousers. Paolo began to describe, at length and earthily, the charms of the new Australian woman who had recently arrived in the town. Nando Tasca cut short the flood of aromatic Tuscan and said:

"You try speak a English. It a good a practice for when you go work on a coconut estate."

"*Non capito.*"

"Why you a always say a that? I speak always very slow, very clear a English. Now, who a this a woman?"

"Fat here," indicated Paolo. "Thin here," indicated Paolo. "Very good."

"I not say a what a she like. I say what er a name."

"I not know."

At this moment Forbes's nightly hammering on the door commenced. The house shook, two beer bottles by Nando Tasca's bed tintinnabulated. The two men lay calm. "Come out!" shouted Forbes of Marmion. "Come out and fight like a man!"

"I think I go fight him," said Paolo languidly.

"That not a bad. But better you a say 'I think a I a go *to* fight a im.' "

"I think I go to fight him."

"That a *much* better. But you not a go a to fight im. You stay a ere." Nando Tasca started on a new bottle. The noise of challenge continued. "E a drink," said Nando Tasca. "E a drink a beer' first and then e come a ere. Very afraid a man."

"Come out and fight, you bloody coward!" called Forbes of Marmion.

"Blad-ee cow-ard," repeated Paolo, patiently, as if merely at a lesson. "What that mean?"

"I buy a you good a book," said Nando Tasca. "Very old a book. Why you not look in a book? I not teach a you all a the time. I an old a man. Get very a tired." But, vigorously, when the thwarted Forbes had shrieked his last challenge and gone back to tend the babies he had awakened, Nando Tasca got up, stroked the creases from his clothes, and said, "Now we go a out."

"*Dove?*"

"Why you always ask a where a we go? We go a out. You a sit a with me and learn a English from a book. Perhaps a too you *listen* what a people say. That a way you learn a English good."

"*Non capito.*"

"If you a listen more perhaps you a understand a better."

Paolo got up from his bed and stood like a boxer in filthy shorts and canvas shoes. "You not a come a out a like a that," said his father. "Where a your shirt?"

"Shirts in bucket water. Today have water. Today wash shirts."

"That not a bad. You work a ard and you learn a good a English. I lend a you one shirt. I very good a father."

So both walked slowly down the road to the town, the father smart though unshaven, the son in a vast shirt that, worn outside his trousers so that it hid their unsightliness, billowed and flapped in the dry wind that had arisen. The father was all sweat and thirst by the time they reached the Kool Kaffi. Paolo entered behind him, a long glum goat's face, shaggy hair, knock-knees near hidden by the great gay garment of his father. The regular drinkers—Fredericks, Crawshay-Davies and his huge meal of a Mongol wife, Frankie with his lipstick, Patrick Ong and his stage Irish—were tonight pushed out to the periphery. Deep whisky-laughs, collar-and-tied officials, the glitter and clink of a fresh round: the eye and ear were drawn towards the centre, where Lydia Lydgate was enisled in wet male homage. "She," pointed Paolo.

"You not a say a 'she'," said Nando Tasca. "You say a 'er'. So," he admired, his piggy blue eyes ashine, sixpences in Christmas pudding dough, "that a er. *Molto bella*." She was much to his taste: he had had his fill of the tiny, the black, the thin-loined: here was a woman with a waist two hands could span, but Venus-hipped, deliriously firm-and-heavy-breasted, with a flame of hair and a smile as sweet as figs, a voice that could ride above the male shouts, a laugh not afraid to show tongue (clean as a dog's) and teeth (sharp as steak-knives).

"What I want to know is," she was saying, "where does he get to? I mean, he must *live* somewhere. Or perhaps he's given up living." The accent was pure but the tone beefy, apt for loud shouts over vast Australian wastes. "I saw him in his office, through a kind of glass wall. But I couldn't get through to him. Do I have to make an appointment or something?"

Nando Tasca had cut through to her side, with a straight firm cut like the cut of a marble-cutting machine.

"We not a meet before," he said. "Nando Tasca. A please to a meet a you."

"Oh, how sweet. You must be Tony Spaghetti." Paolo was in his father's wake. "Oh, how sweet. What a long shirt he seems to have on. Does he wear anything underneath?"

"This a my son. He not a very good boy. You go," he ordered, "to a that a table. You sit a down learn a English. Where a your book?"

"I forget bring book." Paolo gave goatish admiration to Lydia Lydgate, throwing at her the light of his sheep's eyes.

"Oh, isn't he sweet? And can he sing?" The collar-and-tied men round Lydia Lydgate looked sullen or laughed too hollowly. This proximity of unshaven jowls and Southern charm—it killed the cosy chatty Britishness of their evening. Nando Tasca said, "Who a buy a me a one a beer? Very thirsty. Very ot."

"I can sing," said Paolo. "I am a good boy."

"Come on then," said Lydia Lydgate. "Give us 'Sorrento'."

"You go a to a table," ordered Nando Tasca. "You not a sing a good." He took from the counter somebody else's beer, drank eagerly, and said with foamed lips, "You a ear a me a sing." He sang in a hoarse wheedling voice, straight into Lydia Lydgate's green gold-flecked eyes:

"Che gelida manina, se la lasci riscaldar——"

Paolo picked him up on the high notes, an operatic hand on the breast of his vast lent shirt:

"Cercar che giova? Al buio non si trova——"

In horrid competition, an old and a young Rodolfo glaring at each other, they filled the Kool Kaffi with ill-produced tone:

"Ma per fortuna é una notte di luna——" At the same

time they both reached, belatedly, for the hand of Mimi Lydgate, who said, "How sweet," contending *fortissimo* as they sang.

"E qui la luna l'abbiamo vicina."

But, *sotto voce*, in a brief pause for breath, Nando Tasca was able to say to his son, "You wait a till I get a you ome."

Meanwhile, far from the heart of culture, Lydgate sat in an open-air ramshackle eating-shop, under a light-bulb suspended from a tree. He had brought his car to the muddy end of a suburb and then stumbled over duck-boards to this extra-territorial region called Groundnut Village. Here lived the Syrian gamblers. They emerged from their holes at nine each night to gamble till dawn. At midnight, at three, at first light they came to be served with boiled duck or baked fish by a waiter asleep on his feet. Thousands of bucks changed hands; deaths were unrecorded in the annals of the town and corpses never dredged from the near-by stinking river. It was a safe place to visit for a white man anxious to avoid meeting a white woman. Lydgate sat long over warm beer and a kind of pasta that looked like tape-worms, thinking.

He was thinking that it was already time to be thinking of moving on again. He had before him on the table his month's end statement from the bank. His credit balance was a little over one thousand bucks. He needed more. He would continue to send a hundred a month to Wajak, but he would cut down stringently in other ways. He would ration his drinking; he would eat even less; he would buy no more clothes. Perhaps in six months he would be ready to break contract and move on. But was there anywhere left to move on to? The world revolved heavily behind his eyes. There was Borneo. There was Japan. His mind was coloured swiftly with cherry blossom and kimonos: the Japanese girls he had known had been charming, submissive, ready to let a man have his own way. But no, no more women. What then?

He could not think what then. More women meant more pursuits. Wajak would be after him soon. Lydia was already here. The girl in Nairobi was, he was sure, already re-married. Others? He clicked off the switch. But was there really anything except women? He saw his tragedy quite clearly, or thought he did. He expected too much from women, and too little. Heaven, which they could give, was surely a passive thing, static, marble, light, air. But the heaven was enclosed in an irrelevant apparatus with a hellish high-powered will of its own. The trouble with women was that they wanted to be human beings.

Lydgate, brooding over his beer and his messed-up plate, became aware that somebody was standing beside him. He looked up at a tortured grin, lines of agony on the young forehead, thin brittle bird-bones under a shirt bearing a design of boats, fans, flags, jars, treble clefs. Sebastian Hup, carrying no files.

"So here you are, Mr. Lydgate," said Sebastian Hup.

"Yes," said Lydgate and, with the image of bird-bones in his mind, "Sit down. I've got a bone to pick with you."

"Yes, Mr. Lydgate." Sebastian Hup sat down.

"What do you mean by showing my confidential file to other people? I could have you booted out of the service for that."

"At the bridge party, you mean? Oh, nobody actually *sees* it, Mr. Lydgate. It is just useful for reminding people about their sins."

"Sins? What do you care about other people's sins?"

"Other people's sins can be very profitable. We can learn from other people's sins."

"Earn?"

"And earn. But not very much. The U.N. Adviser

163

has just committed a very big sin. But that will not do anybody any good. He allowed a man who had come to Dunia, a very innocent man, to go up-river and lose his head. The man had come to lecture on some subject or other. He gave one lecture up-river and then lost his head. His body, of course, has been eaten. His head is not yet ready for exhibition. Now the U.N. Adviser must pay, but not in money. He has gone to be told off by the authorities. But I suppose we are all sinners," said Sebastian Hup comfortably.

"Oh. So the U.N.A. will not be here when Bastians arrives?"

"No. There again he committed a very grave error, Mr. Lydgate." Sebastian Hup beat his breast three times and looked at Lydgate from sharp suffering black eyes, meagre-fleshed hands joined loosely on the table before him. "And how are your sins these days, Mr. Lydgate?"

"What are you getting at?"

"There are good forces working for you, Mr. Lydgate. There are many people doing their best to save you."

"What exactly are you driving at?"

"We wait, Mr. Lydgate. We wait for you to tell us what you do not want to tell us. It is best to tell your friends, Mr. Lydgate. Do not wait for your enemies to find out."

"Look here, I'd be very grateful if you'd explain."

"Oh, it's nothing, nothing. Just a thought. Look, Mr. Lydgate, I'm on my way to play poker. I find myself just a little short. Could you possibly lend me, say, a hundred bucks? Just till the end of the month?"

"But this *is* the end of the month."

"Is it? So it is. Money goes very quickly, doesn't it? This is an expensive place to live in." He looked down incuriously at Lydgate's bank balance. He probably knew it already.

"I'm afraid I have to give up lending," said Lydgate. "I'm trying to save, you see. One so rarely gets one's loan back."

"Very, very true. Have you managed to save a great deal, Mr. Lydgate?"

"What's that to you?"

"Nothing, Mr. Lydgate. I was just interested. Perhaps we can have a little talk some other time. You must come to another bridge party at Carruthers Chung's. Perhaps the next one. We would be *so* pleased if you would really, honestly, sincerely, tell us everything. We're all *so* anxious to help."

18

Preceded, flanked and followed by cyclists with beards, black mops, and jackboots, Mr. M. Bastians of Colombo left the airport in triumph. He sat with Patu in Patu's crawling opulent car, driven by a richly hirsute driver, waving and showing good Ceylonese teeth in a happy smile. Workers on a monthly wage had taken the afternoon off to see and greet; only the day-labourers kept to their hiding-places. Mr. Bastians was a handsome walnut-juice-coloured man in his sixties, his white hair neatly parted. He wore a well-tailored palm-beach suit of discreet grey. In its inner pocket he carried a letter from the U.N. Adviser (rubber-stamp-signed) informing him that he was permitted to stay in Dunia Town for twenty-four hours and (a bitter touch of Patu's) wishing him well, as also the cause for which he stood. He had also an application to enter the State, stamped "Approved". His passport had been read with interest (a traveller's log-book, unbelievably rich in visas) by the Immigration underlings, and they had decorated it with a square, a ring, and a lozenge, informing him that he had permission to land. His luggage had been found free from cameras, condoms, gramophone records, tape recorders, parakeets, firearms, opium, proscribed literature and scrap metal specifically forbidden under the appropriate ordinance. He was now in, breathing the warm air of an enslaved State.

The police contingent joined in the cheers of "Freedom

from Tyranny!" Mr. Bishopspawn of the Special Branch sat in his roadster, chewing his underlip. With him was his secretary, Mrs. Lydia Lydgate. "You see what they're like," said Bishopspawn. "Let you down as soon as look. No loyalty, somehow. How fast is your shorthand?"

"Fast enough."

"You'd better take it all down at tonight's meeting. It may come in useful."

"Useful?"

"Yes, yes, yes." Mr. Bishopspawn was a peevish beefy young man, easily irritated, still smarting from certain rebukes administered by a defending barrister from Kampala in a recent bribery case. "Bishopspawn," the barrister —a swarthy and clever Jew—had declared, "is a first-class liar. In charity, however, considering his evident lack of talent, one might concede to him a compensatory capacity for fictitious invention which, if he were literate, might carry him far." He had also made fun of his name (an old name, revered in one of the southern counties) and said, "Your move, Bishopspawn." Now, engaging gear, Bishopspawn said, "We want his speech for the files. He's a bad lot. They shouldn't have let him in."

Hibiscus, hibiscus all the way for Mr. Bastians, members of the party cheering like animate black bushes, clean-shaven workmen who wanted (a) the white man out, (b) the Asians out, (c) sinecures, (d) blood for blood's sake, crying "Aaaah." To Patu's house they drove in bottom gear, Mr. Bastians showing thirty-two good teeth to the world, Patu nodding and smiling in hairy satisfaction. Patu's lawn had been set with marquees and long tables: there was to be a tea-party.

Alighting, Mr. Bastians flashed happiness to the flashing cameras. To a reporter from the *Times of Dunia* he gave a brief message: "The workers of Dunia have common cause with the workers of Ceylon. Their struggle is our struggle. My brief visit is a gesture of solidarity. Let us strive together to the end." This appeared in curt National Language as: "Workers Ceylon like workers Dunia. Is one fight. He comes as sign it one fight. He say fight-fight not stop fight."

Then warmish, very sweet, very milky tea was taken, while Mr. Bastians was introduced to many beards. Sickly cakes entered holes in these beards. The beards nodded and nodded, framing gold and ivory engaging green and yellow sponge. Mr. Bastians ate nothing; the cup in his left hand grew warmer. He smiled and smiled, bowed, expressed pleasure and agreement at all that was said to him. Meanwhile party members chewed up soft cakes like the soft bodies of their enemies.

"Unemployment grows steadily. Ten men of Dunia stock could do the work of one expatriate. Throw out all your expatriates and you have more than enough work for all."

"Yes, yes, indeed," smiled Mr. Bastians.

"The uranium company has stopped drilling. It is merely an excuse to throw people out of work."

"Very likely, very likely."

"They are going to start drilling just outside our borders. To evade the heavy dues they rightly pay to the State. Is that fair?"

"Far from it, very far indeed."

"It is like enticing a neighbour's chickens to crawl through the fence."

"A very, very apt image."

"And how do they know the uranium will only last another five years?"

"How, indeed?"

"Geologists, they call them. Another word for liars."

"That is very good. I must remember that."

The tea-pots were drained, the crumbs collected to feed the fowls, the western sky, in green, pearl, vermilion, magenta, warned that the delicious revolutionary night was coming. Time to change and prepare for the meeting in the Chin Chin Cinema. Mr. Bastians was led off by Patu to a cool room with adjoining bath, there to rest, sluice, change, meditate. His thirty-two teeth took their leave, his benedictory arms wide in the sunset. Not his sunset.

The workers in the Mosque, languidly laying the last block of marble of the day, were determined to be present at the meeting. Moreover, they were determined that Paolo should be present. The Indian with glasses stood by the mihrab, the violet sky of Mecca at his back, and spoke with as much fervour as Mr. Bastians of the need for solidarity. Paolo, moreover, was a white man; the word of the white man always carried more weight than that of the brown or black. Let him, at question-time, speak of their grievances—the pitiable wages, the three-times rejected appeal for a rise. Was this justice, was this religion? Paolo said that he did not yet speak enough English to be eloquent. They all laughed tolerantly, their laughter rising to the heights of the squinches on which the dome was set.

"You are a white man, therefore you speak the white man's language."

"No, no, no. I speak only Italian."

"There is only one white man's language." This was not meant figuratively; it was a straight philological assertion.

"And, afterwards," said a muscular Sudu with a rat-tail reaching to his coccyx, "we shall eat and drink together. *We* shall pay. Obviously you, having no wages, cannot pay." In pity a cigarette was given to Paolo, other cigarettes were lighted, the smoke frailed upwards like the thin prayer of a very old imam. Motes of pulverised marble floated slowly down.

"I have no clothes to wear," said stripped Paolo, yet looking somehow overdressed with a cigarette in his mouth.

"No trouble. A tie, a shirt, trousers. Severally we can lend them."

"Better, let him go in rags. It will be more effective. Dramatic even," said the subtle Indian, leaning against the mimbar.

"My father," remembered Paolo. "There is the question of my father." Nando Tasca had taken to drinking in a shop that overlooked the great portals, or workmen's exit, of the Mosque.

"Tell him," said the Sudu, "that a woman is desirous of his company. That some lovely girl is waiting for him in a back alley."

"Disobey him," said a Potok, a cutting hand slicing the air. "Spit at him. He has no right to make you go home if you do not wish to. You owe him no more allegiance."

"But," said Paolo, "I have become so weak. It is lack of food." His face grew longer, more traguline. "And we shall eat and drink afterwards, you say?" He salivated, had to throw his cigarette down.

"Yes, yes. Afterwards."

"But the noise," said Paolo. "He will not let me sleep. Last night he thumped me on the back of the head while I was just dozing off." The singing contest, the evident preference of the Australian lady for the younger and more virile—Nando Tasca had been at his most fatherly, hitting out blindly, using harsh words, raking up the past.

And every day more and more past was manufactured. Paolo drooped, sighed.

"This woman who is fat and thin in the right places at the same time," said the Potok. "The one you were talking about this morning. Say that *she* wants to see him."

"But she doesn't," said Paolo. "It is me she wants to see."

"Have you evidence of that?"

"The way she looked," said Paolo. "Admiration. Lust, almost. At least," he said, in the dispiritedness of malnutrition, "I thought so. I may be wrong." He drooped further.

"I can speak to him," said the Indian with glasses. "I can pass on a fictitious message. I can say—" (his glasses flashed cunning in the last light) "—that she wants him to go to her house. Has she a house?"

"Oh, yes. On the hill. She has just moved into it."

"That she wants him to go to her house and drink with her. There will be a small party. I will hint that she hints that if he will linger on when the others go——"

"Imagination," said a workman who had not yet spoken, a sort of small Abyssinian. "Too much imagination."

"That will do," said the Indian. "He will believe me. He trusts me, I think. I will undertake to keep his son out of danger."

"He will be sceptical there," said the Sudu. "He remembers the night of the broken bottles. It was you who were caught with one in your hand. And you were cheering his son on. He came into the shop and caught you at it. We were all very, very lucky not to be arrested."

"As I recollect," said the Indian, "it was you who had the broken bottle. As I recollect, it was I who was telling you all not to be such idiots. The police car round the corner——"

171

"Your memory's bad. Boozer's memory."

"Say that again."

"Come, come, come. Solidarity."

"I will give him solidarity. Solid from the neck up, that's his trouble."

"I didn't quite like the way you said that. Say it again."

There was one other workman, a fetcher and carrier, a picker-up of dropped tools, a man low down in their scale. He was squat, wrinkled, and of doubtful race. There was a hole in what the National Language poetically called the heaven of his mouth, and he had no obturator. He said, "Hn. Hn, hn."

"He is right," said the Potok. "A timely rebuke. We must stop this wrangling. Besides, it will soon be time for the meeting."

19

Fans set high in the roof of the Chin Chin Cinema cooled, despite their frantic many revolutions a minute, only the bats' nests and the holes of polecats. Polecats, at intervals, came out to walk the tight-rope girders and sneer down at the packed audience. Occasionally they would dislodge a little of their own accumulated excrement, and this would fall as dry dust. In great heat the audience listened patiently to Patu. Patu, his hands resting on the blanket-covered table, outlined the party's programme as he had outlined it so often before, sometimes emphasising a point with a thump of his fist that made the Thermos jug of water dance. Patience, he said, they would be patient. They wanted little for the moment—only a franchise with few qualifications (ten years in the State, less than an eighth of foreign blood, qualifying minimal age of eighteen established by statutory declaration), the creation of a lower house with party government but no opposition, the existing hereditary State Council to be given the status of upper house with no legislative powers, the Caliph to reign as a constitutional monarch on salary, the Europeans to begin their exodus twelve months after the establishment of the new régime, nationalisation of uranium, secondary education in the National Language, free social services. At one point an ape in worker's denims stood up, roared gently, and displayed a mauled picture of Lydgate in New Guinea. "And jobs," said Patu, "jobs for all."

Mr. Bastians gave a speech in English. He apologised for his ignorance of their noble language, he said, but they would forgive the linguistic shortcomings of one who, brought up on the tongue of the oppressor and exploiter, had had to spend most of his political life fighting tyranny with its own terms and its own weapons. Mr. Patu had kindly consented to translate the few humble words of encouragement he would address to them.

Mr. Bastians used the colourful generalities of the skilled demagogue, the gestures, the rhythms, the controlled crescendi, the teeth-baring climaxes, now working his fingers delicately into the mudra of exposition, now thrusting his arms out in crucified agony, at one point smashing the drinking-glass, at another kneeling and praying to a sort of ectoplasmal wraith—Liberty, Progress, the *Zeitgeist*—that he conjured high among the fans and polecats. The ape and others looked up in wonder. Mr. Bastians ended *fortissimo*, suit sweat-soaked, hair raked by agonised claws, teeth and the heaven of his mouth on view, to languid claps and and calls of "Aaaaah". Translation was not merely supererogatory, it was impossible. There was nothing to translate. Mr. Bastians had said nothing and everything. He was a great politician, one whom Patu, with his niggling insistence on a clear programme and a cool plan of action, could never in a hundred years even approach. Mr. Bastians was good value. No wonder the U.N. Adviser had forbidden him entry to the State.

Paolo was charmed by this one-man opera. He called "Bravo," and stamped his canvas shoes on the concrete. "Your time is coming," said the Indian with glasses. "They will soon be asking for questions."

Patu thanked Mr. Bastians for his inspiring performance. He said that the meeting was now open and would speakers please limit their utterances to two minutes. Sweat dripped, Mr. Bishopspawn chewed his lip, the fans spun, the polecats sneered and tight-rope-walked, the huge audience shifted its damp haunches. Patrick Ong, the Hibernico-Chinese, stood up and said, "Speaking as a member of the most downtrodden race in the world——" ("Take his name," said Mr. Bishopspawn. "O.N.G.")

"It's a Chinese," called somebody in National Language. "Who let *him* in?"

"I am not a Chinese, then," said Patrick Ong in heat. His accent was, if not quite Abbey Theatre, at least a good-provincial-amateur-festival-winning *John Bull's Other Island*. "Ong is an Irish name, name of one of the ancient kings of Ireland."

"I knew his dad," said somebody. "Beachcomber, always dead-drunk. Half-caste from Liverpool."

"You can say that to my face," said Patrick Ong. "Come outside and say that."

"Order, order."

"I wanted to make a civil comment," said Patrick Ong. "And all I get from this fair-minded audience is a lot of insults."

"Throw him out. He's a Chinese."

"My father fought for liberty," said Patrick Ong. "He was a sniper outside the Dublin Post Office in 1916." He wiped sweat off his long upper lip, the upper lip of an ape. The ape in denims looked at him, nodding. "And he bequeathed to me, out of his great soul, that passion for the rights of the downtrodden minorities which has been one of Ireland's great gifts to the world."

"Look here," said a workman, standing up, speaking thick and glottal National Language, "if he's not a Chinese he's a white man. If he's a white man he's got no right to speak at this meeting. He's got no right either way. If he's a Chinese *and* a white man, that's twice he's got no right to speak at this meeting. There's too many spies here," he said, looking round. "Who let him in, eh?"

"Order, order."

"Now," said the subtle Indian to Paolo, "is your chance. Stand up. Catch the chairman's eye."

"All right," shouted furious Patrick Ong. "Who has any rights? Just you bloody hypocrites with your four wives and your ten thousand houris in heaven? It's not Christian, whichever way you look at it."

"Order, order."

"Four wives? I haven't got four wives."

"I suppose you'll be saying next that this ape here has more rights than a Christian soul? And that's your idea of democracy, is it?"

"The ape is a worker. And I don't like what you said then about houris."

Paolo stood up, pushed by the sweaty hands of his workmates. "My fader," he said loudly.

"Another white man. Throw him out."

"Order, order," said Patu. "He is a worker. He has no Chinese blood."

"How do we know that?"

"It's the white man we're fighting against."

"My fader," said Paolo, "is a very bad man. But I am a good boy." There were roars.

"What's he talking about?"

"What's his father got to do with it?"

"Order, order," called Patu. "He uses the term 'father' to signify the oppression of paternal white rule. Let him continue."

"I am a good boy," repeated Paolo. "But I not eat. I not drink. All day I work. He give me no money."

These words, delivered in a voice trained to be audible

above a marble-cutting machine, above a father's loud tyranny, were heard and understood by many. This was good English, clear, direct.

"All right," called Patrick Ong, "you let him speak, and he's no better than a bloody foreigner. I claim the right to finish what I started to say."

"Shut up."

"Throw him out."

"Take his name," said Mr. Bishopspawn. "It's a subversive speech. Just write down 'Eyetie'."

"Who?" said Lydia Lydgate. "Young Tony Spaghetti? But he's sweet."

The ape, excited by loud words, began to dance. It lifted the picture of Lydgate in New Guinea high above its head and brought it down on the head of the man in front.

"Order, order!"

There was a tiny tinkle of glass; the man in front rose, framed. "Which of you did that?" he cried in anger. The ape leapt on to a seat-back and, with balancing arms held out at shoulder height, began to walk rapidly along the seat-backs of the row.

"Grab him!"

"Watch out there!"

"Throw him out!"

"Order, order," called Patu. The ape began to climb up one of the structural pillars. Patrick Ong struck the man next to him. The man's mate jumped on Patrick Ong. The ape had reached one of the girders. It clung tight, gibbering. A shower of dust of polecat excrement came down, blinding somebody. There was now a sort of quiet fight. "Order, order," called Patu. "I shall have to declare the meeting closed."

"Right," said Forbes of Marmion. "There he is." Standing at the back of the hall with five of his roadmen, he gave, with a white man's calm, the order to attack. There was a rush to get out, a blockage in the vestibule. Lydia Lydgate screamed.

"Go on," said Bishopspawn. "Get out, quick." The police were nowhere to be seen. In the bright stage-light stood Mr. Bastians, smiling, nodding. He had become the audience. Patu tore his beard and his hair, calling endlessly for order. The ape on its girder forgot, in an atavistic uprush, its proletarian status. It had torn off its denims and these it now hurled at Bishopspawn. Bishopspawn, blinded and surprised, flailed vigorously. Patu's jackbooted stormtroopers fought for order with floating hair, great cries like red grottoes in a dense tangle of beard. Paolo and his workmates fought gamely against Forbes's roadmen. Forbes grinned beerily, seeing it all, and made his getaway while he could. The fight was on outside the cinema. Lydia Lydgate screamed, trying to pass the arms and the cries. In the street, at the dark corner opposite, Forbes saw his wife in frock and lipstick, saw with surprise her being struck pettishly by Frankie the Sudu, also in frock and lipstick.

"You *dirty* little thing," said Frankie. "This is *my* beat and you know it. Get away, you *treacherous* little bitch." The Christian Brothers had taught him good English, emphasising particularly in their courses the importance of *stress*.

"Here," said Forbes of Marmion. "You let her alone." He gave Frankie a back-hander.

"Strike a lady, would you," said Frankie. "Tell this little *whore* of yours to keep to her own part of the town. And take *that*." Frankie had the muscularity of the Sudu: she swiped Forbes's nose forcefully and bright blood looked out, surprised.

"Why you——" said Forbes. But he remembered his

Marmion honour: Frankie was, for the moment, a lady. "Come on," he said to Eileen. "Poor little kiddy, what were they trying to do to you, eh?" His Land-Rover was round the corner. Leading Eileen off, he was prevented by a brown man in a suit. "Excuse me," said the man, "I had arranged to meet her. Fair is fair. You can have her in an hour's time."

"Loonies," said Forbes. "A bloody mad-house. Come on, my poor little kid, I'm going to tike you home."

Drinkers were leaving the Kool Kaffi, Lydgate among them. There were still no police to be seen. Those detailed for duty outside the cinema had scuttled off, seeking cyclists without rear-lights, seeking Moslem drinkers in beer-shops. Duty was duty, whatever it was. Crawshay-Davies said, "I have my P.T. whistle. Supposing I blow that?" Paolo was to be seen, one of the fighting wave that pushed its way out of the cinema. He fought bravely, a good boy. The Indian had lost his glasses, but he kicked and swung with the best. The cleft-palate fetcher and carrier butted low, snorting "Hn" in occasional triumph. Then Lydgate saw Lydia Lydgate. She was crushed in the emerging tide of black working arms, the shoulder of her dress torn. Lydgate ran, dived in, thinking he was doing this for a woman, any woman. He pulled her out, near to a faint, done screaming. Mrs. Crawshay-Davies was suddenly among the fighters, high and formidable, a Mongol terror, cracking down on skulls with her stuffed handbag. Crawshay-Davies, encouraged, blew his whistle from the touchline.

The whistle had some effect. Memories of unseemly scuffles on football-pitches, of the rebuking referee. Memories of playing the game, of not hitting a man when he was down. Also tropical weariness, the loss of too much sweat, thirst. These led men to slink off, nursing their cuts and bruises. "Come on," said Lydgate. "My car's here. I'll get you home."

"Oh, Frank, Frank, it was horrible."

"Yes, yes, I know. You'll soon be all right." The tear in her dress was a deep one: white shoulder shone, the white pectoral swell was visible. Lydgate found difficulty in swallowing.

At last a police van came. But the fighting was as good as finished. Only Patrick Ong flailed still at the air. Bishopspawn came out of the manager's office. "There you are," he said to the police inspector, a wide-eyed Indian. "I've been on that phone for hours. The man at the desk is a fool. He said he couldn't come to the cinema because he was on duty. There's going to be trouble over this, I promise you. Sheer rank inefficiency."

Paolo lay on the ground, a lump already forming over his eye. His mates were trying to lift him. An ape, tranquil, chattering, came out of the cinema. It was trying to climb into its denim suit, trying to re-enter the ranks of the workers. It was very unhandy, whimpering as it fingered the buttons. After all, it was only an ape.

20

Lydia Lydgate's house was not yet a home. The pretty flowered stuffs for curtains and cushion-covers lay on the sideboard; her books and ornaments had still to be uncrated. But there were flowers, there were rugs that Lydgate well remembered. The windows were open, and the clean air of the hill flowed in. A hundred yards away were the lights of the Residency and, nearer, the shaded glow of Mudd's mansion. Lydgate stood awkwardly while, in an armchair, she drank the raw brandy he had poured for her. She gasped and made a bitter face when she had finished it. "That's better," she said. "But, God, what an evening." The bared flesh at her shoulder glowed.

"Well," said Lydgate, "if you're really all right——" If he had held a hat in his hand he would have inched it slowly round with embarrassed fingers. Looking down at the carpet he saw a minute hole. He remembered: in Shurga once his abandoned cigarette had been blown down from the ash-tray by the wind of the ceiling-fan. Why had his cigarette been abandoned? He remembered that too: she had said, "Why do you never want to talk to me? Put that silly book down and come over here."

"Yes, I'm really all right," she now said. "But I mightn't have been. I don't think this Bishopspawn man's much good. He shouldn't have left me like that."

"Well," said Lydgate, "I suppose he thought that he had his duty to do."

"Duty? His duty was towards me first." The old Lydia. She said, "And now I suppose *you've* got *your* duty to do. I suppose your little black girl is waiting for you. And, of course, the black and the white and the khaki offspring."

"One white," said Lydgate. "One off-white. I don't know about the third; that's not mine."

"Poor old Frank. You never do very well for yourself, do you?"

"Oh, I don't do too badly."

"What do you mean," said Lydia, tucking her legs under, as for a good chat, "you don't know about the third?"

"I've not seen it. I've not seen any of them for months. And, what's more, if you're really interested—"

"Oh, I am."

"—they're not coming back. I don't particularly want them back."

"What I'd like now," said Lydia, "is something a bit longer." She held out her brandy glass to Lydgate. "Could you mix me a whisky ginger ale? I'm still a bit shaky."

"With pleasure."

"Really with pleasure?"

"If you like." Lydgate went to the drink trolley for whisky. Knowing one of the hill-houses, he knew them all. Sure feet took him to the kitchen, the refrigerator, the ginger ale. Opening the cool white door he saw tinned beer. That would be for Mudd; Mudd always drank tinned beer. He mixed the fizzing drink and took it to Lydia. "Does Mudd come here often?" he asked.

"Oh, he pops in, pops out again. What are you going to have?"

"I'd really better be going."

"Oh, don't be a fool, Frank. You know you've nothing to go for. No luscious little black girl, no Starkie children."

"No." It was hard to keep his eyes off that rent in the

shoulder of her dress. He could, if he wished, rend it still further. Marital rights. "I'll have a drop of something," he said. "Brandy and water."

"Now you'll have to walk all that way back to the fridge. You *are* a fool."

Lydgate walked down the long living-room, through the ample dining-alcove, to the kitchen again. Opening the refrigerator for water, he thought he would not have diluted brandy after all; he would have a tin of beer. He went back to Lydia with a frothing glass.

"Mud in your eye," he said.

"Oh, Frank, what a silly joke. Now, sit down and tell me about your little abo girl. Why won't you have her back?"

"One gets tired. I don't think I really care much for her. And it's quite certain she doesn't care much for me." He sat down, very deliberately, on the edge of an armchair.

"What gives you this mysterious power over women?" She drank some of her whisky ginger ale, eyeing him. "You're a good deal greyer," she said. "But still not bald."

"I've had five teeth out since we"—He was going to say 'parted'; he said instead—"last saw each other."

"I've still got them all," said Lydia. "For that matter," she said stretching, surveying herself from rent in shoulder to bare curling toes, "I've still got *it* all." She smiled at Lydgate, not without complacency. "Wouldn't you agree?"

"I never said," said Lydgate carefully, "at any time, as far as I remember, that you didn't have your full endowment of physical charms." And then he thought, seeing the events of the evening click into place, 'There's going to be a hell of a row tomorrow.'

"Very nicely put," said Lydia. "A bit too nicely, a bit too pedantically worded. There was a time when you were flatteringly incoherent."

"Why wouldn't you divorce me?" asked Lydgate, twirling his glass round and round, like a hat.

"Wouldn't I? Won't I? I haven't really thought much about it. There was so much else to think about."

"The gay night-life of Sydney, you mean? The big queue of admirers?" Lydgate drained his glass and, unexpectedly, was thirsty for more. "May I?" he asked.

"You may. Harry Mudd will be quite surprised, won't he, when he finds out how many tastes you have in common. Mix me another, will you?" Lydgate went again to the refrigerator. When he returned with the drinks he fancied that the rent in the shoulder of her dress was deeper. But that might just be his imagination.

"And how else have you changed?" asked Lydia. "Are you less selfish?"

"I don't know what you mean," said Lydgate harshly. "As I remember, it was you who wanted everything."

"I wanted what I'd a right to want. Love, consideration—the usual things. That's what one gets married for."

"I did my best," said Lydgate. "I gave what I could. Let's not go through all that again." He drained his chill gassy beer. "I'd better go now," he said. "I've got to be up early."

"It isn't late," said Lydia. "But, isn't that just typical of you? You only think of yourself. You're not the only one who has to get up early. And," she added, "think of what I've been through. Leaving me here all nervy, all shaky. You've no sense of responsibility." She placed her ear to the bared shoulder, as if to hear what ticked inside, pouting the while.

"I've no responsibility to you any more," said Lydgate. "That's somebody else's job now."

"You're still my husband." Lydgate felt a quick throb in his chest, a click in his throat, a metallic thirst. He had a swift reeling image of all the women in the world saying, pouting, "You're my husband." To him. From the very bottom of his stomach nearly came up the reply, in gas and froth, "But I'm not." Whose husband was he? He said:

"I'll have one for the road."

"A lion-frightener we used to call it."

"Yes. And you?"

"It can hardly be one for the road for me, can it?"

"Why the hell did you come here, Lydia?" he asked viciously. "What do you want?"

"I quite like Dunia. It's much more civilised than Sydney."

"What's Mudd after? Is he after you? Is it as simple as that?"

"Why should you be interested? I'm not your responsibility. Gosh," she said, closing her eyes and leaning back to show a full throat with a tiny mole on it, "I'm tired. It was quite an evening."

"But if Mudd's after you, why should he be so keen on our being together again? That's what I don't understand."

"Is he? Don't you?" Her eyes were still closed. "Perhaps he's another who doesn't like too much responsibility."

"What do you mean?"

"Oh, shut up. I'm tired. Put me to bed."

"What?" said Lydgate.

"Oh, all right, I'll put myself to bed." And, standing suddenly, eyes still closed, she began to pull off her dress. It was her old way: scattering the floor with clothes for the servant to pick up in the morning, walking then proudly into the bedroom naked. Suddenly, in a sort of panic, Lydgate saw that that would be the end of the tear in the shoulder. What a frightful waste. Soon he discovered that she was not really so tired as she said.

21

Tins labelled "God in Oil", shaped like mosques, licked with gold paint. The menu that had offered "Fried God in Batter". That was a long time ago. In a canteen some-where in England. Lydgate was in a Land-Rover, bump-ing over beaches, the sea in his right ear, because the road from the capital to the oil towns had not yet been com-pleted. But already he could see the perpetual bonfires on the round horizon, the waste gases being burnt up, a show which the children born there took to be an aspect of the natural world. But the Land-Rover got stuck in one of the small rivers that flowed, after rain, over the sand to meet the sea. The differential was flooded. Crocodile snouts sailed towards him.

Where had that been? The Persian Gulf? Hardly.

"Are you glad I came back?" she asked. His legs were pinioned under hers, heavy warm marble.

"Eh? What? Oh, yes."

"You don't sound very enthusiastic."

"Oh." He was awake. The gas-fires were moving up the hill, cars coming home. His own car would be seen, parked in her porch. "I ought to go home now."

"Home? You haven't got a home. Home is with me."

"Oh, no. It's impossible. We tried it, and it was impos-sible." He wanted a cigarette, and his cigarettes were in the pocket of his trousers that lay, crumpled, over her crumpled and torn dress on the floor of the living-room.

And her heavy limbs held him down. It was a double bed. Why did she have a double bed? That reminded him; he must ask P.W.D. for a double bed. Wajak would be coming back soon, with the children.

"It's not so impossible. You only have to learn to be less selfish. It's easy enough."

"I'll go my own way." No, Wajak was not coming back. He would go his own way. Time to move on.

"You just like to use people, don't you? You never want to *give*——"

"I can't help it. I'd better go now."

"Because, after all, it isn't as though you're still young. You're over fifty, you're grey, you puff and you pant. You're no catch for anyone."

"I know all that. I don't mind nobody wanting me. I'll go my own way."

"Oh, no, you won't. Nobody goes his own way. It's too easy."

"I've finished with women."

"That's easy to say, isn't it? You forget you've finished with them when you want them. Half an hour ago you wanted me."

"I know. I can't help it."

"You've got to *learn*."

"I don't want to."

"Nobody wants to. But they've got to, just the same."

"But it's not too much to ask. (Look, I must have a cigarette.) I mean, just to be left alone."

"Nobody's ever left alone."

The differential was flooded. He would have to walk six miles over the sand to the river outpost with the small P.W.D. workshop. God in uranium. Soon the Mosque would be ready, Bastians calling the people to prayer. "What's that?" he said. "What did you say?"

"You can bring your things in a truck tomorrow. But don't bring anything of *hers*."

"She's dead."

"Who's dead? When did she die? What are you talking about?"

"Eh?"

"All right. Go to sleep. We all have a long, long day."

Ah, Francis Burroughs Lydgate, at it again? Hast thou in thy wasted frame not one ounce, not one teaspoonful, not one drip off the spout of an oilcan of human tenderness? Dost thou disdain to carry on thy back the burden that all but thee accept gladly, knowing it to be the inheritance of all mankind? Not sin only, but the knowledge that taking involveth giving, that we are all members of one another, that the perfect round of man and woman in hardly contrived harmony is a shadow or figure of that heavenly round or harmony in which we are destined ultimately to merge our shrieking selfhood, becoming one with the one with the one with the one with the

Shut up, shut up, shut up.

PART FOUR

22

African morning. A terrible beauty is born. The sun with its claws barely sheathed, a sky nacreous and turquoise, the grass of the playgrounds and coarse private lawns heavily dewed with candy-floss. The children on bicycles or walking, the boys in yesterday's white shirt and trousers, the girls of the Faith in blue wide skirts to the ground, white tunics hiding budding breasts but not the straps of brassières, the Christian girls demure in check frocks, all with books in baskets. The shine of bicycles in the sun, the lurch of departmental lorries. The river with its wharf by the schools, the launches unloading more children. The unlovely trees and the spiky plants showing pure green in the mild light. The cars gleaming townwards. Here and there a pie-dog shot by the Municipal Dog Catchers, lying by the monsoon drains for later collection. Mountains with dense green hair in the distance veiled coyly like the women of the Faith. The women of the Faith off to the market for fish and unsucculent legumes. The tower of the radio transmitter high away on a hill, the polished golden breast of the Mosque. Nando Tasca walking to work.

He breathed heavily in anger. He had expected a lift from Lydgate, but Lydgate's car was not outside his house. Other cars passed him, some of the white executives waved, but no one stopped for a poor old unshaven Italian man. And that feckless son of his lay in bed, his right eye nearly closed, an obscure pain in his right arm, his back aching, a shoe lost. And that Indian liar with spectacles (what did a workman want with glasses anyway?) still to be seen. Nando Tasca had gone to the house of Lydia Lydgate, convinced by that plausible message, and had found it in darkness. Assuming that the party would begin late, he had sought drink at the house of Mr. Mudd. Mr. Mudd's black servant had given him beer in the kitchen and played scales to him on a kind of xylophone. He had gone then, still seeing no lights, to the Residency, but had been turned away from the front door. At a window he had sung an amorous song and had been surprised to see and hear the U.N. Adviser's wife and daughter scream slightly and run away down a corridor. In gloom he had gone to the servants' quarters and become involved in a very lively little party. He himself had sung a Potok song and clapped his hands to the dancing. The U.N. Adviser, he had been awed to note, ordered his beer by the four-dozen case. He had become confused, attempted dalliance with a small slim black girl who eventually turned out to be the wife of the Number One House-boy, and, very late, been sent home. Only when he arrived at his own house to see a groaning Paolo on the bed did he remember the real purpose of his trip up the hill. And the discovery that Paolo had been fighting brought on an attack of rage so violent that he saw a kind of dance of red globules and scarlet spindles and the light seemed to go out. His store of rare dialect words was drawn on so heavily that at last he stood dumb, almost gibbering. And Paolo went on groaning.

African morning, something that Nando Tasca had never really seen before. Rather, he had seen it supervene on night at the maudlin close of some all-night whisky party: then it had been a great gaudy candelabrum light-

ing him to bed. But now it lashed him to work. As he
walked he heard early morning radio music and, as he
neared the Mosque, the quarrel of two radio announcers:

"You're just *awful*. *I'm* to announce the next programme. It says so *here*."

"Get off the air, you nasty thing. What *will* the listeners
think?"

Nando Tasca arrived at the great Mosque, sweating in
the shirt he had worn last night, the fresh sweat re-awaken-
ing the old sweat that lurked, nearly dry, in the shirt's
armpits. Thirst took him to the coffee-shop opposite; there
he drank two large beers and felt better. Perhaps the
workmen could be trusted to get on with the enmarbling
without his supervision. Perhaps Paolo would be able to
work tomorrow. (A doctor, of course, was out of the question. A doctor might order a month's rest and a special
diet.) But time was short. Already workmen were erecting
archways over the streets; already light bulbs—sleeping
now—spelled out on the Government Building a pious
Arabic slogan. No time could be wasted if the terms of
the contract were to be fulfilled. Nando Tasca drank one
more large beer, offered to the world an old man's eructa-
tion, wiped his chin with his hand and heard a sort of
marching sound of stiff bristles, then walked over to the
Mosque.

Inside that huge barn, where bats already nested, he was
surprised to find only two workmen—the subtle Indian
with glasses, the squat moron with the cleft palate. "Where
are the others?" he cried. Echo caught up his stern question: "Others? Others?"

"Ah," said the Indian. "Good morning, Mr. Tasca. I
expected you this morning. Your son, I take it, is still not
very well. That, I'm afraid, is the trouble with the others.
They have gone to the State Hospital, to the out-patients'

department. It is likely that they will have to wait there all day. The doctors will have a lot of work."

"And who started this fighting, eh? That's what I want to know." Sudu, in that *basso* voice, seemed again a violent language. But Nando Tasca added, in fierce English, "What you tell a bloody lie a to me for?"

"I beg your pardon, Mr. Tasca?"

"You know a English. Why you tell a me there a bloody party? There no a bloody party."

"There was a mistake," said the Indian in Sudu. "The party is tonight."

"You a bloody liar. Come on start a work."

But something seemed to be wrong with the marble-cutting machine. Nando Tasca suspected sabotage, yet he said nothing, tugging, heaving, fiddling, groaning, swearing.

"Something is wrong with it, Mr. Tasca."

"I know a there a something bloody wrong." And, in Sudu, he said, "Where is the book?"

The book of instructions was brought from the hiding-hole it shared with plans and sketches and empty bottles. Nando Tasca, who had never seen it before, stared at it in horror. He remembered enough of the German occupation to realise that these portmanteau-words and odd sharp barks were of the German language.

"This," he said, "I cannot read."

"It is written in the white man's language."

"You a bloody fool. This a bloody German."

"Germans are white men."

Nando Tasca threw the book down and tried to kick the machine. "You," he said to the Indian, "go away."

"But there is a lot of work to be done."

"You go away. Him," he said, pointing at the staring man with the cleft palate, "him and me do the work."

"Do I still get my pay? I have a wife and eight children to support."

"You a get a your bloody money. Now go away." And he repeated the order in Sudu.

Nando Tasca and the man with the cleft palate spent the day filling various blanks with cement. But only, of course, on the floor. Nando Tasca knew his work: he had not spent thirty years in the trade for nothing. When the cement was dry he would paint it over with brown paint and a wire brush. It would look sufficiently like marble. What right had they, anyway, heathens with more money than sense, to have their false religion graced with good Catholic marble? But tomorrow Paolo would have to be well. He would have to be kicked out of bed and forced to mend the marble-cutting machine. It was not easy to play this trick on the walls.

"You," he said to his assistant, "not say anything about this to anyone. *Capito?*"

"Hn," said the man. It was an ambiguous answer.

23

Lydgate didn't need a truck. Two trips in the car (the second with the small refrigerator roped to the lower jaw of the open mouth of the boot) and his move up the hill was consummated. Why? he asked himself as he steered up the hill road. Why this weak capitulation? But it wasn't capitulation; he was claiming his rights. A right to servants' quarters, to a fan in the dining alcove, to a garden, to be at least on the same level as Mudd. The rent would be the same: for hovel or tropical Gothic mansion it was the same—ten per cent of basic salary. Then sprang up the real reason for the capitulation. Mudd was not going to ride his mare; he was not going to be cuckolded twice in the same year. And if Mudd did try, if Mudd were caught out, he, Lydgate, would have every right to an even wilder justice than that which Forbes had enjoyed. Lydgate was wresting the weapon from Mudd. Lydia had been brought out to humiliate; what Mudd could never have foreseen was the effect on tired glands of a dress torn at the shoulder in a political scrimmage.

How long would all this last? Till it was time to move on, he supposed. When would that be? When, in the neurotic course of mounting monotony and frustration, he would expect to see one particular image in sleep, a particular and impossible figure moving in the street or entering an office. Then it was time to move on. It always had been. Another six months, say. He should have enough money.

The curtains were up; the cook sang dirty love songs while he mixed batter for a Yorkshire pudding. The split week-end—Moslem Friday and Christian Sunday—saw the ornaments and books uncrated. It was all quite tolerable, even pleasant. Pleasant, if he came home from work before she, to sit in quiet or dull Dunia bird-song while the boy brought beer in a tankard. No noise of Forbes's brats, no duet from the other side—*presto furioso ma molto pesante*. After all, he was moderately civilised: he had had secretaries and telephones, had read certain books, spoke certain languages which had sophisticated literatures: he was entitled to the spinning fan and the bird-song and the vista of purring cars coming up the hill. But at night she cried.

"Why are you so *selfish*? Why must everything be for *you*?"

"I can't help it. You know me well enough by now."

"But you don't even *try*."

He lay back in the dark, silent. How long had it been now? Only just over a week. Inevitably it seemed much longer: the small dram will ring a bell for all last night's alcohol lying quiescent in one's blood-stream, send it racing round again; one is pushed back by a single finger into the long bout of bottles. Why did women want to be people? He felt ill-used, sullenly smoking in the dark, letting her cry.

"We're going to have a party tonight. Before the show."

"What show?" He was driving her home from the office.

"This show for the Caliph's birthday. In the Chin Chin Cinema. I rang up a few people. We ought to have a party, you know."

"Why?"

"Oh, you haven't an ounce of sentiment in you." She

pouted. "Everybody's been expecting us to throw a party."

"Do you mean we've got to have Mudd and Covendry and Brethren and Henryson and Bishopspawn?"

"Not Bishopspawn. Although, of course, he did, in a way, bring us together again."

"Then we ought to have Bastians as well." He was feeling bitter about Bastians: he had been half-blamed for Bastians's illegal entry into the State: he should have suspected something (in a way, he had: that letter had been remarkably literate); he should have checked with the U.N.A.'s office. The U.N. Adviser was in trouble again. Meanwhile Patu produced cast-iron alibis; Sebastian Hup knew nothing. "Or Patrick Ong. Or that blasted ape."

"The ape was rather sweet, really. Don't forget to put on a suit this evening, not just a tie. After all, you are the Controller of Passports."

"So they keep telling me." They mounted the hill. "I do wish you'd consulted me about this damned party. Instead of just slyly ringing people up behind my back."

"You would have said 'no'."

"Too true I would." Shocked by this involuntary Australianism, he turned to her and said, "I beg your pardon."

"I've had to ask one or two of the Aussies. Collie, Clout, one or two others."

"That's going too far. Damn it all, to be called a Pommy bastard in one's own house——"

"How do you know they'll do that? Really, Frank, you are stupid sometimes."

It was a typical Dunia party. The days of the big dinners, the servants many and cheap—these had gone with the British Empire. Now one improvised something at the last moment, hurled cachou nuts into bowls, went out for a meal afterwards or, drinking enough, forgot to be hungry. But tonight everybody had to attend the amateur concert—the lighting of the fuse that led to the sparks of the Caliph's birthday, the great explosion of the opening of the Mosque—and the party must end crisply in a jolly townward procession of cars. Lydia was good, Lydia was excellent. The lights were dim, the gramophone's *musique d'ameublement* continuous and unobtrusive, the boys filled platters with skewered morsels of cheese and silverskins, *kropoks*, olives, Gentleman's Relish on toast.

"She's dinky-die," said Collie of Bridgetown, cocktail beer in his hand. "You know, I don't mind telling you, that a lot of the boys were getting a bit crook seeing you doing what you did to her. Some of them wanted to do you in. But it's all right now," he said, taking one of Lydgate's cigarettes. "They reckon you can be one of the boys now. You've a real bonza kiddy there, old man."

Mr. Covendry, the State Irrigation Officer, keeping up his reputation as the town intellectual, spoke to Lydia of modern literature. "J. B. Priestley," he was saying. "A bit too advanced for me. A bit too consciously clever. You know, style and what not. Give me Hugh Walpole any day. Modern, but not too modern, if you see what I mean."

"Evelyn Waugh?" suggested Lydia.

"With all due deference," smiled Mr. Covendry, "I never really cared for women writers much."

Not all the conversation was highbrow. Clout said that, with the completion of the road linking Dunia Town with the mines, there was going to be yet more unemployment. But even he, in an atmosphere that Lydia's elegance, Lydia's metropolitan accent refined, was led to a sort of puzzled speculation as to the future. In his glasses, with his thin shoulders and stoop, he propounded his doubts almost professorially.

"I mean, you just can't live on uranium, can you? I mean, you can't just sit back and draw sort of dividends from it, can you? I mean, not everybody can, can they? They've got to have some sort of a job to do, haven't they? And what the hell can they do?"

"What did they do before?" asked Mrs. Covendry. She was a compact plump woman who spoke queenlily. She seemed to Lydgate like a publican's wife who, promoted from back street pub to neon-lighted road-house, had now reached her social peak—lady of the President of the local Licensed Victuallers' Association. But on the back of her neck prickly heat flourished, ill-hid by powder.

"Oh," said Collie, "they live in those houses over the water, all of them, fishing through the floor-boards. Now they've been landed, a lot of them, and they can't swim back. A bloody shime, but it's not our look-out."

Lydgate remembered the old days, visiting from Kenya only a few years before—wooden buildings, mud streets, the Caliph carried in a kind of litter, only a few European traders. It was frightening, the speed with which you could build a modern state. You could run the film back as quickly, but you didn't revert to the simple dignity of shacks on stilts with grass roofs. Instead you got peeling stucco, a rusting telephone exchange, carious stone, unexpected craters in the main roads. Five more years of uranium. After that what? An abdicating Caliph perhaps, well able to pay for his suite at Claridge's. Emigration of the Chosen People to other parts of the continent. Fishing and a little maize, the days of Cadillacs and Cinemascope stirred into the pudding of myth. But, by then, he himself would have long moved on.

Mudd had his arm round Lydia's shoulders and she was

giving him the sugar icing of her smile. There was no soft sponge under that icing. Mudd brought Lydia towards Lydgate's group, lordly, proprietorial, giving the bride away. "I'm very happy, Frank," he said. "We're all very happy. It's just like old times, isn't it? Now you try to be a good boy and live happily ever after." Lydgate went stiff as a dead cat.

"Shall I," said Lydgate, "get a peep-hole bored in the bedroom?"

"Oh, Frank," said Lydia. "Please. Not at a party." Mudd laughed.

It was time to be moving. Mudd said, "Who's going with who? There's no point in taking all the cars."

("With whom," corrected Mr. Covendry quietly.)

"Because we'll be coming back after the show," said Mudd.

"Will we?" said Lydgate.

"Lydia says so." Mudd looked round. "Right, Frank, you can take Helen and George. And, Bert, you take Miss Pearce and John can keep her company in the back. And I'll take Lydia. And, let me see. We don't want too many cars. Parking's always a problem down there."

"Oh, Frank," ordered Lydia, "do tell the boys to lay on a few more things for when we get back. And ask someone to go over to Harry's place and get a few bottles of soda. And a bottle of whisky. We're nearly out of it."

"The Pope's telephone number," suggested Mr. Covendry. "Vat 69." Lydia tinkled a laugh, pretending not to have heard the joke before. Lydgate was grim. 'How can women?' he thought. 'How can they do it? Hypocrites, the lot of them.' "I'll come down on my own," said Lydgate. "No point in keeping other people waiting."

It was peace again to be driving down the hill road alone. Should he, he wondered, go to the show? A few quiet

203

whiskies in the Kool Kaffi. And then not come back to the resumed party. People would wonder where he was. Self-pity began to form like mist on the windscreen. He would be the centre of interest. Lydia would be abashed. But, no. That was not it at all. He would meet his responsibilities. Was he becoming a better man for recognising them? He thought not.

He could not see Mudd's car in the parking lot by the cinema. Inside it was dark. The show had already started. He sat near the back, alone. On the stage, in warm lemon-coloured light, stood Fredericks, donating his turn. In silent politeness sat the National Language speakers, uncomprehending. The turbaned elders smoked local shag rolled in strips of young bamboo.

"Oh, you lucky people," pattered Fredericks. "Here," he said, "here. I was speaking to the Caliph the other day, and I said, 'Who was that lady I seen you with last night?' 'That was no lady,' he says, 'that was the Sultana.' 'Sultana?' I says. 'You're lucky. My old woman's a raisin.' 'Raisin?' he says. 'Ay,' I says, 'always a raisin hell.' Here——" The wrinkled patriarchs were impassive. There were European groans. But there came no sound of a laugh from Lydia. "Now then," said Fredericks, "a little song entitled 'I Don't Like Fat Girls 'Cause They Roll Off My Lap'." And, to a scratched record, he moved, with shrugs and œillades, into a slow step-dance.

Frankie the Sudu, in a European gown with a false bust, plastered make-up ghoulish in the dim spots, winked over-blued eyelids at the audience. The young responded in glee. Polite still, with a little wonder mixed, the aged looked on, smileless. Frankie sang, in fair Christian Brothers English, that he was in the mood for love. Lydgate grew restless. Then came Dominic de Cruz, the Inspector of Vehicles, and David Lloyd-Evans, head of the

Municipal Dog Catchers. Both wore blazers. De Cruz had a guitar. They sang a song they had composed for the occasion:

"I'm not in a state of grace.
    It's something far far loonier.
  I'm a terrible case; see the lines on my face?
  I'm in the State of Dunia."

"Well," said Sebastian Hup, sitting down next to Lydgate, "here you are again, all alone."

"Yes."

"Mr. Mudd and the lady whose house you are living in. They did a very strange thing. They came down the hill and turned and went straight back up again."

"How much do you want for that information?"

"I'm not in a state of sin.
    Indeed, I'd very much sooner.
  I'm getting so thin; what a mess I am in.
  I'm in the State of Dunia."

"Oh, I don't think there's any question of paying anything to anybody. Not now, Mr. Lydgate. But you mustn't worry about this lady you're living with and Mr. Mudd. There are far bigger things to worry about."

"Such as?"

"Oh, Mr. Carruthers Chung thinks it would be such a good idea if you came along to the next bridge party and really confessed *everything*."

"What the hell are you talking about?"

"You're such an unhappy man, Mr. Lydgate. People only want to help."

"Went up the hill, did they?" said Lydgate, rising. "Let me get past."

"If you could spare a few bucks, Mr. Lydgate, it would be a very great help. I'm ashamed to say this, but this is one of the very rare nights when I have to get drunk. You see, Mr. Lydgate, there's so much I could say and so much I don't say, and then I'm never sure which country I really belong to, and sometimes I feel so *violent*. I have a lot pressing to get out." In agony he pressed it in, holding his Golgotha skull tightly with both hands. "So, when my friends have finished their turn on the stage there, Mr. Lydgate, we shall go to some little back room and get drunk. Then I can shout my head off. I have to do it sometimes, and it's better that I should—among friends, in a little private room. Shout my head off," he giggled. "That's a very painless way of losing it. Not like that poor man up-river. The U.N. Adviser's always in trouble. Now they'll be wanting his head in the General Assembly, poor man."

> "I'm not in a state of health—
> My voice gets croakier and croonier.
> But I've picked up some wealth, and I've
> done it by stealth,
> For I'm in the State of Dunia."

"Very good, very clever," said Sebastian Hup, clapping delicately. "Don't push me, Mr. Lydgate, I don't like being pushed. There," he said, taking his knees from the chair-back in front and swinging them into the aisle, "now you can get out." He said this smoothly and courteously.

24

The lights glowed in Mudd's house—kitchen, bedroom, the standard lamp of the sitting-room. Mudd's car was in the porch. Lydgate could see all this from the road. He parked his car at the foot of the climbing path that led to Mudd's front door and walked up. The loose flints, disturbed, made a noise of distant marching armies. The front door was not locked. Through its glass panels he could see the decorations of Mudd's entrance-hall—spears to which hanks of human hair were glued; a Potok carving of a sullen monkey-foetus playing a severed head like a drum; long brown cream-speckled leaves in a jar. He turned the handle, went in and, in the sitting-room, saw Lydia and Mudd sitting demurely in easy chairs, she with a liqueur glass, he with a tankard. The fan turned slowly, the regulator at its bottom notch. "Oh, Frank," said Lydia, "it's you."

"Yes. You might have told me you didn't intend to go."

"We did go, didn't we, Harry? But there were such a hell of a lot of people."

"Yes," said Mudd. "We just turned the car round and came back here. It's a wonder you didn't see us. We saw you driving down, staring into space. I tooted, but you just went on staring. Have a drink."

Lydgate sat down, looking from one to the other. No derangement in the dress, no flush, no pallor, no stray strand of hair sticking up and pointing like a thumb to the bedroom. What was going on? He took whisky and water from the small boy and said, "Well."

"Well," said Mudd. "Was the show any good?"

"Yes. No. Oh, it was all right, I suppose."

"Good." Mudd, with much deliberation, screwed out his cigarette in a cloisonné ash-tray. "I'm glad," he said, his eyes on his work, "that we're able to have a cosy chat, just the three of us. You've never been up to see me, Frank, not once since you've been here. I've had the feeling that you don't really like me."

Lydgate spread his lips painfully. "Can you really blame me?" Lydia filled herself another thimbleful of Dom. She said nothing but continued looking at Mudd.

"Well." said Mudd, "I can, really, you know. I've had very good reasons for hating your guts, but I've always shrugged the reasons away. I've always thought you're a good chap but a bit misguided. I've never been unfair to you in our official dealings and I've never said a bad word about you. But I'm afraid you've said a lot of bad things about me."

"Never unfair?" said Lydgate. "The bloody hovel you put me into. The things you did in Shurga. The way you've tried to interfere with my private life."

"For your own good," said Mudd. "You're a valuable man. I've hated to see you go to the dogs. All I've done is to try and chasten you a bit. Now you've been chastened and I think you're a better man for it. If I may say this before Lydia, I've been really sick at heart seeing the way you treated one of the finest women in the world."

"Oh, really, Harry," said Lydia.

"But is that any of your business?" said Lydgate.

"Oh, yes, I think it is. The happiness of people we like must always be our business. Wouldn't you agree there, Lydia?"

Lydia, sipping her Dom, nodded.

"Ever since I've been here," said Lydgate, slumped in his chair, a slight headache making his eyes close, "I've had the impression that people have been fighting for my soul. God knows why. But if saving my soul involves sweltering in filthy little houses, being degraded and insulted, being made bankrupt because I can't afford bribes——"

"It was in Shurga that you went bankrupt," said Mudd. "Not here. And whose money was that, by the way? Was it yours, Lydia?"

"Some of it was mine," said Lydia. "Not all of it. I took my chance, anyway, or, rather, Frank's chance. I'm not complaining."

"Thank you," said Mudd. "I've always wanted to know that. Poor old Frank. He can't do anything right. But that's all over now."

"You know," said Lydgate, quite quietly, two finger-tips on each closed eyelid, "I've never really wanted much. I'm a man. I have certain needs. I like to be warm. I like to have enough to eat, a little to drink. I have certain other appetites, too. It doesn't seem too much to ask, just to be satisfied. I've no great ambitions. Not like you," he said, opening his eyes to Mudd.

"You condemn yourself," said Mudd. "You like to be warm but you forget that we also have to tolerate the cold. You've forgotten what an English winter's like, you've not been home for donkey's years. You take perpetual warmth as a right, but it's not a right."

"The people living here, born here," said Lydgate, "they take it as a right."

"They're not quite human beings," said Mudd briskly. "Only people of the temperate zones can really be human beings."

"Oh, this is silly," said Lydia. "Arguing about being warm. Is that the only reason," she asked Lydgate, "why you've never been back home? Just because you don't like the cold?"

Lydgate thought. "One gets out of touch," he said vaguely.

"It would be much more romantic," said Lydia, smiling, "if you told us that you'd never been back because you committed some dreadful crime and the police were after you."

Lydgate looked at her very sharply. Mudd said:

"You talk about appetites. Hunger and thirst are one thing, but surely sex is another. Food and drink have no feelings, but women are human beings. You can't treat a woman like a piece of steak. Except perhaps prostitutes. But you've never been much of a man for prostitutes, have you? Shall I say this, that you've wanted all the advantages of marriage without any of the responsibilities? You've wanted a meal cooked and the floor swept and your beer brought from the fridge and, after that, the machine that's done all these things for you to smile kindly when you go out to have a couple of drinks with the boys, and then be waiting for you, legs open, on the bed, having turned now from a machine to a sort of receptacle. And that's what you wanted Lydia to be."

"Look here," said Lydgate angrily, "what do you know about it, anyway? Damn it, you've always been too damned selfish even to think of getting married. What right have you got to lecture me?"

"I'm only trying to help," said Mudd patiently. "You're at least ten years older than me, but I still think of you as a child. We want to make a man of you."

"Well, make a man of yourself first," said Lydgate with heat. Then he went too far and said, "It makes me sick, a second-rate amateur jockey setting himself up as a bloody lay preacher." Mudd stood up and said:

"You'd better take that back, Frank. I know all about you trying to get me warned off the course. You said some pretty slanderous things about me in Shurga. I don't like people going round saying that I'm a dirty rider."

"Well, you were. You ought to have been cracked with your own whip. I saw the face of one of the Creole jockeys——"

"Children, children," said Lydia, "this is ridiculous."

"It is," agreed Mudd. He sat down, saying, "He doesn't know what he's talking about."

"All right," said Lydgate. "But you've had that in for me all the time, haven't you? That's at the back of everything. Just because we nearly had you warned off the course. And you have the damned cheek to talk about responsibilities and ideals and morality and Christ knows what. You ought to grow up, little man, you really ought."

"Oh, you're absurd, both of you," said Lydia. "Now, look, can't you forget all about what happened in Shurga and all that you've done wrong to each other here and try to behave like grown-up people?"

"He's been sleeping with you, hasn't he?" asked Lydgate viciously. "Come on, speak out, now that we're being so frank with each other." ('Frank,' he thought; 'Frank Lydgate.')

"I object to that insinuation," said Mudd. "That's slander."

"Oh, Frank, how can you say things like that?"

"Has he or hasn't he?"

"What does it matter to you," said Lydia, with a very sudden bitterness, "whether he has or not? You don't care what happens to me when you aren't actually using me. Except for five minutes every other night, you just don't give a damn. Or," she added, poison in the sugar, "shall we say ten minutes? You're not as young as you used to be."

"Well, if I'm so damned old and so damned ugly and so damned inconsiderate, why the hell did you bother to come back to me at all?"

"*You* came back to *me*," said Lydia with her poisoned smile. "Don't you remember? It's only just over a week ago. But, of course, old men tend to lose their memories."

"Don't bloody quibble," said Lydgate. "Why, why, why do you want me at all?"

"That's a question," said Lydia. "Do you ever stop to consider what you're really entitled to as far as a wife is concerned? You're over fifty, remember. You're entitled to a wife grown grey, lined, stringy or fat, past child-bearing, past sex, a nice, homely, matronly body with two pairs of glasses and a knitting-basket. If you'd married at twenty, that's what you'd have now. You're not entitled to me," Lydia shouted. "I'm young, I'm attractive. Harry here even tells me that I'm beautiful." Mudd hung his head, limp in the armchair. "And," cried Lydia, "you have the nerve to be tired of me, to treat me like some little fourpenny piece you'd pick up on the streets of Sydney. Me," she yelled, her eyes wide open. "Me, me, me! You're a stupid, bloody, ungrateful fool."

"All right," said Lydgate. "You still haven't answered my question."

"No." She became quiet, her nose twitching to keep tears back. "It's quite simple. I thought marriage meant something. I thought if you got married the idea was to stay married. I thought if something went wrong with a marriage you just had to try and put it right. I've been thinking about it all this time back in Sydney. I've felt guilty. I couldn't think of any one thing you'd actually done wrong except not treat me as a human being and sometimes seem to loathe me for being a human being. I thought there must be something wrong with me. Sleeping with other people," she said, "just doesn't mean a thing. I've done it because I've had to do it. I would have screamed if I couldn't occasionally have been in bed with somebody who treated me like a human being. But marriage is different. It's a terrible thing to admit that a marriage has been a failure. I've just not been able to sleep some nights," she said, "with this horrible feeling of guilt. Guilt," she repeated loudly, looking Lydgate in the eye. "Guilt. I don't suppose you know what that word means."

"No," said Lydgate, in loud, heavy, lunatic sarcasm, "no, I've just no idea."

"You've nothing to feel guilty about, Lydia," said Mudd.

"Oh, shut up," said Lydgate and Lydia simultaneously. They turned again on each other. "You," said Lydgate, "can leave me as soon as you like. If it's marriage you're worried about, you can cease to worry. I won't tell you why, but you can. You've no obligation to me whatsoever. You can blame me for everything, every damned mortal thing. I accept the blame, and I'll say that I'm sorry. We can go our own ways, you can try and be happy with somebody else. With Mudd, for instance," he said, doubtfully.

"No," said Mudd, "you can leave me out of it."

"But," said Lydia, "you still happen to be my husband."

"Now," said Lydgate, "listen carefully. Wait," he added. He went over to the sideboard and poured out a very stiff peg of whisky. He came back. "You can hear this, too," he said to Mudd. He drank.

"This," said Mudd, "happens to be my house."

"That's what I mean. Now, listen. Our marriage was never valid. You believed it was, so there's no blame attaching to you," he said to Lydia. "No, don't say anything. Just listen. I married in England, in my twenties. I married a woman already in her thirties. Life with her was hell. Physical hell and mental hell. She starved me of everything. She developed some damned stupid idea about keeping the body pure. No, wait, listen. No sex, no meat, no alcohol. It was murder. She came under the influence of some stupid faddist or other. A Eurasian, he was. I told her I couldn't stand life with her any longer. But she was like you, Lydia; she didn't believe in divorce. She prayed for me, yes, she did, kneeling down by the kitchen table, praying loud enough for the neighbours to hear. She wanted me to be pure, just like her. But I was never the pure type. Please, please listen. I ran away from her. I worked in Spain for a time, thought I was free of her, but, believe it or not, she turned up in Madrid on a holiday. She wanted me to come back to her, she loved me, she said, she'd been praying for me night and day. She'd got a bit of money. That's why she could afford to indulge in her stupid fads, that's why she could afford to stay on in Spain, praying for me. Yes, praying for me even in the blasted office, in front of the boss. I had a friend in Tanganyika, got a job there. She found out and turned up in Dar-es-Salaam. I moved to Nairobi, and damn me if she didn't turn up again. It was hell, believe me. Mind you, in a way I was being punished. I'd married her for her money. It's always a mistake to marry for money. Remember that."

"But you got married in Nairobi," said Mudd. "That's in your confidential file. That was bigamy."

"I didn't think it was," said Lydgate. "You see, when she turned up in Nairobi she was already ill with fever. That made her pray all the more. She began to see visions. Of course, she'd no stamina, living off grass and dandelion leaves. Anyway, they put her into hospital and then she

214

was shipped off home. I got a very reproachful letter from this Eurasian friend of hers, saying that he was writing by her death-bed and that everything was my fault. After that I heard nothing. I assumed she'd died. Believe me, I couldn't feel anything at all except an incredible relief. That may sound callous, but consider what I'd been through. On the crest of the wave of relief I re-married. It wasn't very successful, but that's another story. Anyway, we were divorced. I married you, Lydia, in good faith. I believed I was a free man, I'd taken it for granted a long time before that Agnes was dead——"

"What was her name?" asked Mudd.

"Agnes. From the Latin word for a lamb. A lamb is a symbol of purity."

"Go on," said Mudd.

"But one year after our marriage I discovered that Agnes was still alive. Alive and kicking. There's some sort of vegetarian magazine published in Calcutta. Some sort of vegetarian was staying for a time in one of the rest houses —I forget which one. Anyway, he left a copy of this magazine there and, quite by chance, I saw an article. It was called 'Spiritual Beauty Through Herbal Health' and it was written by Agnes Lydgate. What could I do? How would you have felt? What would have happened to me? I kept quiet about it, and can you blame me? Anyway," he concluded, "there you are. We're not married, Lydia, never have been. We've been living in sin."

"But is she still alive?" asked Mudd. Lydia, mouth open, eyes wide, just stared.

"I don't know," said Lydgate. "I've a feeling that she can't be. I've not heard a thing about her for a hell of a long time."

"Did you know," asked Mudd, "that a herbal health faddist was recently eaten up-river?"

"Good God," said Lydgate. "A woman?"

"A man. A Eurasian. At least his name sounded Eurasian. Nobody actually saw him. It was one of these Domingo da Silva sort of names."

"I can't remember," said Lydgate. "I don't think we got any information about him. I would have known the name if I'd seen it. So that's the man who lost his head," he mused.

"He didn't pass through Passport Control. He came from Shurga in the Information Department's plane. The one that sometimes writes the sky-signs. He just passed through. Nobody bothered about him. The U.N.A.'s in a hell of a row about that," he added. "And you, Frank," he remembered, "are in a hell of a mess." Lydia was now crying gently.

"I don't see why. I didn't know I was doing anything wrong."

"You committed bigamy. That's a terrible crime."

Indignation rose in Lydgate. "What do you mean? We're living in a part of the world where some people can have as many wives as they like. Polygamy's regarded as normal in Islam. Bigamy's very small beer. And, besides, I didn't know I was committing bigamy." He felt curiously light-hearted now, having shed a considerable burden. Perhaps Carruthers Chung's bridge parties were not such a bad idea after all.

"Collusion," said Mudd. "Have you told anybody else about this?"

"Nobody. And, remember, I've told you in confidence."

"Oh, Frank, Frank," cried Lydia, a small handkerchief at her weeping nose, "how could you? What do I do now?"

"You can marry Mudd here. Or any of the other boys who think you're bonza and dinky-die because they don't have to marry you. You're quite free. There's no need to say anything about anything to anybody. You can go to a registry office with a clear conscience any time you like. With anybody you like," said Lydgate.

"But the scandal. This is such a small place."

"The police ought to be told, really," said Mudd. "If you had any decency, you'd go and tell the police yourself."

"Oh, come off it," said Lydgate. "Would you do it, Harry? Of course you wouldn't. For the time being we can just resume the *status quo*. Except, of course, that Lydia's house is now mine."

"No, it isn't," said Mudd. "You're a bachelor. You're not entitled to this class of accommodation."

"A bachelor? Come, come. I'm far from being a bachelor. Very far."

"You'll have to go back to that first house you were in. The second one's been re-allocated."

"Oh, no," said Lydgate. "You can't do that. I'm the official lessee of Lydia's house. I pay the rent. It's in black and white, with no conditions."

"You've got to take your medicine," said Mudd very grimly. "You must go where we send you. But tonight you can sleep at the Dunia Hotel. Send a voucher in to-morrow morning." There was a jolly noise of cars coming up the hill.

"Oh, God," said Lydia. "The party. The party," she cried.

"Cheer up," said Lydgate. "You've got a lot to celebrate."

25

"And then," said George Lim, "you test terminals A and B. If terminals A and B are causing no trouble, then there is only one thing left to do." He read swiftly through the mildewed booklet, mouthing the long harsh German words silently.

"What a that?"

"You clean the whole thing with a stiff brush. That, it says here, should be done every fortnight. Has it been done every fortnight?"

Nando Tasca did not know. But, "No," he said without any hesitation. "My son," he explained, "a very very bad a boy." Paolo's behaviour, during the brief week of Lydgate's second honeymoon and Nando Tasca's re-marriage to toil, had been worse than ever. He had lain on his bed, groaning, refusing to work, asking for a doctor, demanding—unreasonably, thought his father, as he was no longer earning his keep—food and drink. "A very very very bad a boy." Then, fiercely, without gratitude, he turned on George Lim, leaning his bare worker's arms heavily on the reception desk of the Dunia Hotel. "Why a you not a tell a me before you speak a German?" he asked. "Not a possible cut a marble and time a very short and you not a tell a me you speak a German." Because you could not, decided Nando Tasca, enmarble the whole place with painted cement. Here and there it was all right, but not everywhere. And the workmen, all except the cleft-palate moron who was condemned to a vow of silence, wanted to know why they were locked out. They had spent their convalescence playing cards in the courtyard of the Mosque, sitting at the cool base of the fountain, which had now itself begun, though in divine intransitivity, to play. And there the Caliph had found them. The Caliph, trying to enter the Mosque, had met a locked door and, behind it, the voice of Nando Tasca saying, "Nobody not a see this a stage of a the work. This a very secret." The Caliph, having heard about the mysteries of freemasonry, had not insisted on his right of entry. But the workers wanted to get back to work. Or, rather, they wanted overtime. And they wanted to see what was going on. They were intrigued by the incomprehensible pantomime of their cleft-palate colleague—a kind of arthritic ballet with a pendulum arm and music of nasal grunts. They were made apprehensive by the unwonted generosity of paid leave that their patron donated. These were days of prodigies. The sun-whipped earth was settling to another long drought: the brown frogs were going to wage war against the green frogs: heads were rolling in up-river villages: neon lights were coming on all over the town. Had they been Christians they would have crossed themselves; had they been Moslems they would have prayed five punctual times a day; being animists, they tied knots in things, touched wood, bowed before stones, bit their nails, avoided walking under ladders.

"Why a you a know a German, anyway?" scolded Nando Tasca. "It a not a right a Chinese know a German."

Lydgate came in, asking for a room. He had no luggage, not even a toothbrush (he had so few teeth left to clean, anyway). He had not fancied leaving Lydia's house with a suitcase in the midst of a party. Some of the guests might have got a bit crook. Now he would lie on a bed, his drip-dry shirt drip-drying for the morning, and think about leaving the State, how, when, where for, selling his car, getting an exit permit from the Astana, sailings, flights, what friends in Gibraltar, in Macao, in Tokyo?

"Number One-o-one, Mr. Lydgate," said George Lim, giving him a key. Lydgate, clutching the key tightly, for it was a long time since he had had a key, went upstairs. Lydia wouldn't split, but Mudd—— He had been a bit of a fool, he had said too much, he had not taken horse-racing seriously enough. He must think, he must——

"Well, Signor Tasca," said George Lim, "I had to learn most of the European languages, you see, because it was intended that I should be a missionary. A Taoist missionary, taking the true message to the heathen. But I was seduced from my purpose by European literature which, in order to increase my various vocabularies, I was made to read. Dante," he began to say eagerly. "The *Vita Nuova*, for instance——"

"It a not a right a Chinese read a Dante," rebuked Nando Tasca. He himself had not read Dante.

"And so, you see, I entered the hotel business." He had on his desk an Arabic grammar. Soon, with the coming of the distinguished visitors for the opening of the Mosque, the Paraclete would have to hover all day.

Nando Tasca nodded to George Lim truculently and went into the restaurant to drink beer. He had given up protecting his son. His son could be written off. Nando Tasca had already made arrangements with a member of the Italian colony in Shurga to make arrangements with a Eurasian friend on a small banana plantation in Krachucha to make arrangements for Paolo to be appointed under-assistant-manager at a minimal salary. Sixty-six per cent would, by a special arrangement, be deducted from Paolo's salary at source and remitted to Nando Tasca in Tripoli to be remitted, if Nando Tasca could afford it, to Paolo's mother in Italy. That would keep her quiet. But Nando Tasca was disturbed that the jungle war in Krachucha was (Moscow now having other, larger, interests) fast coming to an end. Still, the banana plantations were still, thanks to the Probooba tribes, losing managers at the rate of one every three months. Paolo's chances were good enough. Paolo's mother would be pleased to be the weeping mother of a posthumous hero, and Nando Tasca himself could boast of having freely given his son's life in some cause or other, noble but undefined.

The prospective posthumous hero lay, meanwhile, at home, hungry. He had now a Christ-like beard which brought tears to his eyes whenever he looked into his father's shaving-mirror. He could walk a little now, his bruised temple was healing, he could, perhaps, at a pinch, go back to work again. But he was so hungry. His father had brought him back, grudgingly, an occasional greasy parcel of cold Chinese spaghetti and even the odd duck-head or bone, always, in an ecstasy of self-laudation, with the words, "I a good a father. You a not a work but I a still give a you a food." Paolo had tried to supplement these irregular rations through odd raids on the neighbouring houses. With grief he saw that Lydgate had gone: no more butter or tins of Porkyboy. He had crawled painfully to the house of the two drunken Sudus, but they never had any food. An Indian clerk had given him saffron-tinted rice. Forbes, sometimes standing by the door, backed by motherless children, had snarled strange words at him but not offered further to molest him. But Paolo did not feel he could ask Forbes for a heel of cheese or of mildewed bread. Christ in the wilderness, thirsting and hungering, Paolo sometimes felt that his apotheosis was near—his frame light as the frame of an early biplane, a sensation as of balloon-gas filling his hollows.

Why, he wondered, had he been forsaken? In horizontal crucifixion he lay on the dirty bed-sheet, beard getting longer. Why had those workmen, his disciples, not brought him food, not come to comfort him with dulcet words and threats of new strikes? He had much to learn about Africa, about the good intentions thwarted by indolence, about out-of-sight-out-of-mind. And so he lay, wondering, the naked bulb of light caught in big gathering tears. And then he remembered early images—himself as the Italian Tiger, the Laughing Parricide, the Fearless Thief. A kind of bar-parlour stuffed with old signed photographs surrounded him, though dancing and unsteady like his Lloyd-Triestino cabin in the Indian Ocean. A skull xylophone began to tingle in the distance—a whole-tone scale straight out of Debussy. *"Mangiare,"* cried Paolo, *"mangiare, io devo mangiare."* He remembered an evening when, his shoe full of buck-notes, he had gorged himself nearly ill on Chinese *pasta* and tiny beasts of the estuary. He had stolen, but the theft had harmed nobody. His father's watch was back again on his father's wrist. He must steal again, but what now could he steal?

He looked around the room and, his delirious brain seeing round corners, into the lavatory. The light-bulb, his father's razor, a piece of pumice, a disintegrating sponge, the bed-sheets. They, he felt sure, would fetch very little. Then he saw, in a mound in the corner, his father's dirty shirts and socks and undervests. His father had grumbled that Paolo was not yet able to resume laundry-work. And, of course, somewhere or other downstairs was the electric iron. And, on the landing, was the single wardrobe that his father had appropriated to his own use, locking it, keeping the key in his pocket. Inside, Paolo knew, was a

suit, a suit his father wore when summoned to the house of
the Caliph's Private Secretary to report on the work in the
Mosque. Paolo got painfully up, naked except for the
cerement about his waist, and walked, with many religious
cries, to the landing. He switched on its light, and flying
ants dashed in to dance around it. There stood the wardrobe, locked but fragile. Weak as he was, he found it easy
to open. His father had a long bottle-opener, much prized,
stolen from a Tripoli bar. This hung on a nail beside
his father's bed. Paolo crawled back for it, pushed it into
the crevice between wardrobe-door and jamb, levered and
saw the maimed door fly open. There, cleaned and pressed
professionally, hung the suit. Trembling, Paolo unhooked
the hanger from the rail. He took also a pair of his
father's slacks and a nylon shirt. He dressed himself in
these, and Christ changed to D. H. Lawrence. Then, sitting
on his bed, he felt in the inside pocket of his father's
jacket (there might be a cheque from Tripoli, the odd
ten-buck bill) and pulled out envelopes. He opened them
eagerly. One letter was in English and was signed—Paolo
recognised the name—by the Tripoli whore. Another
letter was in Italian, and this Paolo read with attention.
"Caro amico," it began, but much of the Italian had been
corrupted by long contact with alien races. It was the
Italian of a member of the Shurga Italian colony, garnished
with references to Lighthouse Beer, Pox Road, Murder
Street, some of its asseverations intensified with words like
"bloody". But content began to interest Paolo far more
than style. He read, with horror, that he was not, after all,
to be sent back to Italy after the opening of the Mosque;
instead, he was to be sent to some jungle or other to live
with snakes and lions and leeches. He was to force horrible
black coolies to climb trees and bring down bananas. It was
a trick; he saw that clearly. It was a device to have him

eaten alive by ferocious beasts, never again to see the safe world of *pasta* and Fiats and *Aqua Sacra, gelati* and Sophia Loren. Tears came again. He knew his father was jealous of his intelligence and his virility, but he had not thought he hated him as much as that. Then he felt panic, wondering what to do now. He would leave, he would never return to this bedroom, he would sell his father's suit and buy a ticket to Italy, he would eat, he would get drunk, he would commit suicide. *"Mamma mia,"* he cried, clutching the empty suit to his chest. *"Che faró, che faró?"*

Out on the street, hardly able to walk, he looked wildly about him. A yellow-topped taxi came and, in it, a Chinese youth with sun-glasses who said, "You." Paolo, despite his agitation, his delirium, realised that he had no money and that it would be wasteful to pay a taxi-fare with a suit. *"Aspetta,"* he said. He went back into the house and came out with an electric iron. The youth handled it with interest and said, "Ah."

As they journeyed to the town the youth commented on the festive illuminations that were going up everywhere. "There 355. There 25 blue, 31 yellow. There I not count yet. Tomorrow I count." Alone in the town centre, Paolo looked about, fearful, dizziness coming over him. Everywhere there seemed to be members of Forbes's road-gang, unemployed now, for their road was finished, sneering like polecats, making truculent gestures. He hurried shakily, clasping the suit, down Sir Ernest Sidebotham Road, seeking the shop where his workmates were wont to gather. At a table they sat, leaning against a solid wall of radio music, and the subtle Indian greeted him—"Friend! You have returned to us from the tomb!"—and the rat-tailed Sudu showed gold teeth, and there, to Paolo's numb shock, was his father, sitting at the same table, his back to the street, saying, 'It a too a late a now you go on a bloody strike. Two a week a more, Mosque a open. You work a Sunday you a get a double time. Tomorrow I mend a marble-cutting machine a." And turning bulkily, he saw his suit hanging in mid-air, open mouths of loiterers looking on, and then the suit retreating, legs with baggy trousers beneath it, walking from the knees. *"Ladrone!"* called Nando Tasca. "Stop, you a bloody thief!" But onlookers would not get out of his way, and there was Eileen Forbes saying, "You like, darling? You want quickie, five bucks?"

"Not a now," said Nando Tasca. "Out a way quick, blodoy fool." But Paolo, the suit on his back, had dived, panting, into an alley full of cardboard cartons, cabbage leaves, hens. Sanctuary, sanctuary! He longed, as for his mother, towards some great Gothic cathedral where he would be safe, God on the altar saving him from his earthly father. Weak, he tried to hurry, losing himself, pausing for breath once by a wall. And from that wall, in moonlight, he saw the glory of the Mosque, his home, the one place where he had never seen his father. Moonlight blanched the central dome, the cupolas on their towers, the minaret which poked at the moon. In relief he made towards it, through the filthy back-street gutters, courting cats, the odd stunted scavenger startled by his prayers to the Virgin:

"—*Sede della Sapienza, implora larghezza ed efficacia di mezzi alla stampa cattolica*—"

Over the courtyard, where the fountain played under the moon. The magnificent portico, with its twisted barley-sugar pillars, the oak doors with their stained glass. But locked, locked; the massy ward had been installed, ready for the vast ceremonial key. Paolo looked around wildly, the fountain singing to him. Then he saw the door of the spiral stairs that led up, up to the muezzin's golden cage.

There, up against the moon, among the birds, he would be safe. He took many deep breaths and then, his father's suit on his back, began to climb.

At every turn he had to pause, sit, wipe away sweat with his nylon sleeve. Gasping, after half an hour of aching leg muscles, he saw, through the golden cage round the last bend of the stairs, the moon and the African stars. He dragged himself up, into the conning tower of an alien faith, and felt safe at last. God would protect him; it was, after all, the same God, for there was only one God. He stood, gasping, his hands on the fitted lectern with its microphone, and looked down over the dangerous land. There was the river with lights. There were the fairy clusters on the streets, there the Dunia Hotel, there the Chin Chin Cinema, there the Kool Kaffi. Somewhere below, an angry and agitated worm, was his father. Paolo, light-headed, filling his chest with cold air, laughed. He laughed and laughed and then he cried. He switched the microphone on, and his sobs began to pump themselves, sobs of a giant, from loudspeakers all round the town. God was crying. Then he sang, for a bar or two, "Stardust" in Italian, changing "stardust" to "marble-dust". Then he switched the microphone off, making a pillow of his father's suit, lay down for an empty-stomached sleep. Then, fearful again, remembering some text about "They did it while I slept", he closed the door that shut the muezzin in with his godly wails, pleased that it had a Yale lock. Then, locked in with divinity and the moon and the stars, he lay down once more. God would look after him. He was, despite everything, a good boy.

26

The Honourable Mr. Tomlin received news that Mr. Rowlandson, District Adviser, had lost his head. He was suffering from one of his periodical bouts of dengue when the message came. He sat at his desk, his teeth chattering, forehead hot and feet cold, an obstinate ringing in his left ear, the deafer of the two. The brandy flask rattled against his incisors, and a decollated image of Rowlandson hung in the air, Rowlandson's voice, whining Lancastrian, sounded through the ringing. "Don't send me back there, please. Anywhere but there. There's going to be trouble, honest there is. Please, please." Rowlandson had been compelled to return to his duty, to teaching football and emotional stability to a people half devil and half child. Well, there it was. And now, thought Mr. Tomlin, the authorities would be after him again. He winced at the last rebuke, hearing again odd words spoken in that flat and comfortless voice. "Political agitators in the town— the spirit of unrest spreads easily—keep the head cool and the limbs will dance the right steps."

It was some time before Mr. Tomlin realised that the telephone was ringing. This was because he now had the impression that the telephone was ringing all the time. The line crackled and the voice seemed to come from an immense distance. For a moment, hearing slow monophthongal speech, he fancied in his fever that Rowlandson was chiding him from the world of the dead. But it was not Rowlandson; it was Al-Haji Abu Bakar, Private Secretary to the Caliph, who said:

"He would like you to come up and see him now, if it is not inconvenient."

"But, hang it all, it's nothing to do with H.H. It's between me and my own masters. Moreover, it's one of the Queen's subjects, not one of his."

"I did not realise that the Queen now ruled Italy." The line crackled, the ringing spread to Mr. Tomlin's right ear. "So if you could come up right away——" The line went dead. Mr. Tomlin took another swig of brandy and a couple of Amplex tablets and, with bowed shoulders, left his office. He walked down the stone steps, not pausing to admire the big-breasted female sculpture—recently imported from a fun-fair in Brighton—that personified Holy Living, cynosure of the loungers in the lobby of the Government Building. Mr. Tomlin got into his little car, his wife having taken the official monster to the beach, and drove slowly through crowds that, for some reason or other, gaped towards Mecca. He passed workmen placing floodlamps outside official buildings, under a triumphal arch erected, in honour of the Caliph's birthday, by the Indian community of the town. Lamps, lamps everywhere, though dead in the sunlight, as he now sped towards the Astana. In their corral the royal elephants were being experimentally decked with tasselled headgear and trunk-bells. More bells for Mr. Tomlin, but swallowed by the noise in his ear: there the idiot finger stayed on the button that said "Press". 'Press,' he thought. They must keep Rowlandson's head out of the papers. But perhaps it was already too late: Sebastian Hup had been seen rubbing his hands, grinning in great pain. "Reality," groaned Mr. Tomlin, "come to terms with reality."

The policemen at the Astana guard-room tried to prevent Mr. Tomlin's entering the grounds. Only two days before, a go-getter Bengali commercial—in a car not unlike Mr. Tomlin's—had actually, through some mistake, found his way to the Presence and tried to sell it a gross of lavatory-brushes. But one of the palace servants, holding hands with a corporal, said laughingly that he knew who this was: the Caliph had a picture of him, a picture he seemed to prize. He should be permitted to enter.

The Caliph, black trousers, silk shirt, cutlass in belt, cigarette, flunkey carrying tin and lighter on a salver, received Mr. Tomlin in his dining-room. There was to be an official banquet after the opening of the Mosque, and servants were practising the correct laying of a table. Also the Caliph was supervising the hanging of his pictures on the wall that faced the sunlight of the huge handsome windows. There were portraits of past rulers, including the original piratical Abu standing Byronically on a storm-racked deck, the Caliph's grandfather painted by Sargent, the Caliph's father painted by Wyndham Lewis, four original drawings by Smetana.

"Those," stuttered the U.N. Adviser, "those. Surely you're not going to have those there?"

"The peace of God be with you," said the Caliph cordially. "What do you mean by allowing that young Italian to lock himself in at the top of the minaret?"

"I understand," began the U.N. Adviser. He corrected himself. "Dog understands that the work is going ahead quite satisfactorily. You can't have those pictures there," he said. "I protest. As representative of the United Nations Organisation, I protest in the strongest possible terms."

"Get him down," said the Caliph more loudly. "Get him down at once."

The U.N. Adviser moved towards the pictures. "Dog is

glad that Your Highness is going to be reasonable," he said.

"Listen, can't you?" said the Caliph, so loudly that he coughed. "That young Italian imagines himself to be some sort of princess in a tower. He seems to have climbed up there last night. He will not come down. It is your job to get him down."

Mr. Tomlin's fever was beginning to clear a little. "Dog's job, Your Highness? Dog has no jurisdiction over the Mosque. The limitations of Dog's authority have been made very clear to Dog by Your Highness." ('The bloody young fool,' he was thinking. Still, he had said his say before; he would wash his hands of the whole business; this was the Caliph's pigeon.) "Your Highness is, if Dog may remind Your Highness, sponsor to this young Italian. Your Highness, not Dog, is responsible."

"It has been reported to me," said the Caliph impatiently, "that he is already creating a disturbance. He is shouting abuse down to his father, for one thing. For another, some of the disaffected elements of the town are treating him as a kind of hero. Members of the People's Party have been cheering him. Men with beards have been taking up curries and cases of beer. Beer!" cried the Caliph. "Beer in the holy place of God's word."

"Beer and God can go together, Your Highness," said Mr. Tomlin. "There is a poet called Chesterton——"

"I don't want to hear about infidel poets," said the Caliph. He strolled a few paces, gracefully smoking, angry. "Get this man down."

"Dog is sorry," said Mr. Tomlin, "but Dog would not presume to interfere in a matter involving religion. To Dog's simple mind the presence of an infidel in an Islamic place would seem to be a matter for the religious authorities. Moreover, Dog made it quite clear to Your Highness some time ago that, if Dog had his way, both these Italians would have long ago caught the plane to Tripoli. Your Highness must now bear full responsibility."

"But," said the Caliph, now, in his agitation, with a cigarette in each hand, "I have, under the United Nations agreement, no power to call out the police. I have, under that agreement, no power at all. And here I must sit back and see my Mosque desecrated. Desecrated," he repeated, "because a stupid U.N.O. official will not do the job he is paid to do."

Mr. Tomlin was almost pleased with the Caliph for speaking so clearly, so loudly. Never before had he been able to hear the Caliph so well. But his left eye caught his portrait on the wall, and those of his wife and daughter—heads stilled, in certain ridiculous postures—for ever and ever. He thought of poor young Rowlandson and said, with something like anger, "Don't talk to Dog about not doing his job." (The pension would be adequate; he had money saved; he would receive no decoration on retirement, but still—) "You're only able to indulge in your beautiful Islamic dream because we do the dirty work. Who found uranium? Was it you? No, it was a handful of engineers and geologists, men with adequate salaries but never destined to become millionaires. It's you who've made the real money. And, while you become rich and your lazy Chosen People watch the coconuts fall, people like me and young Rowlandson, poor young Rowlandson, try to give you government, try to show you how to build a modern state, damn it, even try to show you how to build a mosque. Young Rowlandson's dead, and he hasn't even died for an ideal which you, some day, may grow up to appreciate. You've no interest in the aborigines of this State. You're a pirate king, ruling retired pirates, intruders just as much as we are. Now other people are digging out the gold for you and you have nothing to do except turn it into blasted

231

moidores. Don't talk to me about beer being drunk in the minaret. Think about poor underpaid officials like Rowlandson, his head lopped off, his body eaten, in an up-river village." He panted audibly. The Caliph impassively smoked. Mr. Tomlin said, "Dog begs your pardon for speaking like that, but Dog had to say it."

"Yes," said the Caliph, "I see that." Then he said, "I don't think there's any useful purpose to be served by your staying here any longer. We've had the best of you. You're not like the people of the old days that my grandfather used to tell me about—people who really built, who really made laws, people who had visions. You've been a competent little man, but not quite competent enough Soon we shall be rid of the white man altogether. In the meantime, I suppose I shall have to continue to have a U.N.O. official here. But I don't want you any longer. I shall ask the authorities to send me somebody else. Mr. Mudd can, presumably, take over from you till the new Adviser comes. But you," said the Caliph, and in deference to the occasion he put his cigarette down on an ash-tray; never before had he been seen with both hands free, "you have twenty-four hours to leave the State. I will not have my Mosque desecrated."

"I doubt if the authorities will approve of this high-handed attitude," said the U.N. Adviser. "The General Assembly will have something to say."

"This is not a colony," said the Caliph. "Nor do I imagine that anybody is going to be seriously annoyed. There won't be any gun-boats sailing up the river. There'll certainly be no desire for renunciation of the uranium concession. Besides, I know my rights. You can tell everybody that you have to leave at once because you're ill. I shall communicate with your masters. And," said the Caliph, "I shall take down the pictures you dislike so much. If you like, I'll send them to you as a farewell present. They don't really fit in," he said, looking through his dark glasses at the Byronic portrait of his piratical ancestor, a great wind blowing out of the canvas, the waves all black dragons.

27

Lydia still had three boxes of the chic notepaper she had obtained from an expensive stationer in Sydney. She snivelled a little now as she admired its arty heading:

FROM LYDIA GATE

What a waste, what a bloody waste. And what a bloody waste of the best years of her life, or some of them, like being good for a long time and finding incontrovertible proof that there was no eschatological sanction for morality. Now she was back where she had started, Lydia Higgins, spinster, still attractive but not as young as she used to be. She said to Mudd:

"What are you going to do about it?"

Mudd, eager for his noon potion, opened a tin of Lydia's beer over-hastily. There was a gush like an oil-strike, and beer fountained on to the wall. Then, in beer, an octopus painted itself, its legs over-lengthening as it groped for the skirting. "Eh?" He poured the beer and was annoyed to find the glass less than half-filled. "This canned beer isn't much good really," he said. "I shall go back to the old bottle. Trouble is a lot of the local beer's so damned flat."

"What are you going to do about it?"

"Oh, you can't do anything. It's the climate, I suppose. Oh, that, you mean. Well." Mudd sat down. "I ought to get in touch with the police. Then they can get in touch with Somerset House. I can't forgive him for doing what he did."

"It wasn't altogether his fault," said Lydia Higgins. She pouted at her notepaper. "What I meant was, what are you going to do about me?"

"Well," said Mudd, sitting hunched, a jockey for the weighing-in, "well, there are certain difficulties."

"Such as?"

"Oh, the usual thing. People asking questions and so on. It's a bit awkward, really."

"And there you were," said Lydia violently, "in Shurga, and even here, saying how much you'd like me to be yours, but that was impossible, because I belonged to another man and we both felt the same about divorce and so on, having been brought up in good High Church traditions and all the rest of it. Except for that one thing, and that was only not to hurt me, Frank was at least honest."

"Frank Lydgate is a swine."

Lydia felt a twinge of quite unreasonable envy because Frank had the name and she hadn't, but then, of course, he hadn't got the Christian name, had he? She shook her head; how fuzzy the tropics made one's brain. "Well, now's your chance," said Lydia. "Not, of course, that I want to *ask* you to marry me."

"Of course I want to marry you. It's just a bit difficult at the moment, that's all. If you and I were somewhere else— not in Dunia at all; Dunia's a big tract of land but only a small parish—it might be different, because people wouldn't know anything." He sucked in residuary beer-froth with his tongue, as though he were finishing a small advocaat. "The trouble is that I'm with U.N.O., posted to Dunia. I couldn't get out of Dunia if I tried. Not," he added, "that there's anywhere else left, really."

"But if everybody here were told the truth, about Frank and me. I mean, how it was all a mistake—no," she said, "that wouldn't do, would it? I'd feel such a fool. You mustn't tell anyone," she said, with quick urgency.

"Only the police. The U.K. police, not these police. Scotland Yard, or somebody," he said vaguely. "I've really not had any experience of this kind of thing before."

"And what would happen to Frank?"

"Oh, I suppose they'd send out C.I.D. men to collect him. Then he'd have to stand trial and go to prison, I suppose."

"Oh, drop the whole thing, forget it. It's not as though he's committed a real crime." She then said, "But he has. He's ruined my whole life. Ruined it completely."

"He'd no right," said Mudd, "going round and telling everybody I used the whip like he said. He deserves what's coming to him. And to think of the things he's called me. To my face, as well."

"I've got to go, I suppose," said Lydia. "I've been here just over a fortnight. This must be the shortest term on record."

"Oh, I don't know. There was one man who got out of the aircraft and then got into it again. And one P.W.D. man stayed five days. His name, strangely enough, was Jump. We called him Jump-in-and-jump-out. And there was somebody else."

"You're not very anxious to make me stay," said Lydia bitterly. "Still, it doesn't matter. It wouldn't make any difference. I wouldn't like to be in the office when the C.I.D. men come looking for Frank. In any case, this place has been pretty well ruined for me."

"There'll be no trouble about your contract," promised Mudd. "That can easily be arranged. Immediate repatriation, urgent family business. That sort of thing. Mother dying, father an invalid, got to get back at once."

"But they're both perfectly fit."

"Well, something like that. We can think about it later. The main thing is to arrange your repatriation."

"That's right. 'Clear off, Lydia dear, I've had what I wanted.' And what is there for me in that bloody place? Sydney." She shuddered. "A fair cow. And what would you do about it then, with me thousands of miles away? Why," she asked the beer-stain on the wall, "does nobody want me?"

"I want you, Lydia, really I do." He looked covertly at his wrist-watch. "I want you now, as a matter of fact. I don't much fancy lunch." His eyes gleamed in jockey concupiscence.

"Lydia Mudd," said Lydia Higgins. "A comic sort of name. But it'll have to do, I suppose. Unless something else comes along."

"Oh, no," said Mudd eagerly. Blood burned, tongue lent soul vows. "I love you, really and truly. Let me show you how much." He began to get up, or down, from his chair with the rabbity readiness of the small man.

"You randy little jockey," said Lydia tolerantly. "Some other time. Not now. I'll tell you what I'm going to do. There's a job in Aden. I saw it in the *Times*. Teacher in a school for stenographers. I think I could get that easily enough. The Dunia Government can pay my fare to Australia, in cash. That'll get me over to Aden and leave me enough for a few new dresses. I deserve a few new dresses."

"You deserve more than that," said Mudd. If she wouldn't now she would this evening; he kept the loving mood ticking on. "Much more. A bit of affection."

"And then you could come over for your next local leave and tell me how you feel about things. Could you do that?"

"Oh, yes," said Mudd eagerly, "that seems a good idea. I'll fix things up with Treasury this afternoon. After lunch. Though I don't much feel like lunch. You," he said. "I could eat you."

Lydia looked over the parched grass. One of the U.N. Adviser's servants was running towards Mudd's house. "Evidently the U.N.A. wants you," she said.

"That'll be something about that damn fool Eyetie, I expect," sneered Mudd.

"Poor little Tony Spaghetti."

"Poor old U.N.A. I wouldn't have his job for ten thousand a month and a knighthood."

After her Kraft cheese, cold storage lettuce, and Nescafé, Lydia wrote to the man who had, for so long, posed as her husband. She herself posed as his wife, or her notepaper posed for her. She gave him a friendly warning about Mudd. She was writing, she said, to show that there were really no hard feelings, whatever had happened. And to say that this was not really good-bye. They were bound to meet again sometime and, even if she happened to be married—really married—when they met, she hoped that would not prevent their being friends. It would be nothing new; they had lived in sin before. Licking the envelope flap, she felt a certain pride in having been so intimate with somebody who had committed so great an enormity. It made Frank seem quite distinguished. She had met Nevil Shute, she had met Sir Don Bradman, she had met Joy Nichols. And she had actually lived with Frank Lydgate, well-known bigamist.

28

The Imam Mowaffak of Naishapur, vanguard of distinguished visitors to Dunia Town, was himself, though old,
scholarly, gentle, tolerant, not particularly distinguished.
He had come quietly and without fuss to this rather
quaint territory, living quietly in a small hot room in the
local hotel, squalid, its air unconditioned, overlooking the
yard where the fowls were, most un-Islamically, strangled
at all hours. He rose early, prayed, took syrupy Chinese
coffee, spoke a word or two of Persian with the Chinese
clerk at the desk, and then went out and strolled to the
medan to look at the Mosque. Many of the commonalty,
including infidel Chinese and Indians on their way to work,
gaped towards Mecca. The glory came: the stained-glass
windows raged with a score of suns; the golden dome
writhed in an agony of light. The Imam Mowaffak smiled
and nodded, thinking of his fellow-townsman, Omar the
tent-maker, and his witty verses. There was a quatrain
apposite to this dawn moment—the king of day sending a
whistling lariat through the air and strangling the dome;
but *bam*, or roof, made Omar think of *jam*, or cup: the
bam was an inverted *jam*. Either the Cyrus of the day
could not pour wine into it, or else the wine had already
been drained and the empty *bam* or *jam* turned down. He
smiled further as he thought of the naughty Omar making
the bilal cock-crow *"Ishrabu!"* That meant "Have a drink."
There was room for naughtiness in Islam; there was room

in Islam for everything and everybody.

The sun stretched an arm up from the amber blanket. The sun lit a tiny figure standing high in the minaret. The figure raised some kind of drinking vessel to its lips. "Aaaaah," said some of the loitering workmen, "he drinks." The Imam Mowaffak saw a small man he took to be an Arab standing on the verge of the medan. He addressed courteous words to him in Arabic. But the Arab knew no Arabic; he smiled and shook his head. Three generations in this land; he knew no other tongue than the National Language. But then the loudspeakers all over the town belched like a volcano. And through the loudspeakers a voice, like the voice of God, called, *"Mio padre. Molto cattivo.* Bloody robber."

Workmen of the Electrical Department began again their search for the main switch of the Mosque. It was hidden somewhere in a niche behind a marble panel that was supposed to open like a door. The voice cried to all the town:

"One ticket Italy."

The Imam Mowaffak went on his way, shaking his head good-humouredly. They seemed to use the vernacular here. Perhaps the drinking was symbolic. There were, perhaps precedents for all these things. But he had always suspected that the vision of Islam held by the barbarous peoples of East Africa was not a true one. Here one saw the dangers of Protestantism. He walked along the main street, charmed by the strangeness of this exotic country. He murmured to himself verses of the seventieth Surah, about Allah, Lord of the Ascending Stairways, by which the Angels and the Spirit ascend unto Him in a Day whereof the span is fifty thousand years.

PART FIVE

29

This hilltop holiday of sweet air, Franciscan talk with birds and bats, ample cold food and drink, father's insect rage far far below, enforced leisure, gratifying attention from large crowds, was doing Paolo good. His beard flourished and his flesh filled out. There were certain disadvantages, lack of washing and laundry facilities chief among them, but on the whole this was a fine, if somewhat artificial, life. Paolo had as little *pudeur* as the birds about voiding in public, but, being a good boy brought up in a civilised village, he tried to regard the day as a great "ENGAGED" sign; at seven in the evening the sun flushed the sky's basin, leaving to Paolo the blue vacant *gabinetto* of the night. No rain came, and Paolo remained dirty, but every other day he changed from his own clothes into his father's suit. His enemies could not get at him, for he could clearly see who was there down below, ready for the arduous ascension. The men with beards and mops of hair were always welcome: to them he always unlatched the door, taking with gratitude their gifts of curry and beer and cigarettes; but his former colleagues he no longer trusted. Did they not neglect him during his illness, were they not now working for his father? The beards alone were allowed up to encourage him, shake him by the hand, tell him to continue the fight against tyrannical oppression. Paolo, being as innocent of politics as of Protestant morality, assumed in his simple way that it was just a matter of beard calling to beard; he did not know that he had already become a symbol—the prisoner in the tower yelling for justice. Even in Ceylon he was known: Mr. Bastians referred to him in a speech, and the newspapers had brief references to a young Italian fanatic, self-appointed leader of ragged malcontents, emulating Simon Stylites to shame the white men into granting immediate autonomy to Dunia.

Paolo called down to his father several times a day (the main electrical switch had still not been located) words of abuse but also, and more frequently as time went on, a demand for a one-way ticket to Italy. Once or twice his father called back through the microphone that hung above the mimbar, and the town would be loud with snarling Tuscan stichomythia. The father ordered and the son demanded and neither would yield; the town felt as the Trojan heroes must have felt—oppressed by a celestial family quarrel which was no less petty for being divine and ubiquitous.

But the unemployed and the party members cheered when Paolo cried "Italy! Italy!" and they themselves took up the cry and made a freedom slogan out of it. And it was "Italy!" that they cried when at last the police came.

It was a noon of cruel heat and brightness. Mr. Bishopspawn bit his under-lip again and again as he looked at the crowd's proffered throats, as he looked at his squad and the Indian inspector. Nobody was armed. Mr. Mudd, acting U.N. Adviser, had just gone up-river to rebuke the tribe that had lost its head; he had, before leaving by launch, given curt orders that Paolo must be dragged down from his tower bodily—no bloody nonsense about persuasion or threats. The door must be broken in and the prisoner forced back to liberty. However, Mr. Bishopspawn saw that some of his Moslem constables were not too happy about using violence in a holy place, even violence to a door. The fact that the Mosque had not yet been consecrated was neither here nor there; they were faced with a job which, when they first joined the force, they had never expected they would ever be forced to do. Mr. Bishopspawn noted uneasily many beards in the crowd; he saw many small boys who ecstatically grinned "Italy" at him; he felt—as he had felt many times before in his colonial police career —unpopular. He did not want too much trouble.

Mr. Bishopspawn, shy of decision, proffered his own throat to the sun's blade as he looked up at his quarry. Some of the crowd, ready to believe anything of the British, thought that he proposed to climb the minaret the hard way, and there was a murmur of excitement and even sympathy. As he gazed up, drinking the height, his hands on his hips, Paolo's voice suddenly smote him and the whole town with a few bars—in bops and bups—of "Sweet Sue". Mr. Bishopspawn reddened, looked awkward, as the crowd laughed gently, then decided that he had to act. He went over to the Indian inspector and talked to him, occasionally pointing like a general in a news-reel, as though the enemy had many flanks and was to be attacked not vertically but horizontally. It was then, when Mr. Bishopspawn's back was turned, that a nervous constable made a gesture of mock threat at a child—a small boy who had grinned, said "Italy" and put out his tongue. Some of the crowd said, "Aaaah" in gentle reproof, and one of the beards said, "Bully". Some of the constables moved back, and it seemed to Bishopspawn that the crowd was moving forward. He waved an imperious hand at them, other hand still on his hip, and said, "Come on, now," while motioning them to go back. Then he turned, ready to give orders for the ascent of the minaret, but the Indian inspector, with uncommon common sense, said to Bishopspawn:

"I think this is not the best time. Too many people ready to cause trouble. It is better to come back when it is dark and everybody is in bed."

Bishopspawn saw the force of this but said, "They'll think we're scared. We'll lose face."

"Oh, no," said the inspector, who, an Oriental, knew all about face. "We not lose face at all. We lose face only if we try and fail. Nobody is making us go back now. We are going back of our own free will."

"Yes, yes," said Bishopspawn, biting his lower lip. "Yes." 'Subtle,' he thought; 'subtle, these damned Orientals.' "All right," he said, "lead 'em back." The inspector went slowly back to the station with the constables, and Bishopspawn, with a great effort, smiled bleakly at the crowd. The crowd showed teeth in the sun, some cheered feebly. And then, walking back himself, Bishopspawn thought: 'The key. Somebody must have the key.' But that small sun of hope went in; this was Dunia: there would be no key.

Nando Tasca watched with displeasure from one of the stained-glass windows. He had hoped to see his son dragged down snivelling, though he did not want too much violence done to the suit. Anger had been making Nando Tasca work hard these days, working hard had given him an intenser appetite for his beer: he had to guard against softening towards Paolo. He set his jaw *nel modo Church-illiano*, turned towards his workmen, and counted again the number of slabs of marble already laid. They came to a tidy bonus. The work evidently would not be finished on time, but Nando Tasca knew a thousand pretty tricks that would afford temporary satisfaction to all concerned— architect and Caliph included. Curtains could be hung, carpets laid—oh, there were lots of things that could be done. And all the time more blame to be laid on Paolo. "E not a work a ard. I tell im e not a work a ard. I it im.

E run away a ide. E very bad boy. It all a is a fault." A repentant and dirty Paolo could then be made to finish the work after the official opening of the Mosque and before he took up his new and lethal post. A very bad boy. All the world now knew it; it was advertised as openly as the one-ness of Allah.

Nando Tasca gave harsh instructions to his workmen and then left the Mosque for his lunch-hour or beer-hour. He crossed the courtyard by the iridescent fountain, squinting up at the minaret as he went. A tiny figure above shook a fist at a tiny figure below. Nando Tasca returned the salute and walked on towards the Dunia Hotel. He was pleased to notice that he was losing flesh round the middle: he could now squeeze his hand between waistband and belly. His arms felt tired, however; the marble-cutting machine was shaking the fat, to its surprise, back to muscle. But he had a marble-dusty thirst, one not to be sold for a thousand bucks. It was decidedly an ill wind.

Nando Tasca was given letters at the reception desk. He did not sleep here, he did not work here, but the Dunia Hotel had, for many months, been his home and his office. He read the letters over his first and second beers. There were only two of them, one from Tripoli, one from his wife in Italy. The letter from Tripoli enclosed a cheque —Paolo's passage-money back to Italy, representing—as the banana firm would pay Paolo's fare to Krochucha—an acceptable free gift for Paolo's father. The other letter Nando Tasca read closely, twice, sipping his third beer thoughtfully as he read certain passages yet again.

"Mio caro,
I am so sorry that you will not be coming home after your present work is finished. It is such a long time since I last saw you that I am forgetting what you look like and

247

you never send me a photograph. I suppose with all that work and the heat and the foreign food which you will not be able to eat you will be getting quite thin. You must watch your health as you will have to work for many more years yet if I am to stop working which I will have to soon as the sewing machine is past repair and I will not be able to afford another. Lucrezia is a very big girl now but she seems to have forgotten that her father exists. That is because you do not write very often and you very rarely send any money. It is such a pity that they do not pay you more if you work so hard. Lucrezia has had three jobs in six months and has lost all of them. I fear she is not a clever girl and cannot add money up very well and so is not very much help in a shop. I am sorry to hear that Paolo is a bad boy still and lies in bed while you have to work. I think he will work harder and be a better boy when he has a wife and family to look after. And now I will tell you that there is somebody here who will marry Paolo if he wants her to and of course he must want her to. I do not think it is good if Paolo stays in foreign parts and perhaps will marry a foreign woman and we will have black grandchildren. If you send Paolo home he can marry this girl. She is Novello's eldest daughter and she is older than Paolo about seven years but if he loves her and she loves him age is not important. She is not beautiful in her face but I think perhaps her soul is beautiful. She is quite big and strong and I think that is what Paolo needs to keep him in order. Her upper teeth are false but her lower teeth are all her own. Now you know that Novello has now more than two shops he has five with one in Piombino and one in Volterra with managers and he is opening business in Siena. His farm too is bigger. He will settle money he says as he is sick of his daughter's voice and does not want her living at home. So I think this is best for Paolo. If he comes home by ship she says she will meet him in Leghorn if you can say what day he will come. I think this is best for Paolo and for us as you do not seem to earn much money.

> *Molto affetto,*
> Gina."

That, thought Nando Tasca, would be the worst punishment of all. Marriage. Why hadn't he thought of that before? If Novello's eldest daughter were anything like Novello's wife—say, Novello's monumental ugliness and Signora Novello's slate-pencil gramophone voice, together with the thorough and utter bitchiness of the grandmother, why, Paolo would be well served. And he could send money to his mother, plenty, while his poor father languished in Africa. What were lions, leeches and cannibals to a daughter of Novello's? What was tropical sweat, what was prickly heat, what was malaria? Paolo must be brought to heel; he had had too much of his own way, he had got the better of his father—and always by mean tricks and unfilial treachery—much too often. Let Novello's daughter meet Paolo at Leghorn; that would be enough, the rest would follow, he wouldn't be able to get away.

Nando Tasca had another beer, sweating happily under the fan. He thought of his girl in Tripoli. It would not be long now. Africa was too good for sons like Paolo.

30

The Sultan of Lanchap, the Sultan of Dahaga, the Crown
Prince of Lapar, the Raja of Ayut, the Regent of Anchok,
various kathis, muftis and imams, Middle East oil sheikhs,
kings of Arab lands (some soon to be deposed, one
assassinated) and a man from the Mosque at Woking,
England—these were already in Dunia Town when the
Times of Dunia gave, in a note at the foot of the second
of the two pages devoted to astrology, the reason for The
Honourable Mr. Tomlin's sudden repatriation. Mr. Tomlin
had, for a long time, been suffering from slight deafness;
now the condition was deteriorating and, on medical
advice, he was going home. Everybody—said the *Times of
Dunia*—wished him a speedy recovery from his deafness
and a happy retirement. Everybody would probably miss
his charming wife and daughter. He had done good work
for the State, asserted, without specification, the *Times of
Dunia*. No photograph, no departing message. Mr. Tomlin
had flown back at last to reality.

Lydgate read through the paper impatiently, sitting,
after hours, in his office. He was waiting for Dunia Airways to ring him back about flights to Aden. Many
of the regular passenger flights had been cancelled, the
negro clerk had said, because the Government had
chartered so many aircraft for the distinguished visitors.
These were to be flown to the mines and to various other
places of interest in the territory. If, however, Mr. Lydgate

could obtain a chit from the U.N. Adviser's Office testifying that he was travelling to Aden on official business, then some private person's flight could be cancelled and he could be found a seat on one of the regular passenger flights.

"No," Lydgate had said. "This is not official business. Ring me back." Then he fretted for an hour over the *Times of Dunia*. Some disaffected person had written a poem in heroic couplets, beginning:

> "Dunia, the little world of the misled,
> A deadly living for the living dead.
> All mortal sins are venal here; the least
> Of public works officials is a priest
> Ordained by the traditions of his tribe
> For one sole rite—the blessing of the bribe. . . ."

The clerk rang back. "I do not understand, Mr. Lydgate. The Government has already booked a passage in your name for tomorrow."

"Impossible."

"Your name is Mr. Lydia Lydgate?"

"No."

"Oh, I see, sorry, there must be some mistake. I will ring you again."

And then Carruthers Chung came in, together with Sebastian Hup, cheerfully solemn, ready to shake hands. Carruthers Chung had the same James Joyce beard. A late afternoon Dunia cloudscape drifted gravely across his glasses. "Do not be aflaid, Mr. Lydgate," he said. "We come as fliends." They both sat down, Sebastian Hup leaning forward, grinning in costive pain.

"I wonder if it will lain," said Carruthers Chung. "We

play for lain but lain does not come. Our sin must be velly gleat. And soon the flogs will be going to war."

"The frogs?"

"Yes, the gleen flogs and the blown flogs. They sometimes fight duling the dly season. Over the possession of a stleam or water-hole."

"Well?" said Lydgate.

"Well, Mr. Lydgate, I am so much happier that you are now so much happier a man. My whole gloup is happier, too. You look happier, as if you had shed a gleat load. Pelhaps we were plemature before. Pelhaps that was not yet the time for you to confess evelything. But now you have confessed, and you are happier fol it."

"Confessed what?" said Lydgate cautiously. "Who's been talking about my confessing things?"

"Oh, nobody," smiled Carruthers Chung. "Except that Sebastian Hup here said that you looked so much more peaceful, so I assumed, as did he, that you had thlown off a gleat load. One can always tell," he nodded, smiling, Sebastian Hup nodding, smiling, too. "But you must not be aflaid, Mr. Lydgate," said Carruthers Chung. "We are your fliends. And we can be perfectly flank with one another."

"What," asked Lydgate, still cautious, "am I supposed to have confessed?"

"Bigamy," said Carruthers Chung promptly. "It must be bigamy, because it cannot be anything else. We thought of murder, then of lobbely, then of other sins, but then that velly pletty girl flom the London School of Economics suggested bigamy. We discussed that and we all agleed it must be something like that."

Lydgate tried not to show surprise, admitting nothing.

"It was a velly long and instluctive discussion, Mr. Lydgate. The whole blidge gloup was plesent. However, you must not wolly. It is not the quidditas or the quantum of the sin that counts, but the extent of the guilt and the sincelity of the lepentence. I gather, Mr. Lydgate, that you are going to leave Dunia."

"How do you know that?"

"It is velly obvious. You have sold your car. The man you sold it to has sold it to the Government for thlee times the plice. They need many cars now for their distinguished visitors. You have also cashed valious cheques with diffelent people. You have no tlaveller's cheques. That means you are going to some place with no lestlictions on the import of foleign cullency. Where are you going, Mr. Lydgate?"

"That would be telling."

"You wolly too much, Mr. Lydgate. But I suppose you are like Olestes, you have to keep moving on."

"Olestes?"

"Olestes, the Gleek tlagical chalacter. But you need more money, pelhaps. We played blidge the other night, leal contlact blidge, and all winnings were pooled and given to me to plesent to you. Here they are. Not velly much, but it will help." He gave Lydgate about twenty ten-buck notes.

Lydgate was touched. He said, "Why do you do this for me?"

"We are not intelested in justice, Mr. Lydgate. We do not understand light and wlong. Clime and punishment mean nothing to us. We know sin, we know guilt, we know lepentance. That is all. You still have much punishment to come. But not flom law-courts, not in plison."

"I've been punished enough," said Lydgate.

"When you say that," said Carruthers Chung, "that is a sure sign that you have not been punished enough." The telephone rang. "But you will be punished enough," promised Carruthers Chung. Lydgate picked up the receiver. The two visitors stood up to go. Sebastian Hup was

253

acting the part of a man whose vocal cords had been cut out by men of the Mau Mau: he opened his mouth as if in pain, nodding and grinning.

"Don't go," said Lydgate. "Wait. We'll have a drink or something."

"No, no," smiled Carruthers Chung. "We have things to do. There are more blidge parties to be allanged. There are many new sinners in the town." He waved at Lydgate, going towards the door. Sebastian Hup made pathetic dumb noises.

"Thanks," said Lydgate. "Thanks very much."

"Mr. Lydgate?" said the voice from Dunia Airways.

"Francis Burroughs Lydgate," said Lydgate. "Well?"

"We can give you a seat on Tourist Flight LX571. 1405 hours, the day after tomorrow."

"That," said Lydgate, "will do very well. I'll come round in the morning and pay. Thank you." He put down the receiver. He felt, at least, reasonably safe. He had an exit permit from the Astana (a trip to Shurga, he had told the Caliph's Private Secretary, to buy fairy lamps for the Sailing Club, Dunia shops having sold out); his passport was in order; he had enough money; he had a seat on a plane. A few days in Aden, and then to Bombay, where Jock Wragg and Pilsby would be able to help. After that?

He locked the office and walked down the dirty stone stairs to the raging African afternoon. Flags, kites, posters, holiday crowds already. Tomorrow the Caliph's birthday parade, after that the Circumcision Ceremony for the two young princes, after that the opening of the Mosque. If, of course, they could free the minaret of its infidel incumbent. Lydgate looked for a taxi, then remembered that all taxis had been loaned (three hundred bucks a day) to the Government. He saw one now, its yellow top sprayed green to match the body, its number-plates covered with

stencilled boards—H.H. SULTAN OF LANCHAP. In it
a Chinese youth cheerfully catalogued the arithmetic of
the town to an old man with a waving turban and a
dropped jaw—His Highness. The Chinese youth recognised a former patron and democratically waved to Lydgate. Then he spat out of the window and went on. Lydgate had a long walk home. He proposed to break it briefly
at the Dunia Hotel.

Flags, banners, pennants, streamers, triumphal arches,
holiday crowds, sun, no sign of rain, fire engines pumping
up water to the upper floors of the Dunia Hotel. And in
the lobby of the Dunia Hotel an agitated crowd of many
colours, George Lim interpreting like mad, Forbes of
Marmion crying, "And I'll hit the bastard again, just you
let me get at him, just you tike your bleeding hands off, let
me get up those fliming stairs to the bastard." Eileen his
wife weeping, many tongues braying and chittering, hands
eloquent, arms—including those of Nando Tasca—holding
Forbes of Marmion.

"It was all a mistake, he had no idea of his identity——"

"Now you come a with a me, ave a one drink, you a feel
better——"

"Let me get at the sod, the big nasty black bastard——"

"He does not know what he is saying. He has no idea it
is so important a man——"

"*Ilahumma! Astaghfiru'llah!*"

"*Keisatsu-sho made dono kurai arimasuka?*"

"He says he wants the police station. We don't want
any bloody police in here."

"All I want is bleeding justice. Let me get up there and
mike a butcher's shop of the bastard."

"You not a be a bloody fool. That a very big a man.
E ave a your ead cut a off."

"*Hee-ai-lung-tee-kio ma-tah.*"

"What's going on?" asked Lydgate. "Who's done what to whom?" A small brown man, neat in a suit from a Karachi tailor, said smiling:

"This Australian gentleman was looking for his wife and some stupid black boy directed him upstairs to the room of one of these important men from the Middle East—his name I know not—and there most unfortunately——"

"Yes, yes," said Lydgate, "I see." Then the police came, led by a worn Bishopspawn chewing his underlip through to the gum.

"I'm not going to be bleeding arrested. I've done nothing wrong. It was that bastard upstairs——"

"All right, all right, just a few questions, that's all."

"Tike your hands off me, I tell you."

And, in a corner, stood Eileen weeping, poor little kiddy, in her right hand a bundle of strange green banknotes covered with squiggles, an unrecognisable numeral of denomination above the portrait of a fat brown cunning man with a moustache. All flesh the same, and all money.

31

But, of course, a blasted public holiday. All offices closed, including his own. Lydgate woke up early to the fact—at nacreous dawn in his woven sweltering shelter of a house. He couldn't get the air ticket today. Tomorrow morning, yes. Everything would be all right. But he would have felt happier with that ticket paid for and in his pocket. The Caliph's Birthday Parade? He would not go to see it. He would finish his packing. He would wait and sweat, listening for the big boots of Interpol outside his window, nail-biting, starting at the cheep of a house-lizard, a day of purgatory, that the prophecy of Carruthers Chung might be fulfilled. And then freedom. Free as the air, as the birds.

High in air, among birds and bats sleeping upside down, Paolo thought piously that only God and himself were seeing the Birthday Parade like this. He looked down on the town medan—crowds in open square, police with rifles, police band, Sea Scouts, Girl Guides, St. John Ambulance Brigade, the shining cars sailing on to the dry green. Royal salutes, anthems of many nations, outriders on motorcycles, old men waving ancient spears and blunderbusses. No acting U.N. Adviser appeared, but the British representative was given, in its original Elizabethan galliard tempo, "God Save the Queen". Then the tuba-player fainted, not long out of the jungle, unused to this naked brassy sun.

The Caliph came at last, high on an ornate litter, dispensing a sort of Papal blessing. Ox-bellows and goat-bleats of native pipes and bassoons, horrible drum-thumps and tormented gongs. The crowd chewed and smoked, not unduly impressed. The Caliph slow-marched through the open orders, inspecting everybody, and the tuba-less band played "See the Conquering Hero Comes". Then rifles were loaded, muzzles pointed straight at Paolo, and a treble *feu de joie* made the sky crackle like a giant bowl of rice crispies.

Nando Tasca, like Lydgate, was also absent from the parade, also concerned, like Lydgate, with the problems of travel but, unlike Lydgate, only vicariously. Podmore and Company had alrleady told him of a Lloyd–Triestino ship that was due in Aden in a week's time. Three days stay, a turn around, then back to Genoa. He bought a ticket, and to pay out so much money did not break his heart. He would get it all back: Novello should be extremely grateful that his innubile daughter was being taken off his hands by a Tasca. He now had to ensure that Paolo got safely to Aden, there to be closely guarded till his sailing day by reliable members of the Aden Italian community. He could not yet send any cables—either to Aden or to Italy—because the Post Office was closed. Unfortunately also the Dunia Airways office was closed, and Nando Tasca had to spend a thirsty morning going round the drinking shops, searching for a clerk with a mole on his left cheek, on the mole a tuft of fine black hairs.

It was not till near noon that he found him. The cilia of the mole wagged in speech, vibratile in the ceiling fan of the drinking shop. Speech quacked among three friends indifferent to the Caliph's parade. Nando Tasca sat down comfortably and said:

"One a ticket Aden. Tomorrow."

"This is a holiday," said the negro. "No work today."

"This a very urgent," said Nando Tasca. "My son e must a fly a Aden tomorrow."

"Perhaps," said one of the clerk's witty friends, a radio mechanic from a trading company, "he could take off from the minaret."

"I not a want a anyone be a funny," said Nando Tasca, his face beef-red. "Tonight he come a down. His work," he added, aware of foreign smiles, "a finish."

"Teaching the birds to sing?" suggested the witty friend.

Nando Tasca showed muscle under the fat. "You not a be a funny," he said. "I speak a *serioso*. Ave you," he asked the clerk, "one a ticket a Aden?"

"None," said the clerk. "Mr. Lydgate took the last one. He has not yet paid for it, but it is waiting for him to collect. Nothing now available till the visitors have gone back."

"Mr. Lydgate?" said Nando Tasca. "You make a mistake. Mr. Lydgate not a want a go. E stay ere for the *festività*. E not a want to go a Aden."

"But he does. Very urgent business, he says."

"My business more a urgent. You tell a im you a make a mistake. You have a drink a with me," said Nando Tasca. "Everybody ave a drink. And you," he said to the witty friend, "not a be a so bloody funny."

Beer was brought, business was starting. *"Salute,"* said Nando Tasca through the froth.

"It is possible," said the clerk, "it is just possible that the Government might want to book an official passage, and then, of course, Mr. Lydgate would have to surrender his seat."

"Possibile," said Nando Tasca. *"Molto possibile.* And a Government a pay a little bit a more. Ten a bucks."

"Oh, no. The Government has to pay much more than

259

that. In cash, too. The Government has to pay another hundred bucks."

"Fifty, you a say?"

"One hundred. The Government can afford it, you see."

"Bloody robber," said Nando Tasca calmly. "Where a *gabinetto*?"

The negro clerk said he would take him there. In the wet yard, noisy with poultry and tinsmiths, Nando Tasca paid over a hundred bucks in notes. He would get it back. A business in Siena, eh?

"Call in tomorrow morning," said the clerk. "The ticket will be ready. The plane takes off at 1405 hours. I will go round and tell Mr. Lydgate about the Government priority."

Nando Tasca looked at the waving hairs of the mole. A breeze was stirring; would it bring rain? "Perhaps," said Nando Tasca, "e a offer you a more. I not a trust a you," he said frankly.

"Well," said the negro clerk, in no wise insulted, "there is that possibility. But for fifty more bucks I could take you over to the office now and you could buy the ticket. The fifty bucks would be payment for working on a holiday. This is, after all," he reminded Nando Tasca, "the Caliph's birthday."

"Bloody robber," said Nando Tasca. But he paid up.

The ticket safe in his pocket, Nando Tasca went to drink a lonely beer and work out a plan for removing his son from the minaret. It would have to be done quietly. He no longer wanted the police to attempt another perilous ascent. He no longer wanted Paolo dragged down, all filth and hair, crying, to be imprisoned at ground level and await trial for trespass, blasphemy, desecration, or whatever the charge would be. It seemed unlikely now that the police would try again: there had been too much muttering in the ranks. Moreover, the police now were very busy with guards of honour and royal salutes. Orders seemed to have filtered down from the Astana that, if Paolo could not be removed quietly, he had best be left alone till after the ceremonies were over. He had already been passed off as an eccentric watchman to some of the distinguished visitors. Things were never so bad as they seemed. Moreover, the master switch had at last been located, and the prisoner in the tower was no longer vocal. Nando Tasca suddenly came face to face with the horrid reality of the fact that he himself would have to climb those endless stairs, he, an old man. "Oh, my son, my son," he groaned. Then he remembered the rest of David's lament. No, that was far from pertinent. Never, never would he, Nando Tasca, regret that he had not died for Paolo. Dying was Paolo's job. He would die, by God he would. No longer among leeches and headhunters, but slowly, lingeringly in the care of Novello's daughter. It was just. Marriage was the answer to all problems.

32

"So there it is, Lyddy old man," said Forbes of Marmion.
"I won't be seeing much more of you now. I want you to
know that I forgive you for getting that poor little kiddy
drunk that time and that I won't think any more about it.
I want you to shike hands with me." Lydgate took the
dry calloused road-foreman's paw in his. "That's right,
Lyddy. You're still my cobber."

Outside an afternoon procession of decorated cars, honking jubilantly for the Caliph's birthday. Inside packed bags
and palpable heat packed in the basket that was called a
house. "So you're going," said Lydgate. "Is she going
with you?"

"Yes," said Forbes of Marmion. "They're sending us out
of the Stite. It's not bonza justice, the wy I see it, because
it was all that black bastard's fault tiking advantage of poor
little Eileen the wy he did. I did what any decent husband
would do. I knocked his bleeding teeth in for him. Then
all his servants and secretaries and hangers-on kime out of
the rooms along the corridor—they had all that corridor
to themselves, man—and started on me. So I bashed them
about a bit, too, which is only natural. And soft as bleeding
putty they were, man, no stamina in them somehow. Of
course, it stands to reason, considering what they eat. It'll
be a chinge to get back to a couple of fried eggs with a
big stike underneath, which is what we always used to have
for breakfast back home. Anywy, they reckon there'll be

a lot of big trouble or something and they've got to pretend that what I did was wrong. Otherwise, they reckon, there'll be a big flare-up in the Middle East with the Arabs fighting the United Nations, and it'll all be my fault, they reckon. Which doesn't strike me as being a bit right, but there you are, you can't stand out against them, not small fry like you and me, Lyddy old man. So we're going back next week on a boat of some kind or other, all four of us. Or you might sy four and a half of us, because Eileen, poor little kiddy, is in the family wy again."

"Yours?"

"Now, come off it, Lyddy old man, you don't want me to start getting crook agyne, do you? Of course it's mine, bound to be, because I'm the only one she's done it proper with, see? The wy I see it, it must have happened when we were living in the other plice, outside the town. There was only me she saw. She'd come in and do a bit of shopping once a week in the Land-Rover, but she never saw any other men, so I reckon it's my kiddy that poor little kiddy is carrying. Real bucked about it she is too, Lyddy old man."

"So everything's worked out for the best," said Lydgate. "You're sticking to your wife. It's the only way really, the only thing to do. Responsibility. You marry a woman and you stick by that woman." He nodded, believing it for other people. And, in a sense, it was true for him; certainly, none of his false marriages had worked.

"Although, Lyddy, to tell you the truth, I had thought of just clearing out, see, and leaving her to get on with it. I'd even thought of letting her go back to the other bloke, the one who got her in the family wy that time, and I thought once of just dumping the kids on you."

"Thanks," said Lydgate.

"Yes, I had thought of bringing the kids here, while you

263

were out, and leaving a note sying that I knew you'd look after them, having black kids of your own. But it's all different now. We're going back by a nice slow boat, and it'll do my little kiddy good to have a bit of a look at the world. Iden she's very anxious to see. She says, you just sty in some nice little pub or other and look after the kids when we get to Iden and I'll go off, she says, and buy you a nice present, something you can't get in this miserable dump of a plice, because you've been a good husband and you deserve a nice present, she says. A real good kindhearted little kiddy who's been let down by a bad man and been tiken advantage of by a lot of other bad buggers, foreign bastards, if you'll forgive me sying that, Lyddy. Anywy, we shan't be going back to Marmion. I think I've finished with Marmion. My mum and dad have been talking about moving to Sydney, to retire there, you see, where there's a bit of life, and I reckon that's as good a plice as any for me to get a job, me now having the experience I have had. And if little Eileen ever wants to go out and do a bit of shopping or to have a milk-shike somewhere I know she'll be sife. The men are different in Austrylia. More trustworthy, if you see what I mean. You can't imagine an Aussie tiking advantage of a little black girl like that. Although, you know, Lyddy, she has a British passport, do you know that? A little black girl off the trees almost, and, coming from Naraka, you see, she has a British passport. So there's no trouble there. Well, Lyddy, I'll have to be going now. Rotten old dump of a plice thy've put you in here. I notice you've not even unpacked your bags yet, and I don't blime you. You stick out for something better, old man. We've missed you back at the old plice, really we have. There's some Indian or other with ten kids next door now. Terrible row by day and night. Oh, and talking about Indians, I know I had something for you. I'd be forgetting my head only it's fastened on to me." And he gave Lydgate a letter. "An Indian's been round looking for you, says he was given this letter by another Indian. A bit complicated, Lyddy, but, anywy, there it is. Now I'll leave you to get on with it."

The cars still passed, honking holiday joy. Lydgate, left alone, read the letter. It was most literate, the letter of some Indian who, having done great wrong perhaps, or having had some great wrong done to him, was now an exile, Ovid among the Goths, living with books up-river, looking after a P.W.D. transport depot near a Government river ferry. The letter said:

'Dear Sir,

I have not the honour of your acquaintance, but I have been asked to get in touch with you by a man who says that he was asked by somebody further up-river if there was anybody in this uncivilised region who was capable of editing a reasonably intelligent missive to a Mr. Lydgate of Dunia Town. You are Mr. Lydgate; this is, I hope, a sufficiently intelligible epistle. My name, as you will see from the subscription of this letter, is Mahalingam. Mahalingam, as you may know, is Sanskrit for 'large or great or mighty generative organ'—this, of course, having more a religious (through associations of religion and fertility) significance than an anatomical one. Though anatomically and, as I hope to be able to tell you sometime if I am ever lucky enough to make your acquaintance, socially the name has not proved inept. This partly explains why I, a man of some small educational attainments, am here living with savages. But you will not wish to hear this story now. To my purpose. A young Potok lady of your acquaintance, together with three children who it is alleged are yours (I foresee that, when we eventually meet, we shall have much to talk about, having not a little in common) has crossed from a village in Shurga by river and is now esconced in the district of Khras, staying with relatives. This region, as you may have heard, has been much troubled recently with a refocillation of an old and barbarous custom—to wit, man-eating. The young lady is, however, quite safe, and she intends to travel by river up to Dunia Town very shortly. Apparently she has encountered no immigration difficulties—there being at the present time no living white official in the area—and anticipates no trouble at all in achieving her goal, to wit, a happy reunion with you in Dunia Town. She is delayed because, apparently, she has a present for you, but this present is not yet ready. The nature of the present it has not been easy for me to ascertain. The man I met talked unintelligibly about a 'head of mud', whatever that is, but no doubt you will find the present acceptable, coming as it does from one who seems to have a great regard for you and is very anxious to be re-united with you in the near future. I do hope we can meet some time and talk of books, the arts, music, philosophy. Here, as you may well imagine, I am starved of *intellectual* intercourse.

Yours very sincerely,

Mahalingam."

Lydgate put the letter down, closed his eyes, shivered despite the oven-heat. Never pray for anything. Prayer is always answered. Never see visions. Visions come true. The head of Mudd, dried and shrunken, black with smoke, hanging on the wall. "That's a fine specimen. Where did you bag that?" "Dunia. Do you know Dunia?" "Can't say I do." "Let me tell you the story." How long would it be, wondered Lydgate, before his own head would be lovingly smoked and hung up to be admired. "This man once live alongside me. He good man. Then he be bad man. He try to go but I not let him go. We eat his body. Here hang his head. It good head. He bad man but it good head. Worth much money."

The sweat streamed. Oh, come along, come along, tomorrow. Into the wide air, away from it all.

33

The day of the circumcision ceremony rolled up from the hot, dry, parched east, rainless, with no hope of rain. All night long the frogs, field-brown against field-green, had croaked war-chants, hurled deep insults across the drying water-course. With war in the air, few men had been able to sleep. Dignitaries had tossed and dozed in the houses specially built for them up near the Astana (ninety thousand bucks a house, bonus of ten thousand to the contractors for completing the work on time. Perhaps the contractors alone had had a good night's rest.) In the morning, medals, accolades—the Star of Dunia, first class, to the Sultan of Dahaga; the Most Holy Order of the Embattled Oceans to the Regent of Anchok; to the Crown Prince of Lapar a second-class Bearded Lion; long service and good conduct medals to several shifty-eyed rogues, rulers of villages. A procession through the town of the honoured, sweating in slow cars.

Looking up to the tip of the ithyphallic minaret, the people of the town found something missing. Its voice had been silenced now; that tiny presence had been removed. The beards were quick to talk about injustice. Sea-lawyers spoke of habeas corpus. There were crowds round the jail. That symbol of revolt against the tyrannical father-state had been hauled down, like a red flag. Now, in his place, a muezzin tuned up for tomorrow (the key to the door still missing, the latch clicked to ever-open). The muezzin practised the retroflex divided consonants that made up the name of God, an emblem of stasis, of the old order never to be changed—Allah and the white man, *Surahs* and official circulars. Soon banners were on the streets, some saying "Freedom", others "Italy".

"Italy," said a Middle East oil-king in Bedouin robes. He spoke to a Sultan who chewed clear gums, spoke in the accents of an English public school. "It is the name of a country, of course, but it is also a gnomic cypher used on the backs of love-letters. Love-letters of the British lower classes, that is. I remember I had a liaison with a young girl in Oxford, a tobacconist's daughter who lived near Carfax. She wrote me letters, even after I had returned to my kingdom, and she often put 'Italy' on the back. Also 'Boltop' and 'Holland' and 'Swalk'. The Caliph should be pleased that they say, 'I Trust And Love You'."

Paolo was in the *Casa Tasca*, tending his father. His father had strained his old fatherly heart climbing those many stairs. He lay exhausted, fed with beer by his son. His son was happy—soon, in Italy, he would be rolling in the hay with Bice and Violetta, Leonora and Grazia, drinking cheap wine and eating peaches. It was the time of the year for peaches. Peach-juice in thin golden wine. And, before that, adventures in Aden, on the ship. Rich married women. Aaaaah. He shaved off his beard with a new blade, his father groaning on the bed. Little did he know that he had made his mark in Moslem Africa. An emblem of a goat would soon be the banner of the Party; missionary pictures of the Prophet Jesus would rouse a memory, a recognition. And Italy, for others as well as himself, would mean freedom.

"I am dying," said his father from the bed. "You have killed me."

"You drink more beer," said his son. "As you see, they brought me many, many bottles. Somebody," he said solemnly, "somebody down there loved me."

"Yes," said his father, "I will have some more beer. It does some good." He had given up speaking English to his son. At the thought of what Paolo would be returning to, he felt better. "I am getting up now," he said. "Soon we must be going to the airport."

"How do we get there? There are no taxis."

"That is true. And the Airways office has no bus. You must go and look for a taxi."

It took a long time. Paolo, shaven, clean, in the trousers of his father's best suit, striped-shirted, neck-tied for a great occasion, looked in wonder at the crawling stream of cars. At length he saw one he knew. The youth who drove, happy in sun-glasses, a bemused Sultan at his back, said, "You." And then, "That not good lectric iron. Not get hot."

"It cost," said Paolo, "twenty bucks. You take me to airport. *Scusa*," he said, bowing to the Sultan. The Sultan stared with old, bewildered eyes.

"All right," said the youth. "I get tired go so slow. I come to house."

And so Paolo's one small bag was brought downstairs, and also his groaning father. Nando Tasca sat, breathing hard, next to His Highness the Sultan of Lanchap, saying, "E not a good a boy. E nearly kill a is poor old a father. Today e go. I not a see im no a more. Ow many children you a ave?"

"Twenty-three," said the Sultan. "Or twenty-five. I know it is an odd number."

"It a too a many," said Nando Tasca. "I ave a one a daughter. She a good a girl. I ave a one a son. E a bad boy. But," he added, brightening, thinking of Paolo out

270

of his life for ever, "it a no a good be a sorry. A man must a get a married. A man must ave a children. That a life," he said philosophically. "Marriage," he added.

Paolo was pleased to see banners with "Italy" painted on them. He bowed to the crowds, smiling with a goat's clean-shaven face. It was a royal send-off. They sped along the airport road, Paolo saying "Aaaah" with satisfaction. He had been appreciated. He had been loved, if not by his father. The bowing Moslems confirmed him in his convic-ion that, despite everything, he was a good boy.

There were many people at the airport. Raging at the Dunia Airways desk was Lydgate. Raging, crying. The effects of living in Africa too long, thought Paolo. A good thing he himself was going. He shook hands with his father. His father said, "You be a good a boy." He shook hands with the Sultan of Lanchap. Officials bowed to him, awed by the company he kept. He was bowed on to the aircraft. A very pretty Creole air-hostess brought him sweets on a dish. He winked at her. Later, after take-off, when most of the passengers had become somnolent, he would pinch her bottom. Life was beginning again. He sang, in bups and bops, "Stardust" against the engines.

That night the circumcision ceremony took place at the Astana. The guests drank warm champagne and picked at cold curry while, behind closed doors, the *modin* or official circumciser did his work. The two young princes sat on a banana-leaf. Solemnly, the *modin* pulled a prepuce with special forceps, with a razor-knife solemnly lopped. Two lops: the boys had become men. Afterwards, pale, they sat on thrones, were sprinkled with rose-water by hand-maidens. Old synagogue jokes went about among the heartier Europeans. Few, even the least squeamish, could touch the kebabs that were passed round, served with a fiery sauce. More warm champagne was poured; pale and dignified, the princes kept their thrones.

Again, two men were missing. Nando Tasca lay on his bed, aching, lost without his son. There was no longer anybody to blame for anything. He had hardly the heart to reach for the warm beer that stood, in shiny black ranks, by his bed, an old man, a good man, alone in an alien land. At eight in the evening there was a gentle tap at his door. Eileen Forbes came in, smiling, black shoulders shining under the naked bulb. "You want, darling?" she said. "You like?"

Nando Tasca tried to rise from the bed. It was hopeless: he ached so, he felt so tired. Just his luck. "I an old man," he said, and then corrected himself: "No, not a old. Not a very well."

"You like, darling?" smirked Eileen. "I love you, darling." In Aden, perhaps, she would learn more words.

"Where a you husband?" asked Nando Tasca. Anger at his son, now, he hoped, chained up in the Italian colony of Aden, anger at his son's, even in absence, power to thwart, to shame, anger sent adrenalin swishing through his old man's body. He thought he might, if he could only move. But it was no good.

"Other a time," he said. "Not a now. A very ill a man."

"My husband," said Eileen carefully, "drink with Austrylians. In Kool Kaffi Bar and Restaurant. You like, darling?"

"Other time. When I a better. You a go a now." He waved her off. Eileen pouted. A new perm glowed above her Tudor brow, her lips were rich red. Undismayed, she said, throatily erotically, "Good-niiiight, darliiing." Then she clattered down the stairs, the evening short, perhaps her last chance to work this district, off to see the two drunken Sudus.

Nando Tasca, left alone, heard loud Bengali from next

door, unbelievably rapid, wind broken under water. Children cried, there was a clatter of tin mugs, a slap of fat brown flesh, screams. It was different in Lydgate's day. A very quiet a man.

34

Lydgate, ill with frustration, once during the morning physically sick with anger, had waited, with his two suitcases, on the road to the airport. Early, in good time to rage at the Dunia Airways clerk who, at flight-time, entered weights, collected money for excess baggage, made his final check of the manifest. The clerk had sent round a peon that morning to inform Lydgate that he would have to wait at least another week for a flight to Aden, his seat for today's flight having been given to someone travelling on official business. At Dunia Airways office in the town he had found nobody to storm at, plead with. On the hot road, waiting for some private car, some Government Land-Rover to appear, he had been sick once again. At last, very shaky, he had been able to climb into a jeep of the State Information Department, driven by a cynical Sudu who scorned the festive day and said that the Mosque was a load of superstition. The jeep, said the Sudu, was to pick up some fool or other visiting the State, arriving from Naraka at 1350. "Aeroplanes," said the Sudu. "A lot of nonsense. How do they keep up there, eh? You don't know and nor do I. A lot of trickery, if you ask my opinion."

There was no hope at the airport. Regret from the clerk —what could he do?—and no last-minute cancellation. Lydgate felt very ill and had to drink several brandies at the bar. The brandy did its work: nothing to worry about, really. Mudd dead. Bigamy, after all, not an offence that anybody would really want to take up. Only a few more days. A few more days in that fetid hut of a house, Mudd's head everywhere, dripping on a salver like that of the Baptist, black Salome coming with children. But, he thought, with alcoholic sobriety, it takes a fair length of time to prepare a head. As long as it takes to smoke a salmon. He saw a Potok standing by. He asked the Potok. The Potok looked at him strangely and moved away. And then this image of his own head, mummified, black, horrible, like the head of Jeremy Bentham between the feet of the effigy of Jeremy Bentham.

He got a lift back at the back of a Lambretta owned by a junior bank official. He left his luggage at the airport, taking back only the overnight case which held his toilet gear. Let the luggage stay there, earnest of no more frustration. He could buy another shirt in the town. He opened his keyless door, smelling heat and emptiness. He sat down, raking his thin hair with fingers rigid with nerves, and moaned to himself, sorry for the thing that was Francis Burroughs Lydgate, then wondering why he was sorry. Later in the afternoon he went out and, in the empty Kool Kaffi, got slowly drunk. He had a small Chinese meal— spaghetti and prawns, though hardly able to manage the chopsticks. Then he, very slowly, very deliberately, walked back to his house in the circumcising night. He opened the door. Only a few more days, away from it all, nothing to worry about really. The light was on.

"Francis," said the woman, "oh, Francis, Francis, Francis." She held out her hands to him. She was an old woman, about sixty, thin, lined, very brown, dry, hair quite grey, dressed in a costume of striped moygashel, stick-legs planted in mosquito-boots, gold ring on her left ring-finger, fingers like bones. "No," said Lydgate in fear. "No, no, no. I don't know you, what are you doing here, get out."

"Oh, it's been such a long time, Francis. I'm not surprised you don't recognise me." The head could hardly be further shrunken, not even by the most skilled of Potoks skilled in the art of shrinking. But the eyes were sharp blue, the nose Dantesque, the mouth a wide wound, quivering now. The cheeks and forehead were scored and scored, the whole face free of rouge, powder, anything that might show her to be a woman other than her clothes.

"I don't know you," said Lydgate. "I tell you I don't know you. Why don't you get out?"

"And you too, my poor boy. So old-looking, so very old. We're both old, Francis. But thank God I've found you at last. I'm so alone, so all alone. When I think what they did to poor Roderigo." She sobbed and then made a must-be-brave gesture of the head. "I'm punished, punished. I should never have let you go. This is my punishment, but God has turned it into a blessing, perhaps. I've found you. Who would have thought it, me registering at the hotel, then a Chinese telling me there was another Lydgate in the town? Then I knew it was you, Francis. Do you remember your old joke about your initials? You used to say you weren't F.B. but a B.F. And I scolded you for that, because I knew what it meant. But I've learned things, Francis, going about the world, working for our little cause. I've learned to be more tolerant. My poor boy." She came up to him, walking stiffly, gracelessly, her hand ready to smooth his face. "And you're so hot. You're sweating terribly. Have you got fever, my poor boy? Let me feel your forehead."

"No, no, no," said Lydgate, at bay against the soft woven wall. "Don't touch me."

"It's a strange surprise, isn't it, Francis? Almost like a shock. But we'll both get over it. We're husband and wife, after all, and we have a duty to each other. I will never let you go," she said, her voice suddenly sharp, "Never, never, never. You're going to be mine again. I'm sorry, I'm sorry with all my heart that I went with Roderigo, but I swear, I swear by Almighty God that there was nothing sinful between us. I did wrong to you, Francis, just as you did wrong to me. But I can repent, and I can forgive. Oh, I'm so, so happy." Tears tumbled down the lines of her old leathery cheeks. "I'm going to say a prayer," she said, "here and now. I'm going to thank God for letting me find you again at last, and I'm going to pray that He will always keep us together, teach us to love each other purely and sincerely, give us both the happiness that we've missed for so long." She knelt on the floor, her joined hands on the chair-seat, eyes closed. She opened them suddenly, sharply on Lydgate. "Kneel down with me, my poor, poor boy. Kneel down and pray with me."

"No, no," said Lydgate. "No, no, no." He stumbled, fighting air to get to the door, fumbling at the handle. A man stood outside in moonlight, arms by his side. He was just black bulk, small but broad. He pushed Lydgate in again, gently, apologetically, murmuring.

"All right, Daud," called the woman. "He's not hurting me. He's my husband," she laughed, and the laugh was pure metal. "And, oh, Daud, we'll go down later and get the luggage. Just wait outside." The door closed. "That's Daud," she said, "a Moslem. A very good man. He's been with me for, let me see, nearly fifteen years. He looks after me really well," she said. "He won't let anything bad happen to me. I do believe he'd give his life. That's love," she explained, "devotion. Now, come on, Francis, kneel down with me. Let's start our new life really well, really holily." And she began to pray, while Lydgate stood rigid, clutching the strands of fibre that made the wall. "Oh, Almighty God," she prayed, "thank You for sending my husband back to me. Make me the good wife I never was before. Make him the good husband he never was before. Knit us together into one flesh, one spirit. Teach us to do Thy holy will in all things, in the way we behave, the things we eat. Make our bodies pure by virtue of the pure things that alone shall enter them. Give us pure thoughts, strengthen our love for each other and, through that love, our love for Thee. Forgive all my past sins, forgive all his past sins. Make us truly blessed in Thy love and Thy grace, Thou, O God, Who art all things—" her voice grew louder, it began to whine in sing-song—"All things, O God. The moon in the sky and the dog that bays beneath it, the tamarind and the oak, the sea and the sand, the head and the foot, the heart and the cerebral cortex, the man and the woman, the lock and the key, the maker and the destroyer, time and not-time, what was made and what never could be made. All are Thee, O God, O dear, dear God." She bowed her head deeper, breathing deeply like a sybil. Quietly she said, "Amen."

"No, no," whined Lydgate. "No, no, no."

A deep voice outside prayed, *"Amin."*

"Roderigo taught me how to pray," she said simply. "Poor, poor, dear Roderigo. Roderigo eaten. Roderigo without a head. But Roderigo with God." She cried briefly into her hands. She got up smiling, bright, and said to Lydgate, "Well, we must do something about getting my luggage. My poor boy, we must make a home out of this charming, simple house. You seem to have so few things. But you have me now, and I shall look after you. I shall help you in any way I can. We're together again, and I shall never, never leave you. And you will never, never, never again leave me."

"Amin," said the voice outside.

35

Another arid morning, wet nakedness under the mosquito-
net panting in the humid air. The brown and green frogs
had engaged at midnight, hopping into action, brekekek-
king martially. Corpses in no-frog's-land, the wounded
piled up at the regimental aid posts, orderlies bringing
succour to the feebly croaking. The brown staff, the green
staff, each far back at base, plotted simple strategies, sent up
reserves. All night long the deep-chested chorus hopped
into people's dreams and out again. The battlefield was
near the Astana. Lights went on and off all night, fit-
fully, quenched at last by a dry sun replacing a sharp
moon.

The moon of Islam on its banners. The carpet was lugged
to the entrance to the courtyard of the Mosque. A long
tunnel of a marquee, erected yesterday by the Municipal
Dog Catchers, was to bless the entering heads with temporary relief from the sun's blasts and nagging, while the
carpet beneath was to bless the feet with softness. A tented
enclosure for the important was stuck with pennants, a
Technicolor Battle of Bosworth. Tiny metal chairs were
ranged under the sun for the many, many others. The
fountain splashed before the white portico, cooling only
its basin. To early comers the Mosque itself seemed a
crouched leprous sun-beast, bulbous, pillared, the golden
dome the spike-nippled breast of a supine giant Amazon.

It was terrifying and somewhat obscene, like its Semitic God. Loudspeakers solemnly counted in the National Language, testing, testing.

Long before the police with clarinets, the police with rifles, the common people were at the skirts of the court, brown and black, clad in hot orange, scarlet and purple. And then the khaki police for use and the white police for ceremony, and soon the Europeans and the Asiatics and the Africans of good class began to appear, already sweating, their cars parked far away. The metal chair-seats scorched, damp flowered on backs and under armpits, white stone glared, gold burned against hot blue, the fountain cooled itself. Beer-drinkers were soon shod and gloved and hatted in sweat. The ladies, garden-party-attired, fanned their necks with their programmes. The heat, my dear, the heat, the heat. The sun was here no Brighton holiday blessing; it was the enemy, the devil that came long before the world. It climbed, calibrating the long time of waiting.

The first dignitary, mounting the saluting-base and honoured with music, came like a cool wind or tiny cloud of relief. But was it imagination, or was the sweat dryer, did the pennants shake, the apex of the turban at the saluting-base twitch in the air? Some looked up and saw real clouds billowing in, pulled up from the horizons like eiderdowns slipped off the Great Bed of Ware. And then, with human fickleness, people began to fear the big hand on the sun's mouth and the spoilsport clouds. When the Britsh representative stood to six bars of his national galliard, a drop or two struck like thin notes of a glockenspiel. Those near the fountain thought, at first, that it was the fountain. The honoured with salutes ran up the steps of the saluting-base and down again to their sheltered places. The anthems speeded their tempi, the silence between them shrank.

As the rain played its preludial largo, *staccato ma non troppo*, the black Caliph came on in shining robes, blessing all—the police band, the rain, the spectators—under a yellow umbrella. Behind him were elders of the faith, one with the Word on a golden cushion, one with a crozier that had no hook. Boys, youngsters of the faith, marched in, in good time, behind. The Caliph and his entourage reached the portico, stood in stone shelter before the massy doors. The rain attacked its allegro movement, reserving its drums for the climax. Those wet with sweat shrugged humorously, ready to be dressed in a mackintosh, wellingtons, sou'wester of rain. The women mooed and danced, pulped programmes held above their hats. Canvas above important heads began to leak. The loudspeakers crackled and a voice, deep as the voice of a record played at half the prescribed speed, spoke a poem of praise and thanksgiving in the National Language.

Then the rain played *presto furioso* with kettle-drums. The sky gaped stupidly and spewed pure water. All sound else was drowned. On their battlefield near the Astana the frogs still fought and carried off their dead, forgetting what the fight was about. "In the name of Allah the Beneficent, the Merciful," bellowed the rain, "I would that thou wouldst an thou wouldst wouldst wouldst aaaah." An Arabic prayer croaked inaudibly to the drowned world. Then the Caliph asked for the key to the massy doors of the Mosque.

"The key!"

"Who has the key?"

"Where is the key?"

"The key, the key!"

"Does nobody know where the key is?"

"Somebody *must* have the key!"

"The key, the key, the key!"

The rain cracked, hurled and kettle-drummed, vomited like a whole sick heaven over the Mosque and the whole black kingdom, heedless of human time or of any time but its own.